CRIME PAYS

The Darkest Side of Crime

Edited and Compiled by Theresa Scott-Matthews

A HellBound Books Publishing LLC Book
Austin TX

Contents:

CRIME PAYS

God's Wrath
Matthew Wilson

Everyone knows that monsters die at the end of stories, so I decided it would be best to get rid of the worst - Harry Kingdon.

No, the eruption wasn't due till first light, more than enough time to plan and execute the perfect murder, so I called on Harry a little before seven with a six pack and rifle.

We'd been good friends in prison, some stuffy bouncer had given him grief at a nightclub and for punching the officious fool I had gotten six months.

For one punch!

To show his gratitude, Harry had insisted that I live with him when we got out, just until I got back on my feet. Mom had thrown me out for stealing her purse but for a while when we were free, he kept his word.

Until I wanted his wife. Of course I didn't love her - she thought I did - but she was just a little fun. Then she spoke of babies and I backed away.

For spite, she'd threatened to tell Harry, whose temper was legendary, so I preferred to look at it as self-defense rather than murder. For spite, she'd threaten to tell Harry who had a temper that was legendary. I preferred to look at is as self-defense, rather than murder.

For weeks, the TV had warned of a forthcoming eruption of the old mountain and where I'd insisted on a hunting trip, we would be safe, and *I* would be safe from passersby.

The police had arrested many geologist and photographer troublemakers, refusing to get away from the smoking crater but now Harry and I were away from danger, there'd be no busybody TV crews passing by.

"There," Harry said when he saw the deer. The earth tremors had startled many animals away from the mountain and dirtied the stream with ash. The creature slowed as it splashed across the water and I raised my gun.

"Not in the head," Harry demanded. "I want that thing bolted to my living room."

The sun was in my eyes but as I'd loaded both barrels with buck, I swung my weapon at Harry at the last minute and blew his guts out his back.

Done and done.

The deer jerked it's head up in fright and then tottered away to eat its breakfast in peace.

Sadly, the second part of my plan required greater labour.

A good killer does his research - Bundy and others had failed with shallow graves because animals usually scattered their carcasses across great distances. Even if I laid my friend six feet down I could never relax as the real threat of discovery would always be present.

And then God had put fire in his mountain.

At 5am tomorrow, the northern part of the crater would erupt, belching millions of ash into the air and burying the surrounding area in 150 feet of mud.

Driving back to Harry's cabin, I felt nothing as I tumbled his body into the boot of his car and made sure his tracker was activated as I switched on the engine.

A paranoid fellow made sure he knew where his car was at ALL times. When Harry's disappearance was discovered, his worried family would turn on the tracker and see the fool had parked his car too close to the mountain.

You don't think…

I didn't hear any animals as I drove at a calm pace down the old roads. At last I felt something — a sadness for the walks of my youth as tomorrow none of these trees would exist. The land would be destroyed and renewed in a moment, covered in rocks and sludge seven stories deep.

In time, the land would regrow and other children would walk those woods, making memories while killing animals.

Poor Harry and his car would be under it, hidden like dinosaur bones. No animals would be able to pull him up, no hitchhiker would inevitably come upon them whilst taking a whizz.

Soon, he'd be forgotten and I would be free.

The air grew hot as I played the mountain in a game of chicken, its throbbing, cracked crater becoming larger in the windscreen as I put my foot down.

"You're always causing problems, Harry," I moaned when I felt we were close enough to be in what the news warned was the "God's wrath" section.

I killed the engine, got out and opened the boot.

More bloody labour.

At least I didn't have to bleach or burn the car. Tomorrow this spot would be as raw and ugly as the Martian wasteland. I managed to laugh as I pulled the folded bicycle out of the boot and started to put it together with an Alan key.

Sadly my laughter attracted some unwanted attention and I tasted sick when I heard it — the human voice.

I stood straight, thinking myself mad for some said all murderers were mad.

I tried to swallow and failed, feeling my teeth click together as I slowly approached the car.

"Harry?"

"I said can you help me, Buddy?"

My heart jumped in my chest as I turned round and saw a little man armed with a camera.

Thank God. There were no such things as zombies. Only monsters.

For a moment, my mouth flapped and then, finally, words came.

"What are you doing up here? It's illegal to come within twenty miles of the mountain."

The dying sunlight still had enough strength to pierce the woodland canopy and gleam off his bald patch.

"I'm Billy Maston," the fellow smiled with an extended hand that I didn't shake. "The news crews are getting shots from the air but I figured no one else was brave to take pictures from the ground - can you imagine how much money I'd get for these snaps? I could pay my rent for a month. Then I heard your car and wondered if you were here to take pics too?"

I heard a hissing sound, like gas escaping and realised the source originated from me.

Snapper happy Bill had put me in a terrible position. If he told anyone I was here or worse — had taken pictures of me then all my plans would be undone.

More bloody work was needed.

Resigned, I squatted, picked up the largest branch I figured would complete the job and started walking toward him with a fixed smile.

"Come here," I said. "I wanna talk to you."

"Where's your camera?" Bill said, seemingly unaware of the danger he was in.

I would make it painless. One bop on the head and he'd vanish just like Harry in the morning.

"I don't have a camera," I said and stopped walking when he opened his shirt and rummaged under his armpit.

Then something glittered in that dying light, something small but sufficient to strip away my confidence.

"I don't believe you," Bill said, cocking the 32. Pistol. "No one would be crazy enough to be out here if not for making money."

My hands started shaking but I had the presence of mind not to drop the stick, raised like a knight's sword before the dragon.

"What—"

"I've already killed three reporters and broke their cameras - damn snoops," Bill interrupted me, his sudden anger seemed to indicate that he'd had a worse afternoon than I. "They wanted to steal my scoop, to take money out of my pocket by snapping the mountain, but if I'm the only one who brings something back to the network then I can ask *any* price."

My last meal gurgled unpleasantly in my belly.

Maybe madness attracted madness. Was I mad? I didn't think so. *Mad Men* could not construct the plan I had. Now it was being threatened by some balding idiot.

"Show me your camera," he insisted. "I know you have one. By tomorrow you'll be gone, buried under millions of tons of ash."

"I don't like copycats," I said and threw the stick whilst Bill figured he still had the upper hand.

There was an explosion as Bill raised a hand defensively against his face but I still managed to get him in the eye. He screamed womanly and fired repeatedly at me, bellowing his rage and I turned and ran like a coward.

Something hot cut my neck like a vampire's kiss. I clutched the mangled flesh, not allowing myself to feel as I ran on wobbly legs. I took cover behind a tree, assessing the damage and finding it only a flesh wound, I forced myself to think again.

Running away would be a death sentence. By tomorrow this area would be destroyed as if hit by an atom bomb.

Even if I started now I couldn't run thirty miles to escape the God's wrath area — I needed the bike or car to save my life.

I couldn't make it on my feet.

"Paparazzo?" Bill sang and I wished that I'd counted his shots. Was he out? Had he reloaded?

Too many beers with Harry in better times had left me unfit but though I was breathing heavy I still managed to climb the fox piss stinking tree a third of the way up when Bill had the misfortune to wander under it.

"Paparazzi? Bill sang again, his face smeared with blood. Even though his left eye was pouring a milky liquid, he still smiled, tickled by the revenge he had in mind.

I'd hunted with a rifle in these woods as a boy long before this maniac had pointed a camera or pistol at any creature. Poor Bill didn't have time to scream when a shadow fell from the sky.

He just turned his head too late as the sun went out and I fell briefly. I crossed myself once as I jumped, my beer belly adding some weight as I used Bill as a landing cushion and knocked him to the ground.

A rock did the work. I beat his brains out so they pulsed out of his ear.

Done and done.

Now I'd had enough of the place. Night was upon me which I'd planned to cover my escape but this revision of my plans worsened my anxiety and wishing for no more deviations I returned to the car to finish the job.

Where was the Alan key?

I hadn't needed a torch as I'd been so smart — every minute worked out to the last detail. I was meant to be away from here by now.

This wasn't right, this wasn't fair.

I dropped to my knees like a pig rooting round in the leaves as if for truffles.

Dear God, where was the Alan key?

The unfinished bike was unusable — I had dropped the key in the melee.

"Key, key," I sang as I headed to the car and sprang into the driver seat.

Bill had been a cautious killer like myself — the car keys were missing too. A guarantee that I wouldn't work my way around him and hightail it to safety.

Gnashing my teeth I returned to his body, rummaging around his clothing with no luck. The fool must have had his own transport as he hadn't kept Harry's keys.

He had tossed them.

I raged at the moon. I ripped out great chunks of my hair and took Bill's pistol, firing into his unresponsive body until I was sure there was only one bullet left.

Thirty miles to safety.

I couldn't run it. If the worse came then I would have one bullet left — no. I wouldn't think of it.

Miserably I returned to the car, wishing for wings, for any mode of transport to get me away. Where was Bill's vehicle? Where is that needle in a haystack to bring me salvation?

I've rooted so long in this dead vegetation that my fingers are cracked and bleeding, my back is aching and only my soul seems to leave this place, watching over those ugly trees with garish fascination.

Again, I feel something. Fear.

The earthquakes are stronger as the mountain prepares its own death but there are no animals springing into action like that pretty deer from the stream. The only survivor of my day.

I wish the engine was on if only to play the radio, to hear the reassuring voice of another human.

Tomorrow at first light when there is a chance of finding the keys, the sun will be eaten by a black and terrible cloud and it will be too late.

But first there is the A.M, that awful endless night filled with my agonized screams.

How I wish for that radio to blot them out.

And the laughter of my dear friend Harry in the back.

No, there is no such thing as zombies.

Only monsters and everyone knows that monsters die at the end of stories.

The Man Who Was Winter
Matthew McKiernan

It was a cold winter's day in Vindicator City. Melvin Clay really wished he could have spent the day at home. The bitter wind made the stump where his left leg used to be itch like hell. His current peg leg really wasn't working out. Maybe his wife would get him a new one for Christmas; it was just two weeks away. The year was 1900 and so far, the new century hadn't felt any different from the old one.

Honestly though, Melvin was shocked that he managed to make it this long. He had lived to be sixty years old. Not even his granddad or daddy had made it that far. Melvin Clay was a white bearded man who wore a thick orange coat and a dandy pair of yellow pants. He was carrying a huge green vase that shone in the sunlight. He was thinking of hailing down a Hansom cab as he walked by an alleyway and bumped into a Polish man. The vase hit the hard-icy ground and shattered into a hundred pieces.

"You damn goop, do you know how much that vase cost me?"

The Polish man just stared at Melvin as he was being yelled at. He probably wasn't used to men half his size screaming at him. Then again, Melvin wasn't afraid of guys who were younger or bigger than him. He had lost his fear, along with his left leg, at the Battle of Gettysburg. The Polish man bent down and lightly touched the broken glass shards with his ungloved fingers. His name was Casimir Stazek. Melvin had previously met him and his wife a few months ago at the bank when he had turned down their request for a loan.

Casimir was thirty-seven years old, although his clean-shaven face had an almost boyish quality to it. He was six and a half feet tall and was extremely muscular. While growing up everyone told him he had the face of David, but the body of Goliath. His skin was very pale, like someone who was deathly ill, but he was, in fact, in excellent health. He had a head of messy spiky blond hair that was so light it was almost white. Casimir had small pink scars all over his face and hands. His eyes were an intense gray.

He had on a long gray coat filled with countless holes and patches, as well a black buttoned shirt that was missing half its buttons. He wore brown pants, which had a hole in the right pant leg, leaving his knee completely exposed. Casimir finished touching the pieces of broken glass and put his hands in his coat pockets. Melvin stomped his foot in the snow and pointed at Casimir. "I bought this vase for my wife and you're going to pay me back for it, you dumb Polack!"

"You didn't buy that vase for your wife."

"What?"

Casimir sighed and wiped some snow from his hair. "You bought it for your mistress. She's had her eyes on it for quite some time. If you don't want me to tell your wife about your unfaithfulness, you'll let this matter drop and let me be on my way."

Melvin snickered, "Why would my wife believe the word of a complete stranger?"

"Why would a complete stranger lie to her?"

Melvin made his hands into fists as he shouted. "If you don't pay me back for the vase and stay away from my wife, I'll go to the police and tell them that your wife has been working as a prostitute. They won't hesitate to throw her in jail because everyone knows that all Catholic women are whores!"

Casimir removed his hands from his pockets and looked side to side and saw that there wasn't a soul around them. "You fought in the Civil War, didn't you Mr. Clay?"

"Not that's any of your business, you filthy papist, but yeah I did. That's how I lost my leg."

"Good. Then I won't feel any guilt for this."

Casimir grabbed Melvin by his shoulders and tossed him into the alleyway. The icy snow scraped his face as he hit the ground. Casimir ripped off Melvin's peg leg and beat him savagely with it. Melvin didn't even have a chance to scream, not that there was anyone around to hear him. Casimir continued bashing Melvin with his peg until he was a bloody mess. Then he threw it aside and wrapped his right hand around Melvin's neck.

He lifted him up and slammed him against the wall. "My Zofia is no whore! She was going to be a nun and dedicate her life to serving our Lord, but she decided to marry me instead, even though I don't deserve her! You're going to apologize for everything you just said or I'm going to kill you!"

Spit and blood poured down from Melvin's mouth as he responded, "There's no way in hell I am apologizing to a brute like you and I ain't afraid to die."

Casimir sneered and crushed Melvin's windpipe. Melvin's body trembled as life left his eyes. Casimir let go of Melvin's neck, and his corpse slumped to the ground. The snow would cover it before the day was through. Casimir checked to make sure he hadn't gotten any blood on him and then put his hands back in his pockets and went on his way.

***

Casimir felt no remorse for what he had just done. The man was an adulterer; his wife was probably better off without him. Besides, he had given Melvin a choice and Melvin had made his choice. Casimir's knuckles ached from the cold. He worked on the docks, and for some reason they had let him go early today. Since it was close to Christmas, he decided to walk around and look at all the Christmas presents he wanted to buy his wife. He actually didn't have the money to buy them now, but he vowed to get them next year.

That's what he had been promising himself every Christmas in the three years he'd been in this country. However, he was still broke. He and Zofia were living in a rundown apartment, the size of a broom closet. They had a baby due next year and he couldn't imagine bringing up a child in such squalor. Casimir had hoped the church would help him out. However, all the cathedrals and smaller Catholic churches belonged to the Irish and Italians, and they had no desire to aid him because of his Slavic blood. They also wouldn't give the Poles permission to build their own national churches.

The local WASP population harassed and insulted him every chance they got. If he had been a weaker man, someone would have assaulted him by now. His wife was afraid to walk on the street without him by her side because of what she feared they'd do to her. Casimir wished more than anything that he and Zofia were back in Poland, but they could never return, not after all that had happened.

A scruffy dog ran up to Casimir. It was some sort of sheepdog mixture. Casimir bent down to pet the friendly mutt. The dog had a worn-out collar around its neck, and Casimir touched it with his thumb. Immediately his mind was assaulted with images like those movies he and his wife would go see whenever they could scrape up enough money.

He saw the collar being made, delivered to a shop, and then sold to the man who put it around this dog's neck and never took it off.

It was this way with every object that Casimir touched. To him, every man-made thing was like a living creature whose life story he knew as well as his own. That was the gift he had been born with and had been shocked growing up that no one else could do it. Although it wasn't exactly unknown, it was called psychometry, the psychic ability to know any object's history by reading its energy fields. However, it was something that only the spiritualists believed in, while the scientists sneered at it.

The dog licked Casimir's hands and after giving the pooch a nice long scratch between the ears, the dog went on its merry way. Casimir had found the animals of Vindicator City to be far kinder than most of its human inhabitants. This city was a sprawling mass of factories, smokestacks, and skyscrapers. It had several parks, but the ones he could go to were littered with trash and infested with rats.

Casimir passed by an old rundown bar. It had broken windows, dusty floors, and a barely attached wooden door with some flickers of green paint still on it. He touched the broken door, and images of everyone who had ever passed through, or banged against that door, filled his mind. He remembered his youth growing up in a small village in Poland, working at his father's pub, dreaming of inheriting it one day. His father had wanted him to have a better future and make something of himself. Now he was in the land of dreams and opportunities and was far poorer than he had ever been back home.

A black carriage driven by two white draft horses appeared in front of Casimir. The driver was a thin man who had golden buttons on his coat and a dandy mustache.

He turned to Casimir and softly said, "Mr. Fairchild requests your presence, Mr. Stazek."

"Which one?"

"Vernon Fairchild, he's the reason you were let off from work early today. Now may you please step into the carriage sir?"

If it weren't for the bitter cold, Casimir would have sworn he was dreaming. The Fairchild family was the wealthiest in Vindicator City, as well as its founders. Vernon Fairchild was the patriarch. He owned every business, factory, bank, and industry in the entire city, including the docks. A huge philanthropist, there wasn't a hospital, museum, school, or public facility that did not have his name on it. Meeting Vernon Fairchild was something Casimir never dreamed of.

Now Vernon Fairchild summoned him, and since he was the boss of Casimir's boss's boss, he decided he shouldn't be kept waiting. Casimir stepped into the carriage and found it empty. He thought someone would explain the details of the meeting he was to have with Vernon, but apparently, he would find that out on arrival. Casimir sat down on the red leather seat and instantly found it more comfortable than his own bed. He was tempted to give into his own weariness and take a nap.

But Casimir wasn't going to do that. Life had taught him to always expect the worst and always be on your toes. He knew where Vernon Fairchild lived, even though he had never been there. If this carriage headed in any other direction, then Casimir knew he needed to bolt. He had made enemies back home in Poland. Even though he was sure they had not followed him to America, if they had, there was not any trick they wouldn't use to get him. The towers, shops, and apartments all faded, replaced by wide-open green fields. Casimir had never seen so much grass in his entire life. The Fairchild family owned eighty acres, upon which they had built several mansions.

As the carriage went up a hill, Casimir's eyes beheld the grandest mansion of them all. The Fairchild Manor was built in a Châteauesque style. It had a light white roof and was a lovely shade of cerulean blue. It had hundreds of windows with stained glass depicting the entire two-hundred-year history of the Fairchild family and their founding of Vindicator City. Casimir's wife worked as a maid and she had been to the Fairchild manor a dozen times, but her description of it had not done the building justice.

There were armed guards around the mansion and on its balconies. From what Zofia had told him, they were all ex-military and former Pinkerton agents. The head of Vernon Fairchild's security detail was apparently something very different and Casimir was looking forward to seeing if those rumors were true. The carriage came to a stop and Casimir got out. He approached the mansion's big blue door and a servant showed Casimir inside. Another servant came to take Casimir's coat, and another came to take him to meet Vernon Fairchild.

As they walked on the blood red carpet that covered every inch of the mansion's floor, Casimir noticed that there were countless paintings on the walls. They were of women from all levels of society and they were all dead and rotting. Many of them seemed to have had their throats slashed and their eyes gouged out. Zofia had mentioned that Vernon owned a lot of disturbing paintings, but this was far more twisted than anything Casimir had imagined. Casimir asked, "These are really odd paintings to say the least; who painted them?"

The servant replied. "Every painting that adorns Mr. Fairchild's home is one he painted with his own brush."

"I see."

Not much was known about Vernon Fairchild; he never gave interviews and rarely spoke in public. All Casimir knew about him was that he had no children and was a lifelong bachelor. He had plenty of nieces and nephews so he wouldn't lack an heir when he passed.

The servant brought Casimir to Mr. Fairchild's study and opened the door for him. "Mr. Stazek, Sir."

Casimir entered the study. Vernon Fairchild sat in a purple chair facing the fireplace. Casimir had his gaze fixed on the man standing right next to him. Zofia had been correct; the rumors were true. The head of Mr. Fairchild's bodyguards, who was always by his side, was an honest to God samurai. The samurai wore full body armor, consisting of a helmet, sleeve shields, a hinged iron cuirass, and a divide skirt suspended from the breastplate. The samurai was armed with a katana and a Tantō knife, both of which were sheathed in black ivory.

The samurai showed no emotion. His eyes were as empty a dead man. Suddenly, Vernon Fairchild rose up and ran over to Casimir. Vernon was fifty-two years old. He dressed all in black and had a large top hat; his face was adorned with white mutton chops and eyes full of glee. He grasped Casimir's hand and delightfully shouted, "Good evening, Mr. Stazek, I am Mr. Fairchild, and you have no idea how much pleasure it gives me to finally make your acquaintance."

It took a few moments for Casimir to return Vernon's handshake. "I am happy to meet you too Sir and I want to personally thank you for the great kindness you showed my wife. Unlike all her other employers, you let her take breaks and gave her sweet cakes and lemonade."

"Would you like some lemonade? No, it's too cold for that. How about some brandy?"

"That would be wonderful, thanks."

"I must say Mr. Stazek, despite your thick accent, your English is excellent."

Vernon tapped the samurai on the shoulder as he continued speaking. "It's much better than Akira's, and he's been with me for twenty-three years."

"I'm a fast learner." Casimir replied.

Servants spun around Vernon's chair and brought Casimir a chair as well. They sat by the fireplace sipping the finest brandy Casimir had ever tasted. Casimir fingered his glass. "This brandy is way better than anything we ever had back in the old country."

"I'll have to take your word for that since I have never had anything from Poland. Now I need you to hand your glass back to me, because when you see what's behind you, you're going to drop it."

Casimir handed his glass over to Vernon and glanced backwards. He became as white as volcanic ash as he shot up to his feet. "Christ! What in God's holy name is that?"

An animal wandered into Vernon's study. A gigantic feline, who from nose to tail was at least nine feet long and weighed seven hundred pounds. The beast was male, and his fur was a very light brown with faint black strips running through it. He had a small mane of chestnut brown hair and deep orange eyes. His teeth and claws were as sharp as knives; this thing could tear a man's limbs off with ease. Casimir had seen lions and tigers before at the Vindicator City Zoo, but they were like house cats compared to this behemoth.

The gigantic feline strode to Akira and lay at his feet. Akira rubbed the beast between his ears making him purr. Casimir felt the need to cross himself as his gazed fixed on this wondrous creature. Vernon smiled and had the last sip of his brandy. "His name is Heraclius and he's a liger."

"Liger?"

Vernon put his glass down. "You know I own the Vindicator City Circus, right?"

"You own everything in this city."

"True, anyway Mr. Barns, the circus manager had a lion named Leonidas, and one day he purchased a tigress named Alexandria. Now instead of getting her own cage, he decided to put her in the same pen as Leonidas. At first, they didn't know what to make of each other, but then they got along well, really well."

Casimir sat back down and ran his hand over his face. "So, he's a hybrid then. Like a mule."

Akira grunted, "Heraclius . . . is . . . like a son to me. Don't dishonor him."

"Is he sterile?" Casimir asked.

"Yes," Vernon replied. "But he doesn't seem to know that. Which is why I have his sisters in a cottage nearby, so he can satisfy his urges with them."

"I didn't need to know that, but that still proves my point. He's like a mule. Mules serve a purpose; I don't see what purpose ligers serve. I mean lions and tigers don't even meet in the wild, so his existence is unnatural."

A servant arrived with tea to wash down the brandy. While Akira tickled Heraclius and told him funny things in Japanese, Vernon sipped his tea. "You've read the Bible. God gave man dominion over nature and every animal that lives in this world."

Casimir replied. "That authority is to be used wisely."

Vernon took a sip of his tea. "Oh, I plan to use Heraclius very wisely. It's been a while since your wife's been here, but I recall she's a lot younger than you."

"Yes. She's fifteen years younger than me."

Vernon stroked his mutton chops and grinned, "I guess that doesn't make much of a difference. Despite your scars, you look like a Greek god and you are probably as well-endowed as a horse."

Casimir shifted uncomfortably in his chair. "Right, anyway it's wonderful to be meeting you Mr. Fairchild. But can you tell me why you summoned me here?"

Vernon set his teacup aside and placed his hands on his knees. "Okay yes, I guess it's time we got down to business. Tell me, what do you know about *The Sons of Chaos*?"

"Everyone knows that they blew up the mayor's place last month and killed him. They are an anarchist group blowing up all places of authority, both religious and secular, worldwide. They've bombed dozens of churches, banks, and government buildings in this state alone."

"What if I told you that they have a leader known as the Elder One who is holding a gathering in Vindicator City."

"Isn't it hypocritical for anarchists to have a leader?" Casmir asked.

"Indeed, it is," Vernon responded, "I brought you here tonight because I want you to infiltrate their little get together and kill him."

Casimir rubbed his left knuckles against his forehead. "Why me?"

"To me it makes perfect sense to send a terrorist to kill a terrorist. I know you were a top member of *The Winged Hussars*."

Casimir tightly grasped his chair arms as he harshly replied, "We weren't terrorists. We were Polish nationalists and Russia was our only enemy. We only attacked military targets and everything we did was so Poland could be a free country again. The Sons of Chaos have nothing in common with us!"

"Your wife was also a member, wasn't she?"

Casimir was very uncomfortable with Vernon bringing up his wife. Nevertheless, he answered, "Yes, that's how we met. She was a nurse who patched us up when we came back from our missions. She saved lives while I took them. But I bet you already knew all that."

Vernon grinned and tapped his fingertips together. "I always do background checks on those who I conduct business with. I know everything you did for The Winged Hussars and why you joined them. But I don't think you wish to speak of that."

"No, I don't."

Casimir could not bear to speak of what had made him the man he was, but the memories flashed through his mind like venom gushing into a wound. Casmir had once lived a peaceful and unremarkable life as the eldest of seven brothers until his twentieth winter. There were five Cossack soldiers who frequented his father's pub. They never paid for their drinks and tended to break many things whenever they visited. One snowy night they came after the pub had closed for the evening. Casimir had been helping his father clean up when the Cossacks arrived. They drank far more than usual. Casimir lost count of the all glasses and bottles they shattered on the floor. That night, Casimir's father had enough. He demanded that the Cossacks pay for everything they broke.

The leader of the Cossacks just laughed, drew his pistol, and shot Casimir's father in the head. Casimir saw nothing but red, as he killed all five Cossacks with his bare hands. After he came to his senses, he told the village elders what had happened. They advised him to flee until things settled down. Russian soldiers arrived to exact their vengeance. They decided since Casimir wasn't there, to punish his mother for giving birth to him. They raped her on his father's grave and forced his brothers to watch. When Casimir found out, he joined The Wing Hussars and fought the Russians for fourteen years. His brothers joined him at one time or another. Eventually, the Russians eliminated The Wing Hussars. Casimir's brothers were all either dead or rotting in a Siberian prison. As for Casimir's mother, she fled into the woods and no one had seen her since.

Casimir had hoped he could leave his past behind in America. But he now realized that no man could escape his sins no matter how far he fled. Vernon stroked his mutton chops. "You will of course be well compensated for this little errand. How does ten thousand dollars sound?"

Ten thousand dollars was more money than Casimir had ever thought he would make in his life. He could quit his god-awful job at the docks, buy a nice house with a backyard, and fill it with all the things he and his wife had ever wanted. He could purchase the abandoned bar he walked by earlier and have it completely renovated. Zofia could also leave her job and work there. Casimir would let her take off whenever she wished. He also had several friends who wouldn't mind working for him. Most important of all, this money would ensure that their unborn child would live a good life.

Casimir still had questions. "Sounds great. That money will be a godsend to me and my family, but I need to know something?"

"What is it?"

"The Elder One needs to die, there's no question about that. But why do you want him dead?"

Vernon replied, "I am sure you know that I was a huge contributor of the late mayor and I really don't like it when my investments get blown up."

"I'll take half now and the other half when it's done."

A hard look appeared in Vernon's eyes as he responded. "I never pay a cent for a job until it's finished Mr. Stazek."

"Fine, when do you want me to do it?"

"Tonight."

Casimir almost fell out of his chair but managed to keep his composure. "When The Wing Hussars carried out an assassination or any other operation, we always planned for weeks, sometimes months in advance."

Vernon nodded, "I understand, that is why I have done all the planning already. Also, you can take comfort knowing that you will not be carrying out this errand alone. There are three others who will help you. Their code names are agent Summer, agent Spring, and agent Fall. You will be agent Winter."

"I usually tend to know those who I carry out a mission with."

"Yes, that's why your little band of nationalists was crushed."

Casimir sighed and ran his hands over his face. "You're asking me to carry out a mission without any time to prepare and to work with people I don't know. This sounds like it's going to be a complete mess. Make no mistake, I can probably get in and do what I need to do, but getting out, that's always the tricky part. I feel it will be damn near impossible under these conditions."

"Are you backing out?"

"Not a chance. But if I'm taking such a substantial risk, I want double what you offered."

"Done. When you are finished, would you like the twenty thousand dollars in cash, a check, or gold?"

"Doesn't matter. Just give me your word that as long as the Elder One dies, you'll give the money to my wife, if I'm not around to claim it."

"She'll be a well-off widow, won't she? Then maybe she can marry a younger man or an older one, if he catches her fancy."

Casimir could not shake the fact that every time Vernon talked about his wife, his skin crawled. He dug his fingers into the arms of his chair. "So, what's the plan?"

Vernon tapped his fingers together. "The Sons of Chaos are meeting in that unopened warehouse near the textile plant. You know, the one that's going to close down because of the child labor laws that just got passed."

"I know where that is. But how do I infiltrate it? I mean is there a password I should I know or some sort of card or other totem I should have?"

"The Sons of Chaos all have the letter A carved on their right heel. Akira will lightly engrave it on your flesh. By the time you arrive, it will heal up enough that they won't recognize how fresh it is. If not, I'm sure you can fib or threaten your way through."

Casimir took off his right shoe and put his foot on the footrest. "There isn't an inch of my body the Russians didn't leave a scar on, so I have no problem with the bottom of my foot matching the rest of me."

Vernon stroked his mutton chops and grinned, "Every scar on you is like a beauty mark that makes you more desirable. I bet your wife really admires them."

Casimir didn't know how to respond to that. He just let the samurai do his work. Akira drew his knife and carved an A into Casimir's heel as though he was writing calligraphy. The liger lurked and sniffed the air. A quick look from Akira made Heraclius go back to resting his head on his paws. Casimir realized that Heraclius was familiar with the scent of human blood, and he had a suspicion of what Vernon used him for. When Akira finished, Casimir put his shoe back on and paced around Vernon's study. His foot felt no different than before it had been cut. Truly Akira was a master of the blade. "Now, that's done with, what's the next step?"

"You're going to step back into the carriage you came in. It will go to the textile mill and you'll make your way to the warehouse. You get in, you infiltrate, and you terminate. The three other agents will assist and ensure you get out." Vernon responded

"I don't like putting my trust in people I don't know, but it is what it is."

"Akira will show you out. It was an immense pleasure to meet you Mr. Stazek."

Casimir got up. He took a few steps toward the liger, but then turned and headed to the door. The moment Casimir had his hand on the doorknob he glanced at Vernon. "Since you seemingly know everything about my life, do you know about my psychometry?" He asked.

Vernon smirked, "I know all about your talent and let's say I have seen things far stranger."

Casimir left Vernon's study with Akira by his side. While they were strolling down the hallway Akira suddenly spoke, "So was my master everything you thought he would be?"

"Boy, your English has sure improved."

"I don't like the way that foul language tastes on my tongue, so I speak it as little as possible. But I must know, what do you think of him?"

"Mr. Fairchild is very eccentric to say the least. But you've served him for twenty-three years, and you know the kind of man he is better than I ever will."

Akira stopped in his tracks. "A samurai gives his master undying loyalty regardless of what kind of person he is. All I'll say is that in serving Mr. Fairchild I have killed forty-nine men, which amounts to the same number of years that I have drawn breath. Tell me, before you came to this country, how many Russians did you kill?"

Casimir sighed, "Not enough. While we are on this cheery subject, how many lives has your liger taken?"

Akira grinned, which made Casmir shudder because the samurai had the face of one who should never smile. "None yet, but I'm training him for it. Heraclius's first kill needs to be someone worthy of him."

Casimir and Akira proceeded in silence until they made it to the mansion's front door. Akira handed over his sheathed Tantō knife to Casimir. "I heard you are good with knives. I know you'll use it well."

Casimir took the knife from Akira's grasp and a torrent of memories immediately filled his mind. He could envision that Akira's mother had used this knife to kill herself after his father had been ordered to commit suicide and that Akira had kept the knife by his side since he was a boy and never used it in combat. He kept waiting for the day when he would have to use it to take his own life. When the samurai fell, he had almost used the knife to kill himself, but could not go through with it. However, he kept trying to until he met Vernon. Casimir struggled not to toss the knife to the ground. He had been taught that suicide was an unforgiveable sin in the eyes of the Lord since there was no way that one could repent for it. Even at his lowest points Casimir had never considered it an option. Casimir did not hide the repulsion in his trembling voice. "Your own mother . . . and you . . . wanted to? How can the Japanese people take their own lives so easily?"

"So, your gift is true. I'm glad I could see it for myself. You should know Casimir, that in Japan, taking one's own life is the most honorable thing a person can do." Akira replied.

"Where I come from, it's the most dishonorable thing a person can do."

"Well Japan is currently in the process of becoming the most powerful nation in all of Asia. And as you yourself said, Poland isn't even a country anymore."

Casimir tucked the knife into his pants, retrieved his coat, left The Fairchild Manor, and stepped back into the carriage. The horses trotted to Casimir's destination and he leaned back against the carriage seat and sighed. Earlier, he lost control and killed someone who didn't deserve it. Now he had the opportunity to kill someone who did. Casimir knew that would not make things right with his Creator, but at least he could prove to God that his life was not a mistake.

Casimir touched his newly acquired knife. He wondered how he would use it to kill The Elder One. Stabbing him through his spinal cord seemed the best course of action, or he could grab The Elder One and slit his throat. He might just break The Elder One's neck and use the knife to carve his way out. Casimir had killed many high-ranking Russian military officials in such a manner. Most probably they had not deserved to die in such a grisly way, but The Elder One did. Blowing up churches while they were full of worshipers was pure evil. Casimir could not imagine why anyone would do that.

These anarchists were poison and they were making the civilized world a mess. Hopefully, killing The Elder One would weaken them. Casimir knew from personal experience that the only way to permanently destroy an organization was to kill or imprison all its members. That's what the Russians had done to The Wing Hussars. Casimir wondered if America would do the same to The Sons of Chaos. The priest in his village had taught him that all men were descended from Cain. He had murdered his brother Abel before he had any children. Therefore, all men were murderers at heart, even though most men were not killers. There was not a man alive who could not say he wished someone dead.

It didn't matter where one went; it was like that all over the world. Casimir realized how foolish it was for thinking that America would be any different. The carriage went back into the city. It was late at night now and there were few people wandering the streets. Casimir wondered if his wife was at home. He thought she was probably still working. He closed his eyes and got some much needed sleep. He awoke when the carriage came to a stop. He stepped out of the carriage, and as the horses trotted away, he looked at the closed down textile mill.

When his wife told him she was pregnant, his biggest fear was that their child would have to work in a place like that. Now thanks to Mr. Fairchild, that terrible possibility was no more. The frosty night air sent a chill down Casimir's spine. He could not shake the feeling that he was being watched. As he made his way down to the warehouse, he suddenly felt the muzzle of a gun pressed against the back of his neck.

A voice behind him said, "Flinch, I'll put you down."

Casimir raised his hands. "No one's ever been able to sneak up on me before."

"I have quiet feet."

Casimir sighed, "What do you want?"

"Are you Agent Winter?"

"I am. I take it you're on Mr. Fairchild's payroll?"

Casimir heard the man behind him slip his gun back into his holster. "He's offered me something far more important than money. I'm Agent Summer."

Casimir turned around and saw the only man ever able to sneak up behind him. Agent Summer had two colt revolvers in leather holsters and a Winchester rifle slung around his back, a small satchel at his side, and an ammo belt around his waist. He wore blue pants, a red shirt, brown vest, and black boots, all of which were covered in dirt. Casmir had seen homeless men cleaner than this man. Agent Summer was a man of forty years. He looked just as youthful as Casmir, although Casmir had far better teeth. In fact, Agent Summer's teeth were so yellow and misshapen, that Casmir was sure he had never been to a dentist once in his life.

Casimir chuckled, "You look like someone straight out one of those dime store novel westerns my wife and I like to read."

Agent Summer thumped his hand against his chest. "I'm a thousand times more genuine than anything written in those sorry excuses for books. Even the ones written about me were crap."

"So, I take it you're someone pretty famous then?"

"More like infamous." Casimir replied.

From the corner of his eye Casimir saw an ax swing towards his head. He grabbed it and flipped its wielder onto the ground. His would-be assailant was a nineteen-year-old girl dressed in an incredibly ugly dark blue dress. The girl herself had a big forehead and a grubby face. As Casimir ripped the ax from her grasp, a man dressed in a military uniform with a Colt M1900 holstered at his side appeared. The man was about twenty-six years old, had a crooked nose and very badly cut hair. He rushed over to them waving his hands shouting, "Easy, easy now, I believe there's been some misunderstanding. I am Agent Fall and that lass on the ground is Agent Spring. We're all on the same team, so there's no need for violence."

Casimir let the girl get up to her feet as he tightened his grip around the ax. "I have no idea who Agent Summer is. But by God, I know who you and this insane bitch are, Major Lenny West! You're a war criminal who slaughtered a dozen monks in The Philippines! You made them get on their knees and put them down like dogs!"

Major Lenny West rubbed his nose and grinned, "Don't the papers have anything better to print? Those monks insulted me for being a Freemason, so I silenced them permanently. The reason I'm with you all tonight is because Mr. Fairchild promised that he could make all those charges disappear and have me returned to active duty."

Casimir snarled, "That's if you live through this night. Miss Banks, I heard you were in the madhouse. How did you get out?"

Carrie Banks replied, "Mr. Fairchild owns the madhouse, so he just strolled in and signed my release papers. In exchange I'm putting my ax to good and proper use."

Casimir twisted the ax. "You used this ax to murder your parents. You gave your stepfather one whack on the head to finish him off, but your mother didn't even have a face left. My wife worked for your parents and had the misfortune of finding their corpses. She's seen dead bodies before, but never like that."

Casimir seemed on the verge of tears as Carrie tapped her puffy cheeks and responded, "Oh, wait, I think I remember your wife. She's that silly Polack woman. I recall her being as dumb as a cow. So, it makes sense she'd be married to a bull."

Casimir stomped his foot against the ground and shouted at the top of his lungs. "I swear to God if you weren't a woman, I'd rip your damn spine out and strangle you to death with it!"

"I don't think that's even possible." Lenny responded.

Casimir glared at him. "Do you want to find out?"

Agent Summer stepped in with his hands raised. "Whoa, whoa let's all settle down here."

The cowboy swiped out a black ivory snuffbox from his satchel. "Mr. Fairchild gave this to me since he's getting a new one tomorrow. I say we all take a sniff and chill out."

Casimir responded, "You expect me to break bread with a girl who murdered her own parents and a man who executed men of the cloth? I bet you're just a robber who killed people for money."

"I only stole cattle, never cash, and when I robbed, I never took a life. Nevertheless, I've put a lot of men in the ground. I'm a very, very, bad man and I know you are too, pal. Otherwise, you wouldn't be here with us." The cowboy replied.

Casimir dropped Carrie's ax to the ground. As she retrieved it, he walked up to Agent Summer and gently touched the tips of his fingers against his satchel. Agent Summer had possessed it for a long time, and it showed Casimir everything he needed to know. He took a step back and gasped, "Oh my God, you're Billy the Kid. That's impossible!"

Lenny and Carrie stood flabbergasted as Agent Summer grinned and rubbed his stubble. "I haven't been called that in a long time and I'm too old for that name now. You all can call me by my real name, Henry McCarty, and I don't think you've given me yours."

Casimir's hands twitched in excitement and glee as he did his best not to act like an excited schoolboy. "I'm Casimir Stazek and how could you still be alive? Pat Garrett killed you?"

Henry spat on the ground. "That lying rat and his friends say they did. The truth is, by the time they got to where I was holed up, I was already gone. I fled to Mexico, and when Pat realized I wasn't coming back, he told everyone he got the drop on me in order to reap fame and fortune that he didn't deserve."

"Why are you back now?" Casimir asked

Henry put his snuffbox back in his satchel. "Since I fled the states I've been working as a bounty hunter in Mexico. Mr. Fairchild tracked me down and got me to do his dirty work by promising me a full presidential pardon. You know, he's friends with everyone in Washington."

Casimir smiled, "He's friends with everyone. Wait! I should be able to smuggle my knife in, but how will you guys get your weapons through?"

"We will improvise." Lenny replied.

The four of them made their way to the warehouse. As they walked, Carrie sang the *"I'm a Little Teapot"* to herself and Lenny whistled. Casimir could not decide which one was more annoying. Nor, could he believe he was walking side by side with the greatest outlaw who ever lived. If Zofia were here, she would be swooning at the sight. "My wife is such a fan of yours, that if our unborn child turns out to be a boy, she wants to name him Billy or William. Although, I hope I can convince her to give him a good Polish name and have Billy as a middle name."

"You sound almost like you're jealous." Henry responded.

Casimir ran his left hand through his hair and sighed, "I had no reason to be jealous of a dead man. Now I don't know. I'm pretty sure you are not someone who minds going after married women."

Henry gave Casimir a pat on the back. "Yep that's true. But you have nothing to worry about pal. Slavic women aren't my type, I'm a Mexican lady loving man."

It was snowing by the time they made it to the warehouse. Casimir noticed that even though it was a new building, it was poorly made. There were cracks everywhere and missing windows; no one had even bothered to give it a coat of paint. It had a big wooden door, which looked like something that belonged on an ancient castle. There was a gingered haired hobo sitting on a stool by the door. His clothes looked patched together by rags and he had a big unkept busy beard. He was drinking out of a green wine bottle.

Upon noticing Casimir and his comrades, he put his wine bottle down and said, "Show me your feet."

Everyone took one of their shoes off and showed the carved letter A in their flesh. The hobo didn't even bother to check if they were fresh or not. Casimir put his shoe back on. "Are you the only security here?"

The hobo took a sip of wine. "That's right."

Henry said, "You do realize we all came armed, right?"

The hobo replied, "Doesn't matter, The Elder One is waiting. Allow me to let you in."

The hobo opened the door to the warehouse. There was nothing but pure darkness on the other side. The four of them walked inside and the door closed behind them. It reminded Casimir of the sound of a coffin closing. He could not see anything, but suddenly, the warehouse lit up. Two fire pits in the warehouse's center made it as bright as day and The Elder One stood between them. He was dressed in a blood red cloak. He wore black gloves and black boots, and an old chain around his neck, and had iron rings on all his fingers. On his face he wore the skull of a long dead deer as a mask. Casimir could not figure out how he could possibly see out of it. He tightened his grip around his knife. "Why do I have the feeling that we have been set up?"

"Relax," Henry replied. "It's just him and that hobo at the door. I can end all of this with just one shot."

The Elder One emitted a deep and unnatural laugh that sounded like a screaming eel. It made Casimir feel that he was at the start of a nightmare. The Elder One spread out his arms as he shouted, "Welcome to your doom, my friends."

"Yep this was definitely a set up." Casimir stated.

Lenny pulled out his gun. "To hell with this!"

Lenny shot three bullets into The Elder One. They all went through him and found themselves embedded in the wall. He didn't flinch and no blood leaked from the bullet holes in his clothes. The Elder One clapped his hands and blazing blue fire appeared between his four victims and the door. Now they had no way out. The Elder One pointed at Lenny. "You're the first to die!"

The Elder One raised his right arm as though he was conducting an orchestra. Lenny levitated into the air while shouting curses that Casmir was sure that not even the devil would say. When Lenny was almost touching the ceiling of the warehouse, The Elder One moved his hands as though he was stretching invisible dough and ripped Lenny in half. His blood and entrails splattered the warehouse floor. For the first time in his life, Casmir found himself too terrified to move. Carrie screamed like a banshee and swiped her ax at the Elder One. It went right through him, as though she was swinging her ax at smoke. She kept waving her ax at him until she was breathing deeply, and every inch of her body was covered in sweat. The Elder One laughed and flicked her ax from her grasp as if it was a toothpick. Then he put his hands on her head and screamed.

It was like the screeching of a thousand burning bats. Carrie's eyes melted out of her skull like spring snow. Blood seeped out of her empty eye sockets as she fell to her knees, helpless. Henry reloaded and fired a dozen more bullets through the Elder One's cloak and they did nothing. Then Casimir threw a wild punch at The Elder One; he expected it to go right through him, but it made contact. The Elder One was knocked almost to the other side of the warehouse. His mask flew off his face.

The Elder One wiped some dust from his knees and stood up. He was an absolute monster, more horrible than anything that had graced Casimir's darkest dreams. This abomination had slimy dark green skin, an octopus like head, and its face was a disgusting mess of tentacles. But it was the eyes, the glowing red eyes that terrified Casmir the most. There was nothing, but twisted hate and fury in those eyes and Casmir knew that The Elder One was truly something that could not have been created by God.

The Elder One removed his gloves, revealing his hideous hands, including fingernails that looked like the teeth of a great white shark. Two bat like wings shot out of The Elder One's back. The tips of those wings had dark black spikes on them. The Elder One smirked and turned his dreaded gaze to Henry. As he made his left hand into a fist, Henry gasped, "I can't breathe, I can't breathe!"

Henry clasped his hands around his throat and fell on his knees. The Elder One pointed at Casmir and shouted, "You're the one with the blood of the seraphim in your veins. My powers won't work on you. So, I'll have to rip your heart out with my bare hands."

Casimir pulled out his knife and tilted his arm back. It had been a long time since he had thrown a knife, but he figured that creature's head was too big a target to miss. The Elder One charged at Casimir and Casimir threw his knife. The knife flew through the air and buried itself in the center of The Elder One's head. He collapsed onto the ground as dark green blood oozed from his head. His body spasmed a few times, then he lay perfectly motionless in the stillness of death.

His body vanished in a puff of purple smoke and only his clothes and jewelry remained. The fire by the door disappeared. Henry lay on the ground blue in the face; he gulped air and sat up. Carrie just lay down moaning on the cold floor. Casimir retrieved his knife and bent down. His hands shook wildly as he clenched the Elder One's chain and robes. He could not understand what he was seeing. However, he did understand that the Elder One had never been the true leader of The Sons of Chaos.

Casimir let go of the Elder One's things and helped Henry back up onto his feet. "Vernon Fairchild was behind everything. The Elder One . . . whatever that monster was, he somehow created it and every terrorist attack The Elder One ordered was at Mr. Fairchild's direction."

Henry took a few deep breaths and responded, "So, he lured us here for The Elder One to kill us. I think that's kind of overkill. Also, how do you know all that?"

Casimir sighed, "I have a gift, that when I touch an object, I know everything about it. I figured out who you were when I touched your satchel."

"Well that makes about as much sense as what just happened. Why don't we see if that hobo is still around so we can ask him some questions?" Henry replied.

Casimir cracked his knuckles. "Yeah let's do that."

He and Henry walked out of the warehouse. Carrie heard them leaving as she groped for something to touch. She was surrounded by a sea of darkness and there was no way out. "My eyes are gone. Please Casimir, Henry you can't just leave me here. I'll die."

Henry shrugged his shoulders. "It's your call chief."

Casimir stroked his chin and grinned. "Don't worry, Carrie you'll get your sight back when you burn in hell."

"No, you can't do this to me! You sons of bitches, damn you, damn you!"

If Carrie still had eyes, she would have been crying them out. Casimir and Henry left the warehouse. They moved some wooden crates against the door, ensuring that Carrie would meet her end in that ill-starred warehouse. Henry spoke through chatting teeth, "That was a really cold move pal."

Casimir's hands shook. He could not tell if it was from the cold or the horror he had just experienced. "A stepfather is a stepfather, but she murdered her own mother. Maybe God can forgive that, I can't."

Henry laughed and patted Casimir on the back. "I take it you were a real momma's boy, right? Don't worry pal, I was too."

Casimir and Henry went looking for the gingered haired hobo. Using Henry's tracking skills, they found him very quickly. He was leaning against an old burnt down shack, still drinking out of his green wine bottle. Casimir sauntered up to the hobo, snatched the wine bottle from his grasp, and smashed it against the poor man's face. The gingered headed hobo shrieked as he fell to the snow-covered ground. His bloody face had pieces of glass embedded in it. Casimir repeatedly kicked the hobo in his chest. "Did you know what that thing was? Did you have any idea what the accursed creature could do?"

"Stop it Casmir! You're killing him." Henry shouted.

Henry shoved Casmir away and bent down by the hobo. He put a caring hand on the hobo's shoulder. "I think you should start giving us some answers before my friend loses his temper again. Can you start by telling me your name?"

The hobo spat out a mouthful of blood. "I'm Larry Luck and I'm not a member of The Sons of Chaos. Mr. Fairchild said he would make me his grounds keeper if I waited for the four of you to arrive here and disposed of your bodies when it was all over."

"Did you know what The Elder One was?" Henry asked.

Larry nodded, "I knew he was a monster who had some connection to Mr. Fairchild and that it obeyed everything he said."

"And you never thought about going to the police?" Henry asked.

Larry grunted in pain as tears ran down his face and landed on his snowflake-covered beard. He held his broken ribs. "They wouldn't believe me and even if they did, it wouldn't matter. The Fairchild family controls the police; they control everyone in this city!"

"You could have still warned us." Henry calmly stated.

More tears wetted Larry's beard as he sobbed. "Please have pity on me good sirs. I lost everything in the war."

"What war?" Casimir questioned.

"The one against Japan."

Casimir and Henry burst into laughter. Despite how awful this night had been, the absurdity of what Larry had just said made Casimir laugh harder than he had in a long time. It took a while for both of them to stop and catch their breaths. Casimir rested his hands on his knees. "That's the most ridiculous thing I have ever heard! The United States and The Empire of Japan get along swimmingly. The odds of them going to war are about as likely as man flying to the moon."

"You're one sorry lying sack of shit Mr. Luck." Henry snickered

Larry gave a painful sigh. "Well it was worth a shot. Can I go please?"

Henry helped Larry to his feet and dusted the snow off him. "You have until the count of fifty to get out of here."

Larry smiled and started staggering away. After he had taken two steps Henry pulled out his pistol and hollered, "Fifty"

Henry shot Larry through the neck. Larry collapsed on his knees. He pressed his fingers against the hole in this throat. Blood gushed out of it, covering his hands. Larry gave one final gurgle and then died. Casimir kicked his corpse over, while Henry blew on his smoking barrel. "Well it looks like Mr. Luck wasn't that lucky."

"You should have just let me beat him to death instead of wasting that bullet." Casimir responded.

Henry gave Casimir several pats on the back. "There's no such thing as a wasted bullet. I take it you're planning on paying Mr. Fairchild an unexpected visit."

Casimir wiped some snow from his shoulder and nodded. "He is responsible for the deaths of hundreds of innocent lives and he tried to lure me to my death. He created that monster. He needs to die."

Casimir reached in his pockets for his rosary. He realized that he had left it at home and crossed himself while gazing at the starless night sky. "I swear to God and by the souls of my late father and unborn child, I am going to kill that son of a bitch no matter what. Even if it costs me my life."

Henry nodded. "I take it you want my help then?"

"I counted the guards at Mr. Fairchild's mansion. There are at least forty of them and that samurai is more dangerous than a hundred armed men, and that liger! I'm a pretty strong man. To put it lightly, I can take a beating. But I have a pretty good sense that if I go to Mr. Fairchild's mansion, it's a one-way trip."

Henry grinned. He placed a hand on Casmir's shoulder. "It may well be pal, but us outlaws we have a code. If someone saves your life, you owe them one. So, you can count me in. But first things first, we need to get us some horses."

Casimir and Henry broke into the nearby fire station and stole two horses, which they rode bareback. They rode to Mr. Fairchild's estate while the snowy wind blew against them. Casimir no longer felt the cold chill of winter; rage kept him warm. Casimir had never imagined that an American could be so deceitful. Then again, he guessed that if Americans could lie to the Indian tribes and break every treaty they made with them, as well as liberate the Philippines from Spain just to take it for themselves, then it should not come as a surprise that one of them would send him to his death. From Casimir's experiences with Americans, he found Henry to be the most honorable one he had ever meet. He cursed himself for ever thinking that Mr. Fairchild was any better than any of the other WASP elites who ruled this country. In fact, he was the worst of the lot.

When they were on the dirt road leading to the mansion Henry said, "Back when that monster was choking me, it said something about you having the blood of a seraphim. What's that?"

"Haven't you read the good book Henry?"

"After the life I've led, I know I'm going straight to hell when I die. So I don't see much of a point."

"Let's just say if what The Elder One said is true, it explains a lot about my family history and my life."

Casimir and Henry kept on riding until the mansion was in sight. They got off their horses and scurried them way. As they made their approach, Henry grinned and patted his satchel. "Look at what I found in the fire station."

Henry pulled out six sticks of dynamite. Casimir raised an eyebrow. "Why does the fire department have dynamite?"

"Do you really want to know?"

Casimir sighed and shook his head. The two of them continued strolling until they were about a football field length from the mansion, which had six stone columns and two rows of giant shrubs that could be used as cover. Casimir recalled that the guards were armed with Remington Model revolvers and Springfield rifles. At least half of those rifles had bayonets attached to them. He extended his hand. "Light the fuses and give me the bag."

"All of them?"

Casimir nodded as Henry lit the fuses and Casimir threw the bag. It landed in the center of Mr. Fairchild's yard. One of the guards grabbed it; two of his buddies stood right next to him as another two guards passed by them. The guard heard the fuses and tried to the throw the bag away, but it was too late. The dynamite exploded. The remnants of the three guards decorated the yard; the two men closest to them lost an arm and a leg.

Black smoke dispersed, thanks to the whipping wind. All of Mr. Fairchild's men were overwhelmed by chaos as they tried to take up defensive positions while having their vision obscured by the smoke and snow. Casimir and Henry rushed towards them. Henry tossed Casmir his Winchester rifle and drew his colt revolvers. It had been years since Casimir had held a gun, but the rife instantly felt like a part of him. Henry fired his Colts and shot the two coughing guards dead. The bullets started flying as Casimir and Henry managed to get to the columns for cover. The stone pillars chipped apart as the bullets tore through them. Casimir spotted seven sharp shooters on the balcony of the mansion hunching behind several windows. Casimir took them out with seven shots and soon found himself out of ammo. Henry was in no position to give him anymore. It was only a matter of time before they got flanked. Casimir dropped the gun and pulled out his knife. He roared like a wild beast and dashed from cover. A bullet tore across the back of his coat. He threw his knife at the fool who fired it, and the knife buried itself in the in the guard's right eye socket.

Another guard charged at Casimir and thrust his bayonet towards his heart. Casimir jolted backwards and slammed the guard's gun out of his grasp. The guard screamed as Casimir wrapped his hand around his hairy face and threw him against one of the columns. The back of the guard's skull shattered on impact coating the white pillar with blood. Casimir picked up the bayoneted rifle. Two guards fired at him at point blank range, yet all they managed to hit were the tails of his coat.

Casimir impaled one with the bayonet and crushed the other poor soul's windpipe with the butt of his Springfield rifle. Henry leaped from his column and ran to Casimir's side while taking out several more of Mr. Fairchild's guards. Casimir and Henry fired shoulder to shoulder taking out men like they were bottles on a fence. A young blond-haired guard popped up from behind the bushes waving a white flag. "We surrender!"

Casimir and Henry glanced around and saw that only a dozen of their foes remained standing. "Empty all your guns and drop them!" Casimir demanded.

"Then stand in line." Henry added.

The guards complied. They emptied and dropped their weapons, then stood in line like a pack of sardines. Casimir eyed the blond-haired youth, who could not have been a day older than eighteen. "You ever kill a man, boy?"

"No sir . . . I never shot at anyone until tonight." The boy replied.

"See that you never do again. Now go run home and don't look back." Casimir growled.

The blond boy ran through the snow and smoke as though the devil was chasing him. Casimir kept his gun on the guards, but his eyes on the boy until he was long out of sight. He then turned his attention back to all the other guards. Henry rubbed his thumbs against his Colt triggers. A potbellied guard then spoke, "You're going to let the rest of us go too, right?"

Casimir and Henry glanced at one another and grinned. Then they shot all the guards dead. A few tried to run, but they didn't get far before being gunned down. When it was over, Henry and Casimir reloaded their weapons and Casimir retrieved his knife as they made their way into Mr. Fairchild's mansion. All the servants were gone. The empty house filled with paintings of dead women was even more disturbing. Soon they came to the hall that led to Mr. Fairchild's study. Akira and Heraclius guarded the door. The liger growled as Henry and Casimir approached while the samurai smiled. Akira unsheathed his katana. "Well. it took the two of you long enough to get here."

Henry aimed his revolvers at the samurai and scoffed, "Hey yellow man, did you ever hear the saying about bringing a knife to a gun fight?"

"A gun is only better than a sword at five paces, anything less and a sword will win. Also, I don't know why you called me yellow man. I'm not Chinese. I guess we all look the same to you filthy barbarians."

Heraclius sneered at Casimir who found his finger shaking on the trigger. Akira grabbed Heraclius by the scuff of his neck. "I told you, Casimir, that Heraclius's first kill had to be someone worthy of him. He's going to defeat you and devour everything except your heart, which I will give to my master."

Akira bent down and whispered in Heraclius's ear. "This is your moment Heraclius. This is what I have been training you for your whole life. Now attack!"

Akira let go of Heraclius and Heraclius charged at Casimir who fired a bullet that missed and hit the wall. Heraclius tackled Casimir who kept him at bay by thrusting his rifle into the beast's mouth like a giant stick. The liger bit the rifle in two as Casimir rolled away, but the tips of Heraclius's claws cut into his back. Casimir got to his feet. The instant he drew his knife, Heraclius knocked it out of Casimir's right hand and sliced his knuckles down to the bone.

Casimir hissed in pain and punched Heraclius right in the face. Heraclius slammed against the wall. He got up and shook his head. Blood dripped down his left eye socket as he growled at Casimir and prepared to lunge. Casimir also got on all fours. The man and beast roared and attacked with equal savagery.

Henry got off two shots as Akira ran at him and managed to shoot the samurai's helmet off freeing his wild black hair. Akira dodged the other bullet as he swung his sword and cut off three fingers on Henry's left hand, which sent his revolver spinning in the air. Henry squeezed the trigger on his other gun and sent a bullet whizzing by Akira's head as it barely grazed his cheek. Akira bashed Henry's gun from his grasp and slashed his sword across Henry's chest. Henry fell against the wall as Akira swung his sword at him again. Henry used his left arm to block him. Akira cut diagonally through it like butter until his blade was embedded in Henry's elbow. Henry grabbed the blade with his right hand and did everything in his power to keep Akira from pulling it out.

There was not an inch of Casimir's flesh that wasn't bleeding. His shirt and coat had been torn to shreds. As for Heraclius, there was blood dripping from every orifice on his face. Casimir's fists had shattered his rib cage and now he was coughing up blood. Heraclius lunged at Casimir knocking him on his back and dug his claws through Casimir's shoulders. Casimir grabbed Heraclius by his jaws to keep him from tearing his head off. Heraclius's teeth sank into Casimir's hands like needles.

Casimir yelled and kneed Heraclius in his abdomen, knocking the wind out of him. Casimir pushed him away and dove for his knife. The instant he picked it up, Heraclius got to his senses and charged at Casimir who plunged the knife right between the liger's eyes. Blood squirted out of Heraclius's head and got on Casimir's face as he lay dying. Casimir pulled his knife out and threw it at Akira.

Akira sensed the knife coming at him and withdrew his sword from Henry's elbow and batted it to the ground. When he saw Heraclius's lying dead on the floor, he gave an inhuman shriek and rushed at Casimir. Henry picked up one of his revolvers with his good hand and plugged five bullets into Akira's back. Akira collapsed like a piece of timber. He let go of his sword and crawled to Heraclius's corpse as blood flowed from his back. The samurai lay on top of the dead liger grasping its fur between his fingers. Akira wept and then lifted his head and gazed at Casimir. "How could you have defeated him? I taught Heraclius with as much devotion as though he was my own son."

Casimir leaned against the wall. "Despite all your training and giving Heraclius a taste for human flesh, you forgot that animals also have souls, and his was not that of a killer. During our entire fight some part of him was holding back. Despite your best efforts Akira, you couldn't make Heraclius a murderer like us."

"Then I have failed in every way possible. I need the two of you to help me commit Seppuku so I can die with honor."

Henry finished reloading his revolver as he stumbled over to Akira and aimed his gun at the back of his head. "This is America, yellow man; you don't get to choose how you die."

Henry fired and Akira's forehead exploded covering the liger's corpse in blood, brain matter, and skull fragments. Casimir sat down and took in a deep and painful breath. Henry collapsed to his knees and removed his ammo belt. Casimir helped Henry wrap it around his left arm to keep it from falling apart. Henry gave a painful smirk. "Looks like the yellow man and his kitty cat sure did a number on us pal."

Casimir got up and helped Henry to his feet. "We just need to kill Mr. Fairchild and it's all over."

Henry tasted blood in his mouth and coughed and spat on Akira's remains. "Then we better finish that son of a bitch off before we bleed to death."

Casimir picked up the Tantō knife; it was now truly his. He and Henry faced the door to Mr. Fairchild's study and kicked it wide open. Vernon Fairchild sat in the chair at his desk with a glass of brandy in his left hand. He flicked his right hand and a knife shot straight from his sleeve into Henry's heart. Henry fell down dead. It had happened as Vernon took a sip of his brandy; he had not even bothered standing up.

Casimir stood dumbfound. "You killed him. He was one of your country's greatest legends."

Vernon chugged down the rest of his brandy and traced the glass with his index finger. "No, that would be Bigfoot. I haven't gotten to him yet, but trust me I will."

Casimir growled and threw his knife at Vernon's head. Vernon snatched it out of the air when it was an inch from his face. He set it on the desk and poured himself another drink. Casimir pulled the knife from Henry's chest and then experienced what could only be described as hell. He saw the knife being used to kill women in ways only a monster would think of. It wasn't enough just to end their lives; he had destroyed their bodies and removed that which allowed them to create life.

So many women, hundreds of them, and through the knife, Casimir saw all their pain and terror. His body trembled as he cried, "You're Jack the Ripper!"

Vernon put his glass down. "That's just what the London press called me when I got sloppy. I killed hundreds of women. Not just prostitutes, but seamstresses, female factory workers, maids, and plenty of other low-class wrenches that nobody will miss."

Casimir's eyes became almost bloodshot with rage. "Why in the name of God, why did you do that? None of those women deserved what you did to them!"

Vernon shrugged his shoulders. "It's just a hobby. It's not like I have some hatred of womankind. Nor did I do it to satisfy some sort of sexual perversion. Some men collect stamps or coins, others build bottled ships. Me, I like to kill women, remove their reproductive organs, and if I have the time, to and make paintings of their dead faces. Now, enough about my favorite pastime. I'm sure you wish to know what The Elder One was.

"I saw that you created it, how?"

Vernon stood and moved to the front of his desk. "The Elder One was a Tulpa. I was taught how to create them by Tibetan monks. Think of it as a real imaginary friend who does or says whatever you desire. Although, The Elder One was based on something very real, a Tulpa can be anything or anyone you want it to be."

"And you used your Tulpa to mask the fact you were the leader of The Sons of Chaos."

Vernon leaned against his desk. "The Sons of Chaos are just one of many radical groups that the Illuminati have created to fulfill our goals."

"Illuminati?

"We're a secret organization that has existed since the time of the Akkadian Empire. There is not a war or political upheaval we have not had some hand in, including the partition of your homeland. We have some big plans for this new century, war, and death on a scale greater than anything you can fathom. Poland's current state is going to look like Eden compared to what's coming."

Tears ran down Casimir's face. "How can you do such evil?"

Vernon stroked his mutton chops. "You wouldn't understand why. But I will say this. The reason I sent you, the cowboy, the ax wielding lady, and the disgraced solider to kill The Elder One is because a Tulpa cannot be physically harmed by a human. The four of you shared a common ancestor, but your blood is the only one that's pure, and that's why you were able to kill The Elder One. That's why the Illuminati need your heart for one of our rituals."

Vernon pulled out two scythe bladed knives from behind his back. Casimir tightened his grip on his newly acquired knife. Casimir realized he was spraying blood all over the carpet and had to defeat Vernon before he passed out. He pointed the knife at Vernon and gasped, "I'm going to give every last breath I have to thwarting the Illuminati. Even though I'll most likely fail, I want you to understand that there is no way you are leaving this room alive, Mr. Fairchild. Everything that you did to those women, I'm going to do to you!"

Vernon twirled his blades while grinning. "Last time I checked, I don't have a womb for you to remove."

Casimir rushed at Vernon and their knives clashed. Vernon was faster than Casimir anticipated and found himself barely able to deflect his attacks. It didn't help that he had blood running from the cuts on his forehead and over his eyes. Vernon kicked Casimir in his crown jewels. It didn't slow down or even hurt Casimir in the slightest, but it broke his focus. Vernon smirked and stabbed his right knife through Casimir's right leg. Casimir didn't scream. He head butted Vernon, knocking off his top hat. In the split-second that Vernon was dazed, Casmir stabbed his knife through Vernon's left forearm. As fresh blood ran down Casimir's leg, he punched Vernon right in his chest, obliterating his ribs. Vernon flew across the room and smashed into one of his bookshelves. The books collapsed all over him as he writhed on the floor puking blood. Casimir grasped the hilt of the knife in his leg and yanked it out, while Vernon did the same to the blade in his arm.

Vernon scrambled to his feet as blood dribbled from his lips. He smiled the most disgusting smile Casmir had ever seen and charged at him so fast, that Casimir couldn't even see him coming. Vernon pushed Casimir and knocked the weapon out of his hand. Casimir slammed against the wall, and Vernon plunged his knife into Casimir's chest. He gasped as he felt the cold blade slide between his ribs and scrape the bottom of his heart. Casimir found his body motionless and the world suddenly started going black. Vernon pulled Casimir's hair and sneered, "I see the life flighting away from your eyes Mr. Stazek. I want you to know before you go that it's in the best interest of the Illuminate for your bloodline to continue. However, as punishment for killing my two beloved pets, I have decided that after your wife gives birth, she will be Jack's next victim!"

Those words renewed Casimir's strength and he wrapped his hands around Vernon's wrists. The two of them struggled until they crashed through the window. Shattered glass fell along with the snow as Casimir and Vernon plunged towards the ground. Before they made impact, Casimir snapped Vernon's neck and used his body to cushion his fall. When they hit the ground, Casimir saw that he was surrounded by a hundred figures dressed in red cloaks just like the Elder One. However, instead of a deer skull mask, they wore masks of pure gold with expressionless faces. All of them carried daggers with serpent shaped hilts in their left hands.

Suddenly Vernon's corpse turned to purple smoke and vanished into the wind just like The Elder One's had. One of the cloaked figures stepped forth and removed his mask. Once more Casimir found his eyes greeted with the sight of Vernon Fairchild's revolting smile. "A Tulpa can be anything or *anyone* you want it to be."

"No! I killed you! I killed you!"

Vernon laughed as the Illuminati circled in on Casimir like vultures. A hair's breadth away from death, Casimir managed to kill three of them and wound seven more, but soon found himself subdued. Vernon Fairchild grabbed the hilt of the knife the Tulpa had stabbed into Casimir's chest and jolted it upwards, ending Casimir's life. He cut out his heart. When Vernon was finished, the Illuminati left Casmir's lifeless body to be covered by the snow and went on their way.

Spring-Heeled Jim
Steve Stark

Raised voices and increased footfall woke him. He hadn't intended on dozing, but he'd been sitting there for hours, bones numbing to the cold concrete, to the unforgiving door at his back.

A slight tilt to the side cracked his neck, the sound like popcorn in a microwave, easing the tension all the way down his spine and he gasped in relief, breath steaming in the cold night air.

His tattered baseball cap already sat low, its peak shading most of his face. Still he pulled it lower, ever conscious of the cameras above as he gazed through steamy lenses at the bustle ahead.

They were hurrying along now, seeking shelter and warmth. Luxuries he would not afford himself.

Not yet.

Not until he found - *the one.*

A copper coin bounced off the peak of his cap, onto the soggy cardboard he'd made as a temporary bed, and his eyes flicked up immediately yet failed to determine a donor amidst the flow of bodies. He could find no one regarding him with that typical blend of condescension and pity, no one waiting expectantly for his gratitude. Whoever it was they'd pitched the coin without thought and probably only to save themselves the effort of placing the change in a wallet. They hadn't stuck around, or even looked across to see the reaction to their "generosity".

And yet, had they paused for just a moment they might've found something unsettling about the strange giggle it provoked in the recipient.

His disguise was perfect. The coin confirmed that. He pocketed it as a memento to be added to the shrine later and to his surprise found something else had taken up residence inside his coat, something living, squirming. It was clinging to his wrist when he withdrew the hand, armoured body the size of a fat thumb, six spiny legs poised to move, antennae probing busily, and on its rear - the writhing mass of a dozen milky larvae.

He didn't brush it off right away as most people would. He wasn't like most people. Instead he watched, then for a while he amused himself by crushing the larvae individually between finger and thumb. The game was to take out as many as he could without the mother noticing, without it trying to flee, and he scored a total of six before that happened.

But he didn't let it end there.

The mother died slowly on her back with her limbs scattered about her and a matchstick driven into her abdomen. The match was then lit and burned down to the end, its flame igniting something inside the bug which exploded with the faintest pop. Impassively, he watched the last twitches of her antennae fade. Then he flicked the smoking carcass into the crowd's path where it was instantly reduced to a yellow smear on the pavement.

In his eyes they were all insects, worker drones confined to tower block hives and suburban nests, their guts bloated on the nectar of alcohol and processed food.

And at night while they gathered like moths around the fluorescent light of TV, he the Spider wove his web and waited, sometimes days, sometimes weeks, for one of their number to catch his eye, to fall behind, to wander from the safety of the swarm and into his domain.

A clock tower bell chimed in the distance, jarring him from the red dreams once again and he adjusted in his pavement seat, clenching his gloved hands until the numbness faded. A further half hour slipped by and he spared a moment to wipe his glasses. Then at the sound of a voice he quickly reset them on his face, the blurry world coming back into full focus to reveal...

Her.

"Awright lads," she said, in a coarsely suggestive tone, a grin on her red lips for the trio in Stone Island jackets coming toward her.

"No thanks," was the blunt response and she strutted on, head held high.

"Suit yerselves."

Although the Spider had never seen her before, he knew she was the one when his mind replayed those first movements in slow-motion. To him it seemed almost hypnotic, the twirl of her blood-red coat as she turned, the bounce of her platinum blonde ponytail with every stride in those scarlet heels and the wispy smoke trailing alluringly from the lit cig in her dainty grasp.

Giddy with excitement, he stood upright so suddenly that the nearest of the jostling crowd, a bloated grub, flinched in shock before burrowing deeper into the swarm. It caused a momentary ripple, a few heads turned at the disturbance then turned back just as quickly, keen to avoid the gaze of the "vagrant" and any potential requests for change.

The Spider's eyes never left his prey, her red ensemble a beacon amidst the tide of drab clothing in motion, and he commenced the pursuit, tracking her down Market Street, neon shimmering off the wet surfaces around her like some kaleidoscopic dream. Entranced, he followed as she turned off into Market Square where the blacked-out shops and boarded up kiosks were at sleep 'til morning. All that neon vibrancy was gone then, replaced largely by shadow and everything else seemed washed out, de-saturated like an old movie reel.

Only her coat remained clear, that red stain in a world of greys and blacks, and the light click of her heels which echoed as she went, shortly attracting the bloodshot gaze of a genuine vagrant. This one lay slumped against a graffiti-covered wall in a ragged sleeping bag, a dozen empty cans scattered about him, fresh vomit glistening in his beard.

He gargled, "Spare sum change, luv?"

"Sorry," she muttered, not affording so much as a glance in his direction, only quickening her stride while mere metres behind the Spider gathered pace to match.

"'Fanks anyways," the vagrant slurred and even though his senses had been dimmed by litres of piss-warm Special Brew, he recognised the purpose in the Spider's movement, could see that he was following the girl. It didn't really matter to him one way or the other, but when the Spider also ignored a request for change the vagrant felt compelled to call out in spite.

"WATCH IT LUV. 'E'S BEHIND YOU!"

Exiting the square, she must've heard yet couldn't have listened as she didn't look around and actually relaxed her pace soon after. The irony tickled the Spider who, like her, paid the vagrant no mind and continued to stalk her footsteps, an excited grin creeping across his cracked lips.

However, that grin soon sagged when something else caught his eye. In a gift shop window, the word 'Mother' flashing at him from every angle, in pink, blue and purple print.

"Happy Mother's Day" read 'all the banners, cards and balloons, even the bellies of some blank-faced teddies.

In the face of all this the Spider stumbled a little, his head full of soda. Then he shook it off and pressed on with gritted teeth, determined to suppress what was coming.

He only managed to trail the girl for a further block before he felt that familiar pain in his gut, heard that shrill voice ringing in his skull.

You're nothing Jimmy! You're scum, just like your Father!

You're a fucking waste of skin!

A convoy of boy racers buzzed past, bass lines bursting from speakers even louder than their customised engines, and Jimmy realised he'd drifted again. It was happening more and more of late. Panic hit him the way it hits a dozing driver waking to find themselves still at the wheel, and he frantically scanned the street for *her*, finding no trace.

Where are you? he wondered, so preoccupied that he stumbled into a family leaving an Indian restaurant.

"Sorry," he mumbled, the whiff of garlic, spices and booze invading his nostrils as he slipped through their formation, straight into the path of a gang of burly blokes.

"Whose round is next then?"

"It's Phil's round next."

"Fuck off Gaz. It's your round you tight cunt."

Jimmy's first impulse was to give the gang a wide berth, but the pavement was too narrow since the group were walking two abreast and each member looked to have been built for rugby. At the point of convergence one of their number saw fit to strike Jimmy with a bump of the shoulder, which would've been quite a bump had he not seen it coming. However, Jimmy was acutely aware of such moves, the telltale signs as predictable to him as the lyrics to his favourite song, and a swift pivot saw him absorb only the slightest brush on the way by.

Annoyed, the thwarted bully jeered, "Looks like Harry Potter's fallen on hard times," and there was a pause while the drink-dulled minds made the connection, then laughter erupted. It was a scornful kind of laughter often heard from gangs of drunk men; a kind intended to goad a victim into an unwinnable confrontation. Jimmy knew it all too well and simply carried on in silence, pretending not to hear as the wind picked up behind, ushering him along with all the stray trash.

On the horizon a faulty kebab shop sign hummed with the promise of shelter and potential prey, but inside Jimmy found an atmosphere as tense as the prison yard had been. The queue was dense, disorganised and occupied most of the room. Within it lairy men jostled for position, barging and barking warnings at each other like hungry dogs. Around the outskirts others loitered in packs, glaring, posturing. Only a few females were present, all jealously guarded by the men and not one among them resembled Jimmy's lady in red.

He stayed regardless, appreciating the warmth as he weaved through the crowd, probing for weakness the way sharks do. All the while orders were called and collected at random intervals, earning the Turkish vendors either thanks or muttered insults which went ignored in favour of taking the next order.

"One doner an' a battered Mars bar, mate."

It wasn't long before a fight broke out, splitting the queue and sending a ripple of aggression through the room, infecting many of the bystanders. Fists clenched, muscles flexed, threats were spewed yet the vendors just kept on serving. From what Jimmy could gather the quarrel was between the ex and the current partner of a particular woman, who seemed far more interested in a portion of cheesy chips than any of the drama on her behalf.

"She ain't with you, she ain't interested no more. She said you got a little dick anyway."

"That's just what she says to make ya feel better. I've got a nice video of us on my phone if you don't believe me."

Jimmy took his leave before it escalated beyond the standard shoving and name-calling. He wandered on into the night, fooling himself at times that he wasn't looking for *her* any more, and hoping, praying something else might come his way. But to him all the faces he passed from that point seemed the same - blank, vacant, like ghosts, like his own. Worse still, their numbers were dwindling and though this meant it would be easier to pick one off, it also limited his choice.

Eventually he settled on a fat drunk who vaguely resembled a guard that'd once beaten him in prison, and with that memory loaded, he stalked the man for two blocks until a faint, tinny sound of music stole his attention.

It was her.

Twenty metres ahead she'd taken cover at a rickety bus shelter and though the scratched plexiglass between them muted the colour of her ensemble, to Jimmy it seemed even more brilliant than before. He watched while she rummaged in her shoulder bag for the music's source and delighted in the way it lit up her face when she held it to a tattooed ear.

"Hello darlin'. Yeah, I'm all good…yep. At the bus stop now. We're still on."

No buses were coming, Jimmy knew they didn't run past nine in Scarmouth, and she was distracted, vulnerable. But this wasn't the place. It was too open and yet, his gloved hands came out of his pockets anyway, stretching and clenching, stretching and clenching in anticipation. He was almost close enough to touch her then and just like every time before his world slipped into a slow-motion crawl where each footstep resonated like thunder, his own breath whistled in his ears and her words hung stupidly in the air.

"Better get the kettle on," she said and Jimmy imagined a lone person seated at a table, cup of coffee in front of them, another cup unattended at the place opposite, slowly going cold. He smiled at the sad picture and reached out for that ponytail as it danced temptingly on the breeze.

Swish.

Swish.

He would grab it tightly like he used to catch the rats by the canal, yank it in and move to the throat before she could scream. He was within inches now, so close he'd swear he could hear her heartbeat, her eyelids flutter. He would be stopping both forever in mere moments.

So he thought.

"Whoops!"

A solid mass slammed hard into Jimmy's chest, stealing the air from his body, sending him reeling. Rubber soles squeaked and slipped on the wet paving as his skinny arms gyrated to slow momentum, to regain balance, and failed on both counts. Precariously, Jimmy's heels hung suspended off the curb, mere inches from the road and the path of a speeding taxi when suddenly a large pair of hands hauled him back onto the pavement.

"Sorry mate," said a gruff yet friendly voice, those big hands brushing Jimmy's coat off for him. "Didn't see ya there."

To Jimmy, who hated being touched, this felt like getting patted down, a quick invasion of his personal space which could reveal everything about his physique, his intent to someone who knew what to look for. He was grateful then that he'd left the blade strapped to his shin, for it would have surely been detected.

"It's okay, it's okay," Jimmy said, putting his head down and just before he did he'd caught a glimpse of his scarlet woman strutting away down the street, the pendular swish of that ponytail rapid and higher than before.

In the next breath he glanced back to find her gone.

Shit.

The man stepped forward and lifted Jimmy's cap slightly. "Didn't hurt you did I, mate?"

"I'M FINE!" Jimmy snapped, slapping the man's hand aside to reset the cap. "NO HARM OKAY?"

Again the man apologised. It was a weak apology this time, flat, almost goading in a way, and a frustrated Jimmy looked to berate him for it, then reconsidered when he finally laid eyes on the man. The bloke stood a monster, a full head taller than Jimmy and with a neck as thick as most men's legs, shoulders wide as a doorway. More alarming still were his brutish features, which bore the markings of countless old battles and decades of late nights while his eyes glowered behind that gold-toothed smile.

"I-it's alright," Jimmy stuttered, recoiling. "I'm really sorry I snapped there."

"Okay mate," said the big man, still smiling but with what seemed to Jimmy a hint of contempt. It gave him a chill, recalling the manner of someone from the past, although he couldn't immediately picture who that was.

"You 'ave a good night, mate," said the big man, stepping on, big boots thudding the pavement, the steps of a giant.

"You too."

Standing there by the bus shelter, Jimmy watched the man until he was just a speck on the horizon. Then suddenly, a name, one he hadn't uttered in years, came bubbling to the forefront of his mind.

"Derek Renton," he whispered as the memories came flooding back.

It was Derek Renton who'd hidden Jimmy's games kit so he had to play football in his skivvies and suffer the ridicule of all the girls playing hockey on the next field.

It was Derek Renton who'd pelted Jimmy's face with the frog dissected in biology, then later slipped the slimy corpse into Jimmy's sandwich.

And it was Derek Renton who'd once written Jimmy's number on a toilet wall, earning him a breathy phone call from Maths teacher Mr. Selby, a call which didn't have anything to do with maths.

Although Derek's pranks could be considered playful, Jimmy had always seen the real intent behind them, the cruelty, the malice. Oh, the countless wedgies and backslaps. The footballs and trading cards he'd stolen. That day they'd been playing WWF wrestling and Derek had choked him until he pissed himself.

At that time, it was the worst moment in Jimmy's life, lying there semi-conscious, the squeals of young girls' laughter ringing in his ears while the warm wetness in his trousers turned cold.

Prison had been worse of course. Instead of stealing footballs and cards, they stole his food and cigarettes.

And instead of wedgies and backslaps…

Cass O'Neal had been in on three counts of ABH and two counts of sexual assault. A practising occultist and all around psycho, he was Jimmy's cellmate for the duration and Jimmy had never forgotten that rough touch or those bizarre verses whispered in his ear after lights out. Soon O'Neal would be due for parole and Jimmy planned to visit, repay all those late night kindnesses. But he knew that would have to be one of the last because it probably wouldn't take long for someone to make a connection, not with their history. Then some of the others might start to add up too.

Ah the others, he recalled them so fondly. First there'd been the skeletal junkie who tried to talk him down. So eloquent and heartfelt were the filth's arguments that Jimmy briefly allowed her to believe they'd succeeded, hesitating just long enough to raise a toothless smile of relief before turning it into a grimace of pain.

Next there'd been the old dear who surrendered without struggle, then the young mother who never saw it coming.

And what about the little whore? Her life wasn't worth shit and still she fought tooth and nail even after six stab wounds. Lucky number seven did the job, although he gave her twelve more for the trouble, cutting so deep in his frenzy that he actually blunted the blade on her spine.

Suddenly Jimmy found himself back on St Catherine's street where he'd left her, his legs carrying him automatically, obeying some subconscious command. On cue the weather calmed, almost as if to welcome him and from there he proceeded like a sniffer dog on a trail, drawing short, hungry breaths through his nose.

The smells weren't as pungent as last time. The weather then had been warm and dry and the bins had been out for three weeks due to the dustman's strike. Jimmy remembered it being so quiet that night, so quiet that he'd heard her from a street over, yakking into her mobile phone.

She'd sounded drunk and like a slut, just like all those slutty girls who'd rejected him. Just like his own slut mother, whose nightly pantomime orgasms he'd endured through the paper-thin walls of their apartment.

Harder, harder. Yes, YES!

Standing where she'd fallen only a few weeks prior, Jimmy remembered her bloody face staring frozen at him from that very gutter and shortly felt a warmth building in his groin. After checking the coast was clear he slowly peeled the leather glove from his sweaty hand, started to rub himself lightly, over his jeans at first until he could resist no more.

"You bitch, you bitch," Jimmy panted, rapidly jerking himself while the sounds of that last horrific dance echoed in his mind. He was already approaching climax as they were joined by other sounds; the faint click of heels, and a voice, a familiar voice nattering loudly.

"Yeah, I know…yeah he is…I'm not far now, mate."

Jimmy swung round just in time to catch a distant glimpse of the scarlet woman disappearing down another side street, that mobile phone still pressed to her pale face. Adrenaline hit him hard, his thin fingers crawled back inside the glove and he tucked himself away as he began to jog in pursuit, tracking by the sound of her heels and vacuous chatter.

"Yes, yes, yes," he chanted, vaulting walls and fences to cover the ground.

Brambles snagged his coat in the second yard he cut through and a sensor light dazzled him in the third, forcing him to dive blindly into the nearest hedge for cover. Like a lizard he crawled on all fours through mud and growth into the freshly clipped lawn of the next garden where he was faced with a final wall over ten feet high.

Most would turn back from it, find another route. Jimmy had no intention of either. He'd lost her too many times already and wasn't going to risk it again.

Clinging to the shadows he gathered himself, catching his breath before making the dash, fast as he could, straight at the wall. During his formative years he'd often peeped at people from their gardens and many times had needed to flee, to overcome obstacles quickly. As is often the case necessity and will made Jimmy quite the urban gymnast. Back then he was doing moves free runners had yet to name, back then he cleared walls like this without breaking sweat, but that was back then. Twenty years was plenty of time for the body to forget.

Partway across the yard Jimmy skidded on the wet grass, slowing his pace, then he met the wall a stride before anticipated which threw off his timing. He leapt at it anyway and braced his foot against the brick to propel himself further. To his delight the tactic worked regardless of the poor set up. It lent his leap the height required, although he didn't anticipate the broken glass cemented into the top of the wall where his hands clasped hard. A bolt of pain shot through both palms and down his spine. His eyes bulged from the shock, yet through sheer hateful will he managed to cling on and haul himself up and over, snarling and spitting through his teeth all the way.

Dropping clumsily into the next street Jimmy collided with an overstuffed wheelie bin, losing his glasses amidst its scattering contents, and a dog barked at the commotion. It was a deep, cutting bark which resonated loudly in the alley, seeming to surround Jimmy while he scrambled to locate his lost specs. In brightest day he could see only blurs without them, so in the shade of that alley at night he was virtually blind and as the barking became louder, nearer in turn the search became more desperate. Without qualm Jimmy delved through mounds of wet boxes, bones with rotten animal flesh still clinging to them and cans stinking from the dregs of stale alcohol.

Come on, come on. Where are they?

Already the source of the barking was in front of him. Jimmy's hazy sight caught the bulky silhouette of the animal and he fell backwards onto his haunches, arms crossed over his face in defence. There was a preceding growl then the animal darted in close and all Jimmy could do was shut his eyes and cower in wait of those teeth.

Please God.

The next thing Jimmy heard was a light clinking sound of metal on metal and then…

Nothing.

Seconds passed, which felt like minutes, while Jimmy waited to be mauled. That was too long. *It should've already happened*, he thought and his muscles were just starting to relax when the barking erupted again. On reflex Jimmy's arms crossed tighter than before while he cringed in anticipation. The animal was close, close enough he could feel its hot, stinking breath and thick spittle against his bare wrists, but still - no bite.

"Don't worry, mate,' went a gravelly voice. Then there was that metal sound again and the beast fell silent. 'I've got him."

Cautiously, Jimmy uncurled from the cocoon of his own limbs and forced his eyes open as a large figure emerged from the blurry murk to place something light and wiry into his hand.

It was his glasses.

"Reckon ya dropped these, mate."

Donning his mangled specs Jimmy squinted and looked up. The man standing before him was huge, as big as the Derek Renton lookalike from earlier, possibly even bigger, and the dog at his side was a large bull terrier, one sharing more traits with the banned Pit than the legal Staffie. Its head, bigger than Jimmy's own, levelled so that those blank, black eyes were staring right into his and a rising growl resonating in that deep chest shortly erupted into another torrent of barking.

Jimmy flinched, throwing his arms up once more, but the big man yanked the choke chain with an authoritative order of, "Shut up, Tyson," and the beast was silenced once more.

"Thanks," said Jimmy, rising to his feet while the dog eyed him like a honey-glazed ham, a quivering snarl hovering above its vicious teeth.

"No worries," said the man. Then he tugged on the leash, snapping the animal out of its killer stare to lead it away up the street, that chunky choke chain jangling as they went.

I've killed dogs for less, Jimmy thought, dusting himself off, shedding mouldy chips, pulpy tissue and flakes of cod. Blood was streaming thinly from under the cuffs of his gloves, down his wrists and when he licked them he tasted the sharp tang of bin juice, causing him to spit in rapid succession like a child imitating gunfire.

On inspection those cuts to his palms weren't so bad, the blood already drying, and didn't sting when he pulled the gloves back over them. Sharply he turned to leave, almost tripping on the spilled trash which he kicked in frustration, sending a beer can ricocheting off the nearest wall. Almost defiantly that can came rolling back to where Jimmy stomped it flat, killing its tinny melody the way he wished he could've killed that girl's phone conversation.

The girl, she had to be long gone now. Jimmy ran after her anyway. As fast as he could he rounded the corner at the end of the alley and emerged just in time to catch a flash of that red coat, a swish of that blonde ponytail, before the colours were swallowed by the blackness of an unlit underpass.

"Come to Daddy," he panted, taking after her, no longer showing any caution. He saw no need when the streets now stood deserted, populated solely by parked cars, wheelie bins, and with the underpass providing a prime opportunity to strike unseen. He only slowed at the ramp leading down to the tunnel's mouth, treading lighter where the echo might telegraph his approach.

On into the darkness Jimmy crept, following her footsteps while his gloved hands groped blindly, eager to touch her soft body but finding only air. Her strides shortly drifted out of earshot or stopped, leaving him disorientated, stranded in the throat of the tunnel and he felt the wall to navigate a bend, glass crunching softly underfoot. There was light around the other side, something flickering, an erratic strobe. He moved toward it.

Yes.

There she was, not far ahead. Like some cinematic fantasy her slim figure stood illuminated by a failing street lamp and framed by the dark semi-oval of the tunnel. She wasn't moving any more, just standing there, gazing back, the breeze teasing her hair in that way he found so enticing, so arousing.

Could she see him?

No. Jimmy read no fear on her face just yet and couldn't wait to change that. Swiftly he drew the blade from under his jeans, not minding the sting of the tape stripping the hair. Then licking his lips in excitement, he lunged from the shadows to attack, knife gleaming as it met the light.

The very instant the girl saw him she recoiled, her eyes wide in alarm, mouth agape as though to scream, yet for some reason she didn't. She didn't run either, didn't do anything. Her gears must be stuck somewhere between fight or flight thought Jimmy. He'd seen that happen before.

Then she said the strangest thing.

"Come on."

Jimmy barely had time to process her words before a skull-splitting blow struck the back of his head and the floor came rushing up to his face. The next thing he saw through his freshly cracked lenses, was the starry sky and a large figure looming into view.

"Sorry mate," said a familiarly gruff voice, and it had no undertone of anything this time. This time it was as dry as a saw going through bone. "I really should learn to watch where I'm going eh?"

It was the big man from earlier, the Derek Renton lookalike, now brandishing a steel cosh, one of those retractable types the police use.

"Kettle's boiled," he said, turning back to the girl. He pointed with the cosh. "You can go now, luv."

Her ludicrously long false lashes didn't blink, not once, her gaze fixed on Jimmy. She was clearly disturbed by him, yet also intrigued in that perverse way gawkers are by crash scenes.

"Nah, I'm stayin'."

The big man shrugged. "Suit yerself. Just stay back alright."

During their brief exchange Jimmy had thought about sitting up but that was all. He felt drunk almost, his head swimming, and there was a wetness about his neck. Had he fallen into a puddle?

Idly he wondered where his cap had gone. Then with a pained effort he rolled onto his front, into a press-up position and saw blood, his blood patting the paving in a steady flow.

"I wasn't doing anything," he whimpered, the whine in his voice echoing, amplified by the tunnel, while somewhere nearby a dog began to bark.

"Yeah right," the big man snorted and he kicked out one of Jimmy's arms to put him down again.

"I'll come quietly," Jimmy slurred, woozy. "Just want a solicitor."

The big man frowned. "A solicitor?"

"I know a good one," went a second male voice and it was accompanied by the dog barking.

Jimmy had seen them before.

"*Tyson*," the man hissed, yanking the chain to silence the dog. Then he nodded to the man with the cosh. "Alright."

The man with the cosh tapped the end against his wrist, gesturing to a watch that didn't exist. 'What time do you call this?'

"Steady on, Derek," said the dog handler. "I was just keepin' back 'til the time was right. Tyson woulda scared 'im off."

Derek? thought Jimmy. *Not Derek Renton surely*? But in hindsight the resemblance seemed too close for him not to be. Of course, it'd make sense for a bully to join the police force, getting paid to follow those natural sadistic impulses. Jimmy wondered then, *Does he recognise me*? and reached for Derek's boot.

"I'll come quietly, come quietly," he promised, patting the steel toecap, effectively tapping out.

The big men laughed and Derek withdrew his boot to leave Jimmy's hand stroking the concrete.

"We're not pigs, mate," said the dog handler as Derek then stepped on those outstretched fingers, grinding his heel. Tiny bones cracked under the weight like ice.

"An' you're not goin' anywhere."

Jimmy's eyes bulged, his breath stuttered, less at the sharp pain in his hand and more at those words, each syllable like a hammer tap to the nails of his coffin. He couldn't be sure at that point whether he'd be able to stand, much less run, but he'd have to try. They weren't bluffing.

It was then the girl piped up, her voice full of raw, tearful rage. "Yer fackin' done," she screamed, starting toward Jimmy, inadvertently providing the very distraction he needed. Derek wheeled to stop her and the instant his foot came off those fingers, Jimmy sprang up and fled, bolting toward the tunnel.

"Fackin' 'ell," said the dog handler, sounding almost impressed.

"Better stop 'im then," said Derek, gesturing to the dog.

Tyson was already fully primed, his sixty lbs of pure muscle, taut and straining at the leash. He shot forward like a stretched elastic band the instant his handler released the catch.

"GET 'IM," the girl screamed.

"NO," Jimmy shrieked, hearing that light yet rapid scamper closing behind. In the next breath he felt those jaws clamp around his right forearm, all two hundred and forty lbs of bite pressure, bringing him down just in front of the tunnel and for the second time that night Jimmy's face kissed concrete, a sound of raw meat hitting the butcher's slab.

"YES," Derek cheered, "get in there boy."

Jaw locked, Tyson thrashed his bulk, snapping Jimmy's ulna like a breadstick to draw a blood-curdling cry.

"GET HIM OFF ME."

In response the two big men only laughed, booming, coarse, full-bellied laughs at the ongoing mauling, and as his body eventually went numb, as his bowels gave out, this laughter followed Jimmy into the oblivion of unconsciousness, melding with the laughter that forever haunted his dreams.

Pissy pants, pissy pants...

...pathetic, like your waste of a father...

Turning his head with a pained groan, Jimmy's eyes cracked back open to find Tyson's black-eyed glare within kissing distance, that foul breath blasting his face. The dog appeared to be gnawing at something, like one of those chewsticks. It made that hollow crunching noise as he worked it over between slavering jaws.

"Come 'ere," said the handler.

Metal glanced off metal and Jimmy recognised the sound of the dog being leashed. He felt grateful for it. But when the handler started to lead Tyson away Jimmy found himself going with them a little. A moment later they stalled and started again, this time dragging Jimmy further.

And further.

"Fuck's sake, Tyson," hissed the handler. "Let go."

The dog growled and there was a sense of a physical struggle from the frantic rustle of clothing to the handler grunting. It went on for some moments and culminated in the sound of a wet snap with Jimmy's limp arm flopping to the concrete just after.

"Christ," went Derek.

"He'll be 'appy now," said the handler and it sounded as though he was chaining Tyson to something nearby. That hollow, grinding chew stick noise started again.

"See? That'll keep 'im quiet."

Laying there face up and too weak to move Jimmy saw Derek loom into view, bald head eclipsing the moon. Without specs Jimmy couldn't be sure, but he got the feeling the man was grinning.

"Looks like you won't be gettin' much use out of your wanking arm now, mate."

"Whu-what?" Jimmy murmured. "Whu d'yuh mean?"

"Yeah, we saw you earlier," said the handler. "Funny place to go for a wank right where Tasha got killed."

"Very suspicious," Derek chuckled. "Still, it's not like you're gonna be doin' much more a' that...'less you're ambidextrous."

The meaning of the words and the horror of the situation finally dawned on Jimmy. With a strenuous effort he managed to turn his head and saw the hazy shape of his mangled arm, bent completely at the wrong angle and flattened as though parts were missing, parts that would sound not unlike a chew stick in a dog's mouth.

"NO," Jimmy gasped, his rapid sobs adding a few syllables to the word, then he cried out with an anguished howl.

"Shut it," Derek snapped, moving quickly.

A firm tap from the cosh was enough to prevent Jimmy making such noise again and he lay silent awhile, listening to the gut-churning sound of Tyson's determined gnawing, the steady trickle of his own blood running out.

"But why?" he eventually asked, which provoked the girl to storm across.

"You killed Tasha," she snarled, still coming, a look of furious intent on those tattooed eyebrows. "You killed her, you little cunt."

Derek quickly put an arm out to hold her back and she pressed against the muscular barrier, red lips baring teeth, painted fingernail aimed at Jimmy.

"You're fuckin' dead, mate," she warned and Derek put himself in her way, started talking her down in hushed, soothing tones.

"Easy luv, we've got him. We've got him."

"Twenty times he stabbed her, Derek. Twenty fuckin' times. She was my mate."

"I know, I know."

"Cunt's gotta pay. He's gotta suffer."

"Does he look like he's 'avin' a good time to you?"

Jimmy listened in fear, wondering what was to come next, what else they had in store and it soon occurred to him that this might be a chance to get away, now while they were distracted. But could he still move? He wasn't sure. He noticed some feeling remaining in his crushed fingers and tried to flex them only for the dog handler to step on them hard, in the process proving that he was, as suspected, slightly heavier than Derek.

"See Sadie 'ere works for us," he said and he continued to explain the situation to Jimmy in the casual tone in which a tradesman might detail a piece of work. "She's one Jof our girls. Tasha was too. Now Sadie rang us when she clocked you followin' her. At first we thought she was just jumpy cos of what 'appened to Tash, an' we 'ad you down as a basic weirdo. Then we saw you wankin' an' we knew. So she led you 'ere where there's no cctv, no one to mind while we 'ave our way with you."

"I didn't…" Jimmy whined.

The dog handler grinned, flashing chipped teeth. "Yeah, you did, mate," he said wryly, seeming amused at Jimmy's protest of innocence. "My only question is why'd you do it? You 'ate women or somethin'? You one a' them types?"

Jimmy said nothing.

"Maybe it's cos he's got a maggot dick," said Sadie and the men broke out in fits of laughter which echoed through the underpass tunnel, carrying into the deserted street beyond.

The dog handler had to take a seat he was laughing so hard. "Maggot dick," he sighed, clutching his side.

The helplessness, the humiliation, to Jimmy it felt like the playground all over again. Again? Perhaps he'd never left it. Perhaps he'd always be that lonely boy who spent his break times terrorising the ant nest at the edge of the football field.

No, Jimmy refused to accept that. He *had* changed. He was the Spider. He was cunning and deadly and he'd demonstrated his power time and again. *Show them*, he thought, *show Derek and his whore the truth, show them what lurks under the disguise*, and from somewhere deep in his tortured soul Jimmy summoned the strength to raise a bloody grin and loose a gloopy, malicious cackle, like a blocked drain, which killed their laughter dead.

"Okay, I did it," Jimmy gasped, spitting blood with every consonant. "I KILLED THAT LITTLE BITCH!… an' there's NOTHING you can do to change that!…She's not the only one either…you have no idea you fucking…*insects*."

Silence dangled, the two big men staring at Jimmy throughout, heavy brows frowning, jaws slightly agape in primitive confusion. Gradually these dumb expressions faded, first giving way to smirks. Then the men began to chuckle intermittently, the sound soon building to another eruption of full belly laughs. In turn that hideous grin melted from Jimmy's face as a fresh shadow fell upon it, the very shadow which had tormented him all night long, tormented, teased and tantalised.

Sadie stood over him now. To Jimmy her long, lean legs seemed to go on forever. They were elegant pillars in fishnet, the extensive trackmarks peeking through only added to that sense, creating a marbled effect on her alabaster skin.

Moving to grab her Derek warned, "Shit-careful luv," and ignoring him, she raised one of those knees to her chest in an impressive display of flexibility, which drew a gasp of awe from Jimmy. Her stiletto heel hung suspended for a moment, the dirty price sticker visible underneath, before it came down fast onto Jimmy's face, the dull point driving deep into his eye socket to produce a squelching sound, like wet mud underfoot.

"Fackin' 'ell," said the dog handler.

Jimmy thrashed fitfully as a worm on a hook while that heel remained embedded in his skull, Sadie leaning on it with most of her weight. A further crunch soon signalled the socket's collapse and that heel entered Jimmy's demented brain, putting a stop to his thrashing, a permanent stop to his anything.

"Faaack," said the dog handler, wincing.

Jimmy fell still and Derek slowed his rush to dust his hands together, a sound like sandpaper on wood. "Well that'll be that then," he said, casual. "You can get off him now, luv."

Emerging from her bloodlust, Sadie slowly turned to move and nearly fell, having to windmill her arms to keep upright due to her heel remaining lodged in Jimmy's head. After she recovered, she tried again to the same result and on the subsequent stumble Derek caught her in his arms.

"Stuck," she said, not outright asking for help, but the distressed look on her face said otherwise.

"I'll get it," said Derek and he crouched to Sadie's foot, allowing her to lean on his back while he performed the most gruesome recreation of the Prince Charming pose. The heel was firmly embedded due to a suction effect which forced Derek to recruit more muscle than he expected, and it was here while bracing one hand against the corpse's forehead that he made a surprising discovery.

"Don't believe it."

"What?" said the dog handler.

Derek looked round sharply, a bemused grin on his big features. "Reckon I went to school with this one y'know."

The dog handler shrugged while Sadie looked on weary, and Derek returned to the task at hand, chuckling to himself.

"Small world or what?"

Thanks for the Night
Roger Lime

Rory stood at the corner of Glade and Grambling wearing a tight black shirt that barely reached his navel and equally constrictive skinny jeans that were torn deliberately at the knees.

He did not want to work tonight. The weather was sweltering, Glade-Grambling was empty, and Rory was still sore from the prior night's shift. Moreover, he had awoken that morning to find an ugly hickey, red as a rash, swelled under his jawline. Rory had painted it over with white makeup earlier, but the touch-up had begun to melt away in the heat of the humid night. The client who had bruised Rory had been a fit young man with close-cropped hair and a stiff, regimental posture. He spoke softly, but authoritatively. He had seemed like a soldier, so Rory called him *Sarge*. Sarge had been passionate and angrily forceful with Rory. And Sarge had cried when they finished.

As Rory continued to wait for prospective buyers, idly attracting business like a streetside mannequin, he noticed a car parked further down Glade turn its headlights on. It stood out rather glaringly as, other than the faintly flickering streetlamp next to Rory, the headlights were the only lit part of Glade Street. None of the other parked cars were occupied; none of the other streetlamps had working bulbs; none of the closed-up shops along the street kept their lights on. After hours, Glade was a dead zone with an otherworldly darkness that obscured one's vision of anything further than ten yards away. The vehicle, an ugly colorless Lancia Dedra, was almost a half-block away from Rory. The hustler paid no mind to the machine, turning his attention back to his immediate area. Playing hard to get was his lure.

Minutes went by, and the mangy Italian compact car continued to burn in Rory's periphery. The driver was not taking the bait. Anxious and annoyed, Rory turned his head to gaze at the vehicle, staring into the headlights unblinkingly. After a while of Rory's staring game with the invisible and motionless motorist, the car backed out of its spot and began to drive up Glade toward Rory's post. It moved slowly--no faster than 5 mph.

Finally, when the car was directly adjacent to Rory, it came to a gliding stop. The passenger side window rolled down and Rory saw, obscured by the shadows of the dark car interior, a bizarre figure sitting in the driver's seat. The curb-crawler wore a mask--a Venetian *Volto*--that veiled his entire face. The eyes of the false face were fringed with gilded lozenges with deep angles that dipped downward to lips chiseled compactly like a small, golden heart. A wave of unease came upon Rory, submerging him in a bog of nausea.

"Are you one of Pontrelli's boys?" a voice inquired from behind the mask.

"What?" Rory had not meant to ask for clarification—he had heard the driver's question and understood exactly what he was asking. What was simply a nervous response, an impulse triggered from the surprise of seeing such a frightfully weird character.

"Do you work for Pontrelli?"

There was something cold about the way the man asked this question. It sounded as though his inquiry was made with serious purpose. Rory wondered why the stranger would possibly wish to confirm the identity of his employer. For a moment, he considered that this strange man in a mask could be a cop—an undercover vice officer inquiring about the identity of his pimp, Lou Pontrelli, to build the foundation of a case. But policemen dress down. They wear threadbare coats, raggedy caps, and aviators that scream, *I am a plainclothes policeman; don't engage me*. This guy looked like an escapee from a Parisian opera house. This guy was no cop.

"Yeah, I work for Pontrelli," Rory said.

From the shadows of the unlit car interior, a wad of paper bills emerged. "I like Pontrelli's boys." The man's voice was noticeably lighter and the severity in the air subsided. Rory took the money and began counting each dollar. He was careful not to look up as he calculated the payment, though he could feel the hollow black eyes of the mask watching him as he did.

"I know his rates," the man said, "Unless something's changed, that's enough for the night." $1,500. "It is," Rory assured. Not wanting to kill the paying customer's mood, Rory smiled a sexy smile, reciprocating the stranger's false face with his own, before walking around to the passenger door.

"What is your name?" the masked man asked as Rory entered the car.

"Rory."

"Rory?" he said, cocking his head to the side, "Whorey Rory. Whorey Rory! Are you called that?" There was a manic childishness in the man's ever-changing tone.

"Not really," Rory said. It was a lie; bullies had called him Whorey Rory throughout his time in school and his friend—a fellow hustler named Mickey—called him that as a term of endearment. The john's petty pet name was anything but original.

Mister Pontrelli had coached the boys to chat with and butter up their clientele. And Rory had become quite adept at this. Ordinarily, Rory--who was certainly no extrovert--could look at a john, estimate his personality, and adapt his banter as necessary. He'd talk sports with the crop-tops, books with the bookish, and weather with the bland. But he could gauge nothing with this one. This john was literally covered from head to toe. His face was masked, his hands were gloved, and even his neck was wrapped with a scarf, despite the hotness of the dog day. Not a single shred of identity was exposed to Rory. Rory could discern neither age nor ethnicity nor geographic origin. The man was just a living costume--a disembodied voice produced from the emptiness within his bundles and layers of outwear. The invisible man.

And so the two sat in uncomfortable reticence, with Rory staring at the cashmere lining of his john's black lambskin gloves while the driver stared ahead with the vacant expression of his listless mask.

"You aren't much for conversation, are ya,' Whorey Rory?" the man finally said, breaking the silence of the joyless ride, "You seem nervous. Let me guess. You are wondering why a man would solicit a boy while wearing a mask."

"That did cross my mind."

"I can assure you that I am not a serial killer. I am not driving you to your death and this will not be your last night on earth," the driver said. Rory did not respond. He was not satisfied with the dry assurance, and the stranger, sensing this dissatisfaction, continued.

"I am a very prominent conservative running for a very high public office at the state—no—federal level. A sex scandal like this would surely ruin my campaign. I am the CFO of a very large business, and I know that the exposure of this seedy proclivity would hurt my company's public image and, moreover, upset our shareholders. I am a devoutly religious man. Hmm, a deacon even. If this sin were to be uncovered, my spiritual community would be profoundly disrupted. Or, perhaps I am simply a husband whose poor, betrayed wife would be shattered by the revelations of such a seedy affair. And so, I ask, why wouldn't a man solicit a boy while wearing a mask?"

"I guess," Rory said.

Just then, the Lancia Dedra turned down Ketchum Road.

Ketchum Road spiraled through the Alice District--a neighborhood that made Cabrini Green feel like Park Avenue-- like a racetrack buttressed by crooked palisades of rotting warehouses. The Alice District's poorly planned and abandoned skyscrapers, intermeshed with poorly preserved brownstones, formed a black, rambling skyline of broken towers that jutted skyward like the thorny spikes of barbed wiring. To outsiders, the slums of Alice appeared as a monumentally labyrinthian and endless sprawl of serrated roofscape. It seemed truly infinite. To its denizens and insiders, like Rory, the Alice District was very much a prison. The tightness of its buildings was a claustrophobic nightmare that inspired feelings of lostness and isolation in even the most traveled natives of the city.

Ketchum Road was a dark place illuminated only by the moonlight, an occasional dim street lamp, and the distant glow from Midtown--a faraway carnival of loud signage aflame with cackling neon tubes wrapped along art deco high-rises that raked the heavens with their bulleting spires. Inexplicably, there was a constant music on Ketchum Road-- a looping Hi-hat drumbeat that echoed ventriloquist jazz against every nook and cranny of the underworld. No one knew where it came from and the mystery drummer's percussion, joined with the iron clangor of the nearby Factory District, was referred to with cynical affection as "the anthem."

After countless unprovoked threats, three muggings, and one especially vicious rape, Rory had adapted well to the three tenets of Ketchum Road: keep your head down, camouflage in the murk, and wear your ugliest snarl. The twisted strip was an orchard of bad apples and a graveyard for shops that had long been exsanguinated by extortionists. Every window was boarded up to keep out the wolves, who would come out from the woodwork in nightly droves to infest their favored hunting ground. Even the sick indigents who panhandled on most other roadways were too afraid to seek help on Ketchum Road; and too sensical to expect any semblance of charity.

The Calico Club--named for the area's infamous infestation of feral felines--was the beating heart of Ketchum. Reprobates, gangsters, and closeted debauchees from all over the city would brave the wilds of Ketchum Road to make it to the Calico and its surrounding venues. The activity centre was a dense bazaar that offered every fathomable fetish and vice. Back-alley pharmacies; old-timey opium dens; depraved sex clubs; toy stores for the trigger-happy; and libraries of secrets and bad deeds where anyone could relive the worst thing they had ever done. More than any red-light district on earth, this evil zone was the place to peddle poison and make deals with devils. But there was no debate that the Calico Club reigned as the supreme attraction. Every night, crowds swarmed the dancehall to rendezvous with its rogues' gallery while listening to the somber crooning of the Calico's cabaret of blues singers.

With Rory's instruction, the john parked across from the Calico and killed his engine. The two men got out of the car and Rory noticed his client took with him a leather attache case from under the backseat. Attached to the Calico was their final destination--the Hotel Fiero. The Hotel Fiero had once been an ambitiously lavish place that, shortly after its blissfully ignorant grand opening, learned the hard way not to overstep its caste. Like all of those who settle on Ketchum, the exorbitant inn quickly fell victim to a ferocious battery of shakedowns, senseless vandalisms, and other felonious messes that had left it a cruel parody of its original blueprint.

Since it became cursed with self-awareness, the Fiero had steadily decayed into a den of discontents--embracing its role as room and board for wrongs and wrongdoers. The management, resentful at the indignities suffered by the hotel, adapted their outlook and strategy to the cynical standards of Ketchum Road. The personality change transformed the Hotel Fiero into a ramshackle getaway for fugitives, drug dealers' mall, and hooker headquarters. Everything changed. No more room service. No more IDs at check-in. In fact, even the decorations had undergone a Jekyll to Hyde transition, converted from a retro fanfare of Warholian kitsch to a diamond-checkered slaughterhouse festooned with strings of sarcastically festive holiday LEDs and gory reprints of Francis Bacon's liquified crucifixions. It was *abattoir chic* at its most pessimistic--the raw dreamscape of a woman-wearing deviant.

On their way through the front lobby, Rory and the john passed a long-legged, ladylike creature with a bulging Adam's apple. He or she looked like the Nagel Woman; he or she was beautiful with pale eyes, hair as black as soot, skin bleached so chalky white that she seemed noseless, and lips died bright violet--a stark paint that she constantly refreshed with frequent new smears. Though they had never spoken to her, Rory and the other inhabitants of the Fiero took to calling this crossdresser Tracy. Tracy was a regular here and he or she had been long before Rory had started living at the Fiero. Every once and awhile, Tracy would come to the Fiero just to sit in the foyer and take in the ambience. He or she never bought a room and no concierge ever came to ask if he or she needed anything. Lou didn't like her one bit. Said she seemed ghostly. The boys were kinder. To them, Tracy wasn't ghostly. She was forlorn. They figured she came here awaiting the return of some long lost love. *Tracy's like Delta Dawn, waiting for her mysterious dark-haired man*, Mickey would say. *He's a-meeting her here today to take her to his mansion in the sky.*

Courtesy and maintenance and other artifacts of the past were replaced with an ever-present storm cloud of reckless angst that led the Hotel Fiero to self-mutilate. No longer did its ownership bother to reapply adhesive to the Fiero's aeriated burgundy-checked wallpaper, which now peeled and hung off the walls like gluey red trimmings of flayed skin. No longer did a maid service vacuum the zig-zag patterned carpets, which festered with dried pools of puke, dirty footprints, and cum stains. A tidal discord of sensual moans, profane rows, and insane laughter flooded the building--unreported and unstopped--and the perishing bulbs of flickering wall lamps remained unreplaced, heatedly blinking darkness at Rory and his disguised john as they made their way through an infinite twist of blank crimson halls.

Mr. Lou Pontrelli owned the fourth floor of the Fiero and had singlehandedly converted each of the thirty rooms to parlors for his boy whores. Room 416 of the 4th floor brothel was Rory's place. It was where he lived, officed, and reclused. With a worn key, Rory unlocked his room and opened the door to the masked man.

Rory's home was an undecorated room specially designed for working sluts like him, complete with a carpet dark enough to hide stains and a heart-framed love bed with solid bars that were perfect for handcuffs. Once the door closed behind the two men, Rory tossed his keys onto his nightstand and turned anxiously to his nocturnal guest. "So. What are you into?" he asked, doing his best to disguise his nervousness.

"I would like you to shower," the john demanded curtly, "It's hot outside and you've been standing outdoors. I abhor the taste of sweat. Go. Wash off, Whorey Rory."

"Yeah, sure man," Rory said, noting that the man's imperious tone presaged another rough night at the hands of a dom. As he marched to the bathroom, Rory wondered how the Phantom of the Opera would compare to Sarge.

While Rory kept his bedroom presentable to guests, his bathroom was a pigsty of unlaundered clothes, crumb-filled wrappers, and cosmetic products strewn all over. The aroma in here was a fetidly fusty blend of shit-stink and stale marijuana (Pontrelli didn't want clients disturbed by weed smells in the fuck zone, so Rory was accustomed to hotboxing in the bathroom).

In his shower, under a weak jet of water that smelled like it was poisoned with rust flakes, Rory conditioned his hair, douched his asshole, scrubbed his pits, and lathered his balls in two handfuls of soapy water. He was careful not to let the water touch his jaw and rinse away the makeup he'd caked over Sarge's hickey. He flung his long wet bangs back and rinsed the water out of his eyes.

And he saw the masked man staring at him through the blurry folds of the shower curtain.

Rory jumped back. He choked out an asphyxiated gasp through fright-clenched teeth and caught himself just before he slipped and fell. The john did not react to Rory noticing him. He kept still and continued to watch. *This is what he wants*, Rory thought. *He's into surprise shower play. Humor him.* He bit his lip and braced himself for some bruising foreplay.

The john swung open the shower curtain. He leaned in close enough to kiss Rory. "Give me back my money," he said. Rory saw the glint of steel from the man's thigh. He was too scared to look down and see what is was. But he could guess. But was it real? Was this still his game? "Give me my money. Now," he repeated. He raised his gloved hand to Rory's cheek, pressing the edge of a long straight razor against the boy's face.

"Okay," Rory whispered.

He crawled out from the tub onto wet porcelain tiling and across the bathroom to his crumpled pile of street clothes. As he did, Rory prayed for the john to make his move, desperation hoping that he would come through and prove that this was nothing but an elaborate roleplay for a man with aggressive tastes. But the john stood still, watching sexlessly as Rory dug into his jeans and found his night's earnings for him.

"Now, call Pontrelli," the john demanded, pocketing the money in the inside pocket of his jacket, "There is a conflict over your rates. Now your client is refusing to pay. Call him here to settle the dispute."

"It's...it's okay. You can keep the money.

The john suddenly lunged forward, grabbed Rory by the nape of the neck, and flung him out of the bathroom onto the carpet. "You've already given me the money. I've asked you to do something else. Call Pontrelli, or I will kill you. I won't ask again."

Rory went to his phone and dialed the boss-man's number. It took him longer than it should have to punch the number because of the spasmodic way his fingers shook. He was scared the john would lose his patience and murder him because of the delay, which made Rory's fingers shake with even greater intensity just before he finally hit the call button

The phone rang and rang and rang and rang. With each ring, Rory felt his life coming closer to a grisly end.

"He's not answering," Rory said.

"Liar," snarled the john.

"He's not!"

"Leave a message. Tell him to come here to the room. Tell him that your client is refusing to pay, and that he needs to come to the room and settle things," the john said.

The phone rang three more times before an automated operator instructed Rory on how to leave a voicemail. At the tone, Rory immediately left his SOS. "Lou. It's Rory. There's this guy--a client. He refuses to pay. I need you to come up and resolve things."

"Tell him I'm becoming belligerent and that you fear for your life. Convey urgency. Whimper a little bit," the john said. Rory did as he was told and looked at the john for approval. The john nodded for Rory to hang up. He did. "You had better hope for your sake that Pontrelli's greed brings him here," the john said, "If he doesn't come by the end of the hour..."

"He'll come. I swear he'll come; he always does."

"Hmph," the john mumbled distrustfully. His tense posture eased up and his grip loosened around the straight-razor, allowing it to rock loosely in the cradle of his fingers. "I apologize if I was discourteous," he said, pacing away from Rory, "Admittedly, I have been known to suffer from mood swings and irritability. I believe that my inappropriate temperament derives from irregular exercise as well as a lack of B-vitamins in my diet. You have been very cooperative with my requests, Whorey Rory, and I by no means wish to imply otherwise. Please excuse my undue harshness."

Rory could not tell if his assailant was being sincere or jeeringly sarcastic. "What do you want with Pontrelli?" he carefully asked.

The john scoffed at the question. "Well, I am a famous celebrity who, after soliciting the affections of one of your coworkers, now finds himself blackmailed by Pontrelli. The pressures of this extortion have led me to undertake drastic measures. I am a former business associate of Pontrelli's who served several years in prison after he testified against me in court. I have sought bloody vengeance since my release. I am a religious fundamentalist who has been commanded by God to cleanse this city of sin by purging those who peddle vice and smut. Or perhaps I am simply deranged? Perhaps I simply derive gratification from the spilling of blood?" The john finished his runaround with a dry giggle.

"Listen," Rory pleaded, "I called him. I left him a message. Pontrelli will come. I promise, he'll come as soon as he listens to his voicemail. I know he will. You don't have to do this. You don't have to keep me here and you don't have to hurt me. I'll leave forever. I won't tell anyone what I've seen here. Please. I'm begging you...I'm so afraid. I don't want to die. Please..." Unable to help himself, Rory began bawling, blubbering hysterically like a scared little child. His vision became glazed over with tears and, through this blurred lens, he watched as the john came toward him.

"Stop it. Please, stop crying. I'm not--Don't look at me like that. Oh, please. *Don't you look at me like that. This is nothing. NOTHING.*"

The room became silent.

Rory held his breath and stared at the john. And the john stared back. Rory could hear him breathing rapidly. He could see his shoulders bouncing up and down and his chest heaving. In spite of the expressionlessness of the Volto, Rory could tell that the stranger was crying.

The john, frustrated and ashamed, turned from Rory, running his glove over his scalp and slumping against the door to the room. Rory brought his knees up and defeatedly buried his face in his lap, surrendering to the fact that his fate was in the hands of an obvious madman. He was out of tears to shed.

"You can put your clothes back on," the john said, "I won't look." Rory had forgotten he was still completely naked from his interrupted shower. He was surprised to find that he wasn't too scared to be embarrassed. Awkwardly cupping his genitals in one hand, Rory shifted off the floor and carefully made his way back to the bathroom.

In the bathroom, Rory looked for a way out of this nightmare: a hiding place or a weapon. He searched his clothes for anything he could possibly fashion into a shiv. Nothing. He felt along behind the toilet for a hollow spot of drywall from which he could perhaps break through and tunnel into the next room. Nothing. For a moment, Rory considered shattering the bathroom mirror with his hairdryer and weaponizing a shard of broken glass. Certainly, the john would hear the commotion and rush in. But perhaps Rory would be fast enough to impale him through with his piece of the mirror. But what if there weren't any knifelike shards? What if the mirror just broke into tiny little pieces, hardly thicker than sand? What would Rory tell the john then? *I tripped and fell into the mirror and it broke.* Rory felt his aggressor would not hesitate to slash his guts out for such a stupid excuse. Defeated and hopeless, Rory crouched down on the wet mat next to the tub.

"How old were you when you first started working for Pontrelli?" The inquiry came from just behind the bathroom door.

"I don't know," Rory whimpered, closing his eyes and wishing that he would finally awaken from the nightmare. He felt so stupid. Why hadn't he turned this creep down when he had the chance? There had been such obvious bad vibes. The prowling. The mercuriality. The hateful teasing. The mask. The red flags had been so infinite, so overt. And it had been entirely in Rory's power to say no. And yet, he didn't. What was it that compelled him? What sordid hypnosis brought him here now?

"I was fourteen," the john said. Rory opened his eyes. "I bet you were around the same age, yeah?" he was asked.

"I was... I was about to turn sixteen." Rory said.

"Were you born and raised in the city?"

"Yeah."

"Not me. I grew up in a commuter suburb, which I despised. My father was a brutal alcoholic who would come to my--I'm sorry. That's a lie too. I wish my father had been an abusive alcoholic. I wish my mother had been a neglectful whore. I wish that we had been starvingly poor. My series of wildly bad decision-making would make so much more sense if I'd had a wildly bad childhood. But, no.

My upbringing was very healthy. My parents, both of them, were loving and supportive people. There was nothing remotely abusive or dysfunctional about my family. I even got along swimmingly with my brother and sister, which I understand is more than most people can say. It was just an ordinary middle-class family. And *that's* what I resented. Every single thing was so hideously ordinary, stable. There was never any controversy or conflict. When you live in a comfort zone, life is a vacuum. Where there is nothing to fear or provoke, there is also nothing to care about or look forward to. It is existence without a beating pulse. Without anything at all. There was no question that made me angrier at the dinner table than, *What did you do today*? Nothing. Of course I did nothing, mother, because there was nothing to do in our nothing town. Nothing, nothing, nothing at all."

"My boredom there was immeasurable and I longed for the adventure of city life. My dreams were filled with dashing monorails, street performers, and impossibly high skyscrapers. I dreamed of danger that would give my life purpose and finally liberate me from my prison of pillows. Finally, after the tedium of my home grew intolerable, I left. I didn't even pack anything, or leave so much as a note. I just came to the city with nothing but some money I had stolen from my parents. And I loved it. I loved the Riverwalk; Wylie Park; the museums at Exhibition Square; watching the cargo freights take off at the harbor. I loved it all, and not just the touristy parts either. I even loved the Alice District. The homebodies from my town had always warned me that urban life wasn't nearly as glamorous as it seemed in movies. They always liked to point out the differences between visiting the city and living in it, and how the roughness of day-to-day living eventually would eventually bring me down. But I loved the roughness. It was the grittiness of it all that felt so wonderfully real to me, totally unlike the phoniness of suburbia. Finally, for the first time in my life, I felt home."

"Of course, it was never easy. There was no work for a fourteen year-old runaway. Nothing legitimate anyway. At first, I just panhandled, picked a few pockets, shoplifted a little bit. I was a real street urchin. But I became increasingly fearful that I would be recognized by a passerby from my parents' missing persons report and dragged back to my suburban hellhole. I tried to balance minimizing my exposure with making enough to sustain myself. It was a challenging game of survival which, while fun at first, eventually became so incredibly exhausting. Then one day, when I was out panhandling, I struck up a conversation with another kid, Kirby, who was only a couple years older than me. He told me about a man who fed, housed, employed, and--most importantly--protected lost boys. No questions asked."

"Lou Pontrelli," Rory whispered from the bathroom. This part of the story was familiar to Rory. He even vaguely remembered hearing the name Kirby years ago. *Kirby used to...Kirby'd always...Kirby'd never...*

"Lou Pontrelli," the john continued. "I was Oliver Twist, brought to Fagin by the Artful Dodger. And, just like that, I had a home, gainful employment, and a new family. Lou was like a father and the other boys were like brothers. We would do anything for each other. Their enemies were my enemies, and vice versa. I loved them. I lived here, Whorey Rory. Not in this exact room—but in a room very much like it. And I imagine some of the younger ones are still here now. I bet you love them as much as I did. I was happy. And everything seemed like it would be okay. I should have sensed something was wrong when the Artful Dodger went away."

"When Kirby disappeared, I only asked Lou about him once. He told me Kirby had gone to work someplace else. And that was that. That is until about a year later when Lou told me that he'd sold off my contract and that I was going to go work somewhere else. Just like Kirby. I told him that I didn't want to work anywhere else. He said I didn't have a choice. You see, with Lou, the merchandise depreciates. Like a used car. Youth is everything to these freak buyers. They can't ravage with their strapping young nephews, or their sons' buddies, or their daughters' boyfriends, so you're their next best bet. I knew you were one of Pontrelli's boys the minute I laid eyes on you. His market likes your kind—smooth skin, big eyes. The 'twinky teen' type. But, like I said, it doesn't last. You put on some muscle. Your laugh lines deepen. Your hairline recedes a little bit. And, just like that, you don't look like anybody's teenage nephew anymore. You go on the clearance rack and, soon, you become a liability to manage. Ah, but Lou—he doesn't pay severance and wish you well. No. He just sells you off someplace new. Like a used car."

"I fought him. And that—that's not a lie. I fought him. I swear I did. I hit him right in the face with a bottle. He hit me back and we went flying over the bar, beating each other senseless even as we cracked down onto the floor. But the other boys, the ones I had come to know as brothers, joined in. They wrestled me off of Pontrelli and held me still while he bashed me into unconsciousness. I was betrayed by my new family, just as I had betrayed my old one."

"I awoke to find myself in a dark place, tied to a crusty chair beneath a single hanging lightbulb. I was encircled by a group of five libertines, each wearing a uniquely grotesque, porcelain face. There was a heavyset man in a monochrome *Bauto* masque, whom in my head I called Billy Gruff for his gravelly voice. There was a woman—the only woman—who wore a black *Moretta* and a veil and a ballgown. Of course, I called her the Lady. There was a tall, lanky, quiet one disguised by the beak of his ridiculous plague doctor helm. I knew him as Father Grim because I thought his cassock made him look like a clergyman. There was Sad Clown, who wore the morose motley and *Arlecchino* of a suicidal Harlequin. He was the gentlest of the lot, though he was sadistic enough to qualify for sure. And finally, there was the Marquis, who wore a grand aristocratic wig... and a gilded *Volto*. Ah Marquis—he was the worst of them all. This was the Masquerade."

"*Welcome to the Carnival of Venice*, the Lady declared. And, with that, a yearlong of festivities and rituals began. They quickly proved even more abusive than I had feared. The Masquerade prohibited me from wearing clothes. They used spiked bindings to keep me from sleeping and they forced me to stay on all fours at all times, like a naked dog with my knees and shinbones painfully leveled by the soiled, cold concrete floor. But all of this was to be expected. Of course, they controlled me. Of course, they beat me. Of course, they raped me. For what other purposes would someone purchase another human being? And yet, their imagination was as boundless as their sadism. They whipped my back with barbed floggers, lashing and lashing away until there was hardly any flesh left. They'd wait weeks, sometimes months, for the skin to grow back. Then they would whip it off again. They suspended me, laying me out against the wall, and hammered spikes into my hands and feet and fingernails. That—that was what they called *passion play*. They forced juiced castor down my throat and smeared me all over with my own sickness. They poured burning oil onto my chest and watched my flesh fizzle, bubble, and pop. Oh, I was thoroughly branded. They pressed a sizzling iron against my back, searing me with a great big *M*; and they ran long needles through my tongue, taking turns to stitch each of their initials inside my mouth. I can still feel the sting of their embroidery prick the gumlines against my cracked teeth. I want to tear it all out. But there's nothing really there anymore. The thread fell out long ago. There's nothing there but invisible scarring and phantom pain."

"And of course, there were varying rituals of imaginative abuses that I cannot begin to describe—that I do not even understand. They used tools that seemed to be from other worlds. The Sad Clown took pictures and filmed everything. He captured my pain with movie-grade cameras, the type of equipment professionals use. I think they were selling the tapes. They recited chants in alien languages. They mutilated every conceivable inch of my body thrice over. All except my face. *Not the face*, they would say if a blade or flame got too close. *He has such a pretty face*. At first, this ground rule confused me. They relished in the ugliness of their sacraments. They obviously did not value beauty. It took quite some time for me to solve this riddle. They didn't want to preserve my face for its beauty. They wanted to preserve my looks of pain. What good was the torture if my face would not twist and contort for them? Without my screams and my agonized expressions, I was nothing but an inanimate slab of meat to slice. They didn't want to objectify me. In spite of all the degradation, suffering, and mutilation, I was to be kept minimally human. My value as a plaything was in my humanity. And, with all this, my face was the only thing left that humanized me."

"Worse yet, they gave me updates on the happy little family that I had left behind. They told me about my sister starting her studies at Edmundson College. My brother's wedding—which I know, in a better world, I would have attended as best man. The layoffs at my father's work. They stalked my family and they told me terrible fantasies of how they would bring them to my dark place. How they would hold a knife to my mother's neck and force my father to do things to..." His voice trailed off. He struggled to produce an end to his sentence. Finally, he choked out three words—*my baby sister*. "These were the traditions and the ceremonies of the Masquerade."

"And then, one day, Pontrelli came back. At first, I thought I was just seeing things. Like a mirage. But it turned out to really be that old, fat, traitorous toad. What the hell was he doing there? I wondered if it had all been just a cruel, sick joke. Or a nightmare that was finally coming to an end, just before a wonderful return to normalcy. From the confines of my prison, I eavesdropped and from his negotiations with the Marquis, Pontrelli revealed the truth of my circumstance. He was leasing me out. Once again, after all this time and torment, I was nothing but a used car. And yet, with this revelation, there was hope. I knew this trial period would determine everything for me. My entire future. I resolved to vandalize myself, to become damaged goods. So I went to the red room, where they developed the Sad Clown's pictures. They assumed, like Pavlov's Dog, that I had been thoroughly conditioned against any and all escape attempts and, consequently, they trusted me to stay put. But, in my incredible desperation, I proved them wrong. I broke free from my psychological bindings. I went to the tray of etching acid where they burned serial numbers and toned our negatives. And I dipped my face into it."

"Oh God, Rory. I felt everything. I cannot even begin to describe the unspeakable agony of slowly disintegrating myself. Imagine forcing yourself to slice open your eyeball; to drink boiling water; to flay your gums; to smash your teeth down onto a curbside. Imagine the anguish and the fear it would take to compel you to inflict such tremendous pain unto yourself. And I was still a *boy*. The nightmare was horrible enough for a seventeen year-old to willfully melt his face—eyelids, lips, nose, and cheeks—away in caustic chemicals. And that nightmare awaits you, Rory. Don't think for a moment that I was just one of the unlucky ones. I was *lucky*. I was the sale that never went through. I was the one who got away."

"So please, I beg of you—don't look at me like that. I can't stand it. Please don't look at me like I'm a monster. I'm not a monster. I miss my mom and dad," the john cried, his voice cracking with pain, "I wanted to go to my big brother's wedding. I wanted to go to my little sister's graduation. I wanted...I want my family. I want it back and I miss them more than anything. But it's all gone, Rory. It's all gone and it's *all his fault.*"

Rory opened the bathroom door to find the pitiable phantom, weeping against the wall. One hand continued to grasp his razor. The other clutched his face. The Volto. The Marquis' Volto.

Knock, knock.

The john went quiet.

"Rory!" a voice called out from the hallway, "You in there? Ror?"

The masked trick looked at Rory up close, perhaps wondering if the boy would call out and warn his employer of his impending doom. But the boy just stared at the Volto, speechless and witting. For the first time all night, Rory noticed his client's eyes, which were bloodshot and shadowed behind the mask.

The john rose from the wall and moved to answer the door, gripping his razor in his hand like the most imposing barber in the world. His pace was fast but measured against the rhythm of a silent metronome.

"Rory? I'm fixing to kick in the door. Open the hell up!"

Suddenly, the john stopped in his war path at the front of the door. With his back to Rory, he reached up to his jaw, took off his mask, and placed it on the dresser. Then he opened the door.

Rory could see Lou Pontrelli's grimace turn pale as he was met with a face from hell.

"What in God's—"

With the grace of a dancer, the john swung his arm out at Pontrelli. From the precision of the swipe, it was clear that he had done this before. His blade swiftly disappeared into Pontrelli's neck before reemerging seamlessly from out the other side, bringing with it a trailing ribbon of gore. Instantly, a curtain of red fell down the front of Pontrelli's throat, painting him down from his fat jaw to his ugly brown bowling shirt.

For a moment, Pontrelli stood there, processing what had just transpired. Finally, after seconds of stillness, he raised his fingers to his dissected gullet. He tried to pinch it closed to keep in the cascades of blood that were now rushing out of him like a sprinkler system. The attempt at stoppage was to no avail--the blood merely began seeping out from between his sausage-link fingers.

Pontrelli recoiled back into the hallway, still clutching his opened esophagus. His eyes were white and wide with fear. As he backed into the door of the adjacent room, Pontrelli let out a sickening gargle that echoed from deep within his sodden gorge. His lips rapidly opened and closed. From inside the room, Rory could see his boss was trying to desperately mouth something. *Jason*.

"If only we'd had more time," the john said as Pontrelli began sliding down the door to the floor, dragged down by his dying weight, "There was so much I wished to include in our farewell."

Rory wasted no time. He leapt off the bed and, as soon as his bare feet touched the carpet, he lunged out of the room. He raced past the john gleaming with carnivorous vengeance, past the pimp sputtering his wet final breaths, and past rooms 415-430. He sprinted and sprinted and sprinted. He didn't look back until he reached the end of the hallway. His feet did not stop as he glanced back to see if the john was after him. He saw that the killer still loomed over Pontrelli's body and that he still faced the wall, apparently too unbothered to turn in the direction of his escaped captive. The profile of his face was nothing but a sliver of a vaguely red blur, too far down the corridor to make out.

In the lobby, Tracy the Lady-Thing, applying another layer of lipstick, watched as a frenzied young man, shoeless and shaken, ran past her, out of the Hotel Fiero and into the night.

In the month passed since Rory's encounter with the john, the weather finally cooled down. Rory did not return to the Hotel Fiero. He did not return to Ketchum Road. He did not return to the Alice District. Instead, Rory returned to his mother, who lived in a studio apartment along the Haeckel River. He flung his arms around her and cried into her shoulder, begging for her forgiveness. And she cried too.

Rory spent the rest of that summer crashing on his mother's couch, working at Birdee's—the sports bar his mother co-managed--, and practicing for his G.E.D. exam. He met with counselors at the local career center, who mapped out and helped price their yearlong HVAC technician program. His mother helped him buy an entirely new wardrobe for his new life, replacing tight shirts and torn skinny jeans with polos and slacks.

On one frigid Tuesday morning, Rory exited his mother's apartment for his 6 a.m. shift at Birdee's and nearly stepped on a manila packet left in front of their door. The envelope had been placed right in the middle of the welcome mat. An address sticker had been stuck to it. *For Whorey Rory.*

With a deep breath, Rory tore open the flimsy paper wrapping. Inside it was $1,500, and a note that read, *Thanks for the night.*

It Comes in Threes
Nick Swain

Richard could see her. She was driving the Mercedes, merging into the carpool lane of the terminal. The windows were dark. Too dark. "Tinted" is what they call them when they're that dark. He didn't like them but they'd been her idea, and he'd never been able to say "No" to her. Ever. She wasn't the kind of woman you said "No" to. Through the shaded glass, he could see that abundance of garnet-hair he'd loved for so many years. When the sedan came closer he could even see the rubies dangling from each of her lobes; earrings he'd given her just last year as an anniversary gift. They were perfect for her. Even now. He thought they might look pretentious on other women; like they might be attempting to project an image of Romanian royalty. But never on her.

His stomach churned, but he'd already chewed up his last roll of Tums.

She parked beside him and emerged from the car. She was smiling. She looked just as he'd imagined she would. Red feathered-hair, her buxom features obvious even under that fur-coat. Her heels rapping against the concrete as she trudged the short distance around the grill to him.

He embraced her hug. Inside, a cruel, intangible hand tightened its grasp, twisting his intestines like a carny might a thin balloon. "Hello, Rita," he breathed into her ear.

"I've missed you so, dear. Happy Birthday!"

He held her tighter.

"How was your flight?"

"Uneventful. But I thought of you the entire time."

This seemed to please her, and she tugged him by the jacket to the car. He tipped the skycap and shrugged it off when the young man pointed out that he'd handed him a twenty. Richard climbed behind the wheel and when the boy was finished loading his bags he waved them off.

"I've made our reservation at Brannigan's and reserved our table. And Sean is going to meet us at The Pierre tonight. I tried to keep you to myself, but it seems everyone just *had* to see the birthday boy. But I'll get you alone later."

She kept her hand on his leg the entire drive to Brannigan's. When they arrived a pretty young hostess showed them to their usual booth at the window. He enjoyed watching the sea. In all the years they'd been dining there, Richard spent most of his meals taking in the ocean-line and the docked fishing boats where the gulls constantly perched, providing only the dutiful grunts of awareness as his beautiful wife carried on one-way conversations.

Tonight, she had all his attention. Rita told him all about her doleful weekend; of the lonesome idle hours, spent rereading the last erotic paperback she'd snagged from the bestsellers rack, and having her hair colored a month early to spend an afternoon in the rush-hour of salon gossip. But mostly just missing him. Waiting for him to come back.

He knew she was lying.

He ordered the Salisbury steak, extra potatoes and onions, along with a Molson. Rita had the salad. She always had the salad. Of course she did, she had that enticing figure to worry about; the same maintained shape that had won him over so many years ago. He'd wondered in the last few days, on top of everything else, if he'd still love her if she were to become fat. Or even too gauntly. He thought, yes, he would.

He would always love her. She would always be his.

Richard took the final bite of his steak, and almost as though they'd been lying in wait, a group of waiters appeared and broke into a painful falsetto: *"Happy Birthday to you! Happy Birthday to you!"*

He smiled at her the entire time. When the waiters finished they left a small chocolate cake with a scoop of melting vanilla ice cream behind, a single candle burning in its center. He wondered at what point they stopped using the exact number of candles for the recipients age.

He cut pieces for the two of them. She ate hers, but he could only glare down at his.

"Excuse me, dear. I won't be a minute." He wiped his mouth and rose from the table.

"Hurry back, Richard. I'd hate to eat all your birthday cake."

He sauntered to the back of the restaurant and into a dim corridor, past a short fellow who turned out to be the only one in the men's room. He was glad. Richard stared into the same mirror he must have used countless times before and smiled at himself. He couldn't hold it anymore. He turned around and lunged for a stall, retching into the bowl. Once more, and then he gagged on his own sickness for about a minute. He kicked the stall-door shut and sat up against the wall. He flushed the commode and listened out for any others coming in as his thirty-five-dollar dinner literally went down the drain. *"Pull it together, man. Pull it together."*

Disgusted by his own nerves, he spat the thick, acrid taste into the bowl. Why should he be so shaken? It was going the way he'd thought it would. She hadn't seen him coming out of the cab fifteen minutes ahead of her at the airport. She didn't know that he'd been back since the day before. She hadn't seen him. He'd seen her. Watched her as she went to *his* apartment; she'd been carrying champagne with her the last time, as though that final night of his supposed absence had been something to celebrate. But that hadn't been when he decided to kill her. He'd decided to kill her back home, in Little Rock. That last day before leaving when he hadn't caught any fish. He'd caught three the day before. He thought about the three that entire last day; maybe that was why he hadn't caught any others.

His legs were still trembling as he pulled himself up. He knew he needed to do it soon or it would never be done at all. The gun was in his bag. A .38 he'd picked up in a sporting goods store back home. The portly hillbilly who'd sold it to him had kept insisting on the magnums. Richard declined each time, unable to explain how he didn't want something that would completely annihilate his beautiful wife's face. He couldn't tell the man that though she'd betrayed him in the worst way possible, he wanted her punishment to be instantaneous; without pain. Not too much fear. He wanted her to know he loved her, but that he was disappointed by her, and that he would be in so much more pain about it than she would be. And then it would be over.

But he had to do it now.

After paying the check they climbed into the Mercedes and Richard pulled onto the highway and started uptown.

"You just missed our exit, dear," Rita said.

"I've got my own little surprise. I thought we'd go somewhere. Just for a bit."

"I thought you wanted to meet Sean for drinks?"

"I do. And I will. It's early, he'll be there forty minutes from now. Come on…you can't refuse the birthday boy."

"Oh, Richard, you're trouble."

A few miles down he took an exit to a town called Julton. If it meant anything to Rita yet, she didn't let on. Richard pulled into the first service station he saw. "Would you mind getting me some cigarettes, dear. My stomach is acting up."

"I wish you wouldn't smoke so much."

"Last pack. I promise."

He watched her strut into the store and then he slinked out of the car and popped the trunk. He'd forgotten the exact shirts he'd hidden the gun between and had an internal moment of panic when it wasn't under the first one. But he found it towards the bottom. He didn't look at it. He watched the station door as he dropped the revolver into his jacket. He climbed back into the car and flipped on the radio; somewhere in the Atlantic a hurricane was forming and meant trouble for Florida, and the shrill, overly-enthused voice of the stations commercial speaker promised an upcoming round of the most influential love songs from the Home of The Golden Oldies.

Now, he thought. If it's not now, it'll just go on. And that would be worse than anything. It can't go on, not with *him*. Maybe it could've been anyone but him: Ed, the lanky four-eyed numbers man from the office he brought around the house for poker nights. That would certainly be humiliating, but it would be different than her being with *him*. Or maybe even with Zach; the self-proclaimed ladies' man who seemed to have made it his mission in life to let his buddies know he could have any woman he wanted if he felt like it. Maybe. But it wasn't.

A minute later, Rita came back out with his cigarettes and they drove deeper into Julton.

He only found the dirt road because the ramshackle remains of the old house still stood at the end of the long, vacant highway, watching over what had been regarded as Lovers' Lane for anyone who could find their way there and got a kick out of the ghost stories surrounding the place. There was supposed to have been an old couple that lived in that house up until the twenties. The story was, their son enlisted in the first World War and came back cold, bitter, and missing half of his face. Some people said the gas the Germans used made him crazy. They said there used to be neighbors (though no one knew where they were supposed to have lived, as there was only one house around) that would see the disfigured veteran roaming aimlessly up and down the lane as though he were waiting for something to come along. One night, no one exactly knew when, the man killed the couple with his trench knife and then went down the dirt road by the house and cut his own throat. His specter supposedly haunted the place; murdering any lustful teenagers unlucky enough to screw around on his land. Richard and Rita had been there every other day for months at a time when they were first dating. Before either had their own place out of the dorms or had even considered moving in together. They never saw anything supernatural on that road, but the excitement was there each time. A sense of isolation. Of danger.

She recognized the macabre scene of their early romance and was delighted.

As he pulled onto the road, her hand was back on his leg, inching its way to his inner thigh. She was almost touching the gun in his pocket.

When they were down the road and the mouth of sky disappeared from where they'd come from, Richard parked the car.

It was quiet, aside from the radio. And dark. The headlights offered the only light, other than the ghostly eye of a great white ball peering down at them from the sky like a steady, omnipotent spotlight. Waiting. Expecting. Urging.

"Richard…"

From the radio, mellifluous words of love and wisdom sounded out from The King: *"…wise men say…only fools rush in…"*

The sickness inside of him seethed. His hands numbed the way they did when he vomited. The worse he felt, the louder the music seemed to become.

"...but I can't help, falling in love...with...you..."

"Richard, I really have missed you. I know those fishing trips back where you grew-up are good for you, but these last few days I've just really wanted you back here with me."

If it had been anybody else. Ed, Zach, the cable guy, the fucking maid, Jesus. But not him. Not his best friend. Not the sensitive, successful artist who'd been with them since college. The only one who'd been with them from the beginning. The two humans he trusted implicitly. It was unforgivable. It was so serious that in the beginning he'd denied it. Smiled and drank away the pain, silently. But after that was over, he followed her. It was true; every time she went out she went to *his* apartment. And she'd always lie about where'd she'd been. Every time, so easily. He'd almost hired a Private Detective to follow the both of them, but what would have been the point in that? He'd caught them. He didn't want anyone else to know how'd they hurt him. It had been going on for a least a month. He watched *him* greet her at the door once, but that was the most he saw. He didn't want to see anything else. He imagined them in that apartment — he'd been in it many times himself. He wondered if *he* fucked her in his studio on top of a blank canvas, their nude bodies drenched in paint, laughing at him; snickering, lecherous fiends indulging in a loving husband's ignorance. On the other side of his best friend's apartment door Richard imagined loathsome acts of perversion carried out in a deliberate means to shame him. Every time she kissed him he thought the worst and had to brush his teeth.

"Richard? Richard, what did you have in mind?"

If it had been anyone else.

He thought about the steelhead he'd pulled out of the river that first day in Little Rock; the three of them. Lifeless, ugly, alien corpses that had been deceived with a hook, and caught with the same. There were three of them: Sean, Rita, and Richard.

The best friend, the wife, and the cuckold.

"Listen, Richard, we'd better start out soon. Sean is certain to be at The Pierre by now."

Her saying *his* name did it. She'd said it earlier in the night, maybe more than once even. But never while he'd been thinking of them…together.

He jerked for the gun. He'd planned on telling her that he knew, and that he loved her, but didn't forgive her. He'd planned on slipping the short muzzle of the revolver around the back of her seat and in between the head cushion. He'd planned on her not having to see it coming. But when she said *his* name then, he exploded. "Sean is certain to be *in the fucking ground tonight!*"

Rita watched her husband take the gun out; the hammer only briefly snagging, ripping strings out in the fabric of his jacket. And then suddenly it was in her face. *"Richard!"* He pulled the trigger and watched the hammer rise and fall just before he shut his eyes. *Click.* He opened them; Rita's own were crossed, staring into the black-eye of the .38 in her face. He pulled the trigger again and she flinched. *Click. Click, click, click.* Each time the hammer dropped and the cylinder spun, each time Rita jumped and blinked in rapid successions, never taking her eyes off the guns' barrel. Each time it dry-fired.

And Richard remembered the box of shells he'd hidden inside a pair of dress socks. They were still in his bag. He never even loaded the goddamn thing.

He took the gun away from her, gawking at it as though it had betrayed him. Rita's jaw bounced up and down like a ventriloquists' stuttering dummy.

He knew it was too late. He dropped the gun and pounced on her before she could speak. He didn't want her to talk to him. Snarling and cursing, he wrapped his hands around her neck. He was strangling her, and just before her tongue jutted from her mouth for good she managed to croak: "Ri…why…"

"*Because I love you too much!*" he screamed in her face.

Her eyes bulged in their sockets, her hands clasped onto his as they choked her, her feet put up the most struggle behind him until one finally stilled against the dash; her heel had caught on the volume knob and was cranking the music up and down. "…Ri…"

"…like a river flows, surely to the sea, darling so it goes, some things are meant to be…"

"Because I love you too much. And *he* can't have you!"

Her hold on his hands weakened. And finally, her foot dropped to the console, spinning the volume all the way. And he knew she was dead. Not so much because her body went limp, but because he'd watched something go out of her eyes. She didn't look afraid anymore.

"…take my hand… take my whole life too…"

He opened the door and fell out of the car. The love song went resounding into the night, and his dead, slumped-up wife watched him crawl in the dirt, crying, gagging. He wanted to let the sickness out of him but there was nothing left. And so he gagged.

"…for I can't help falling in love with you…"

Still on his knees, he lifted himself. Gawking into the cold light of the moon hanging above him, still, watching. Showing no gratification. Only knowing that there was more, telling him he wasn't finished. That if he could do that, he could do anything.

"I know. I know."

There was more, but the worst part was behind him.

He spoke to the sky, "I haven't forgotten about you Sean."

***

Sean was waiting at the bar when Richard arrived at The Pierre. The artist stood out amongst the slew of stockbrokers and lawyers. Instead of a double-breasted suit with cuff links he donned a leather coat and a pair of black Brutinis. Rockstar length hair curling just above his shoulders was another crowd-only. Sean had often told him that he'd spent most of his teenage summers with his mother in Hell's Kitchen; a part-time slum kid, who'd taken his daddy's offer to pay for his schooling, only to drop out half way through after impressing a gallery owner who knew all the right people. He'd long since been bumping shoulders with the best of them, and still he dressed like that. Maybe that rugged individualism had been what lured Rita to him. Or maybe the way he never seemed to have a thinner or thicker shadow of bristle on his face had been what won her over.

He'd shoot him through that face.

He spotted Richard from the bar and raised his glass; no doubt a soda-pop. As a successful artist, Sean was obliged to a life-long substance abuse problem he could conveniently fly off the rails of.

"Richard, you old-dog, you already losing track of the hours? If this were whiskey I'd have drowned by now."

Richard sneered and patted him on the shoulder. "Whiskey Sour," he told the bartender. The gun in his pocket clanked against the bar as he took his stool, but no one seemed to notice. He'd been sure to load all five chambers this time.

"Get the birthday boy a double, on me," said Sean. "So, how was the motherland? Catch anything decent?"

"I wouldn't say decent," Richard spoke into his drink. The liquor burned going down, at first frothing bursting bubbles of pain in his stomach, and then all at once numbing him completely.

"Where's Rita? I thought she'd be here tonight? As a matter of fact, she told me she would."

"She wasn't feeling well. I dropped her off at home."

"Really? She said that?"

How dare he. "You two talk a lot while I was gone?" It came out before he could think better.

Sean looked to him like he'd been lightly slapped. And then he grinned. "You've always been a funny guy, Dick. This time it wasn't so funny."

"I guess I didn't realize I was trying to be."

"You're serious?"

Richard took a drink.

"So, what, one of the three amigos ain't allowed to speak to the other now? That it?"

Richard still didn't answer him.

"You're a funny guy, Dick," he tossed a bill on the bar and stood.

"Hold on, Sean." He stopped him before he could walk off. "I'm just tired. I…I didn't mean anything."

Sean didn't speak. But he didn't leave.

"Come on. Sit down, let's have a good time."

Sean moved back by his stool. "Rita really said she was sick? I talked to her just a couple hours ago about you two meeting me here. You obviously got the message."

He wanted to yank out the .38 and plug him right there. Questioning his word about the whereabouts of *his* wife. As though that were any sort of rightful business of his. "Tell you what… how about we go to my place. We'll have a drink…or a soda…and you can see her for yourself."

"Well actually," Sean said, "I've got something I want to show you. I guess it's kind of a surprise."

Richard's face tightened. "Here?"

"Yea, that's right."

"You've got a surprise…for me…"

"Don't look so forlorn, Oldman. I think you're going to like it."

"A surprise."

"Now he's catchin' on." Sean stood and gestured for Richard to follow.

What could he say? No Sean, *you* follow *me* because I've got my own little surprise. That's right, just over here into the parking lot; that's where he thought he'd do it. Pop the trunk and allow the ghastly, transfixing sight of Rita's corpse to prod him with a harsh surge of reality just before he blew his head off. He'd topple over into the trunk, Richard would shut it, and then he'd be on his way.

Only now he was taking *him* somewhere. He followed Sean to the hotel elevators, the shaded-glow of the lobby lights gave the sandy-marble walls of the vestibule a haunted, almost orange tinge. They loaded into the car with a group of others, the young operator never took his eyes away from the panel of buttons. Richard stood in the corner, his hands in his jacket pockets. They got off on the fortieth floor and the blood began pounding in Richards ears, he knew where Sean was taking him, and he hated him for it. He was taking him to the same suite that he'd proposed to Rita in right after graduation. Sean had been there. It had been a place of ceremonial significance between the three of them; he and Rita because of their engagement, and Sean simply because he'd been their closest friend; the best man. He'd been the one to pop the first cork when she said yes, showering them both in Dom Perignon.

And now he was taking him there. Richard couldn't understand why. And then it occurred to him that this could be it; Sean's stand. Maybe Rita *was* supposed to be here tonight. Maybe they were going to stand up to him. Say, this is it, Dick, old boy. We're leaving you. We thought it only right to end it where it began in a sense.

As they moved down the corridor Sean was carrying on about the after-party of his first art show; he was going on about the old days. Richard wasn't listening. Richard could only think about how he couldn't wait to kill Sean; actually *couldn't* wait. He'd kill him in that room. Soon as he opened that door. It couldn't wait for outside, it had to end here. He'd let off a single shot, Sean would fall to the floor, and then he'd shut the door and walk off. Maybe he'd make it to the elevator and down to the lobby, maybe he wouldn't. Right now, that didn't matter. All that mattered was that Sean died.

They were there. In front of the door. Sean fished for his key and grinned at Richard. "Close your eyes."

"What?"

"I promised someone I'd make you close your eyes."

"Oh."

"Now keep them closed until I tell you."

He never shut his eyes, and when Sean turned around and unlocked the door Richard pulled out the revolver. It snagged quietly (much the way it had earlier) in his pocket and then its short barrel was pushing against the back of Sean's head. He jerked the trigger as the door opened; the blast was louder than he could've imagined, a bullet went ripping through the back of Sean's skull and exploded out of his forehead and into the ceiling.

"Happy Birthday!" the room of guests sang out as they were stippled in Sean's blood. And then they were screaming. Sean crumpled to the floor and Richard could see them. All of them. It was a surprise party alright.

There was: Ed and Zach, they were up front with Richard's young secretary, Mary Ann; and then there was Stan and Jill Penzler, the older couple from the apartment next door; Richard's Director from the office, Mike Sultan; there were nearly a dozen others, co-workers, neighbors, plenty of friendly-faces that were now contorted in an ugly blend of horror and incredulity.

Richard was aware of his friends, crying and brushing past him — mindful of the blood pooling around the sprawled out figure by the door. But he wasn't looking at them, he was looking at Rita. There, in the center of the room, displayed proudly in the middle of where the crowd had been gathered, she looked to him; her brilliant blue eyes a soft pastel, no larger than the size of quarters. She looked to him with all the love and vivaciousness she'd demonstrated throughout their marriage. There was no hate and no fear in her eyes. She watched him from an ornate-honey frame, her face flecked in spots of blood like ominous crimson freckles.

The world seemed to stir; lucidity surfing the dizzy waves of a brooding sea just ahead of a storm of devastating comprehension. Richard's skull felt more like a shaken soda-can. And the sickness had never been worse.

For over a decade — long before the troubles — Richard had pleaded with Sean to paint Rita's portrait. It had begun as a breeze-shooter, but gradually transformed into an obsession. Sean had always refused, telling him that if what he created did not live up to the expectations of a naturalistic, mirror image of her, he'd never forgive him. Richard had always assured him that this wouldn't be so, but Sean still wouldn't hear of it. This kept up for years until Richard had given up altogether on pressuring Sean to do the deed. But he never let him forget about it.

Or Rita. Rita had known. He'd often brought it up in front of the two, in the hopes it would incite Sean into going through with it.

He finally had. And Richard couldn't help but admire the work of his two closest friends.

Other pictures began to take shape; one-by-one, like stark puzzle pieces in Richard's reeling mind. Simple things like: why Rita might've been spending all that time in Sean's apartment (where he happened to work) and why she would lie about it. Why Sean had stopped inviting him over. Why she'd never seemed to spend the night there, even that last night, when she thought he was out of town… with the champagne…maybe they'd been celebrating the completion of something after all.

Simple things. The driving forces of murder.

Richard moved deeper into the room; mindful of his best friend's body, but not bothering to avoid the pool of blood. He looked down at the artist, the only sensation even remotely relatable to relief was that Sean hadn't seen it coming. But Rita *had*. Rita had suffered at *his* hands. He thought of her in the trunk of that car down in the parking garage as his shoes squished lightly along the carpet, a red trail of footprints followed him to the bar by the window. He poured himself a bourbon, not troubling with ice cubes or a water chaser, listening to the formidable reverberations of sirens belting along somewhere down below. He knew it was too soon, but he couldn't help but feel that they were coming for him. He gulped down the last of his drink and sauntered back over to the middle of the room and stood in front of her. He felt like she had the right to watch. He shut his eyes, the steel of the muzzle was cold beneath his chin. A minute later he opened them to hers and pulled the trigger.

Dorchester
Bill Davidson

Tom Button was driving a stolen Audi with fake plates, impossible to trace back to him. Still, he wore gloves and followed an old school paper map, with handwritten directions. He would burn that when he arrived at the hotel in Dorchester, a small town in rural Dorset. The county town, it was described as.

It was December, a few days before Christmas and just after mid-day, overcast, but Button slid his aviators on as he came to the outskirts, pulling his baseball cap low. If this car was ever found, he didn't want a CCTV image showing him driving it.

He paused only briefly at traffic lights, but long enough to see he was about to cross an old stone bridge into the town. To left and right were snow covered fields, the road ahead rising turning into a picture postcard. Old sandstone houses and what looked like a church with a big clock, a tower of some kind. Christmas decorations hung across the street, nothing lit up at this time of day.

It made Button feel like an alien, a city dweller arriving in some ancient and sleepy backwater. He breathed out an irritated hiss. Who, in a comfortable old place like this, needed killed?

The phone on the passenger seat still hadn't vibrated, a message coming through to show who the target was, which was frustrating. That phone would go off Westminster Bridge as soon as he got back, the contract completed.

Button drove past a gentleman's outfitters that looked like something from before he was born, tea rooms and the Shire Hall, all the way to the Top o'Town roundabout where he took a left, doubling back down a narrow street of real cobbles and into the car park of the Casterbridge Hotel. He stepped out and put a lighter to his map, letting it burn on the ground, then took his suit-bag and hold-all out of the boot, the loaded Glock easy to hand in there.

The hotel didn't look much from the rear, cramped between other buildings and so old it's worn sandstone blocks seemed to sink into the ground. He could stand a night in someplace like this, though, for a contract worth fifty grand, his biggest ever pay-day.

He needed it. A pay-out like that, he could be very nearly square with Big Eddie. Enough to give him time to breathe, anyway.

He walked out of the cold, taking his aviators and hat off as he went. It was as gloomy as he had expected, but clean and only slightly musty. The furniture in the lobby was heavy and grand, in a faded way, tinseled up for the season and with a ram-packed tree in the corner. The background music wasn't Christmas though, it was muted classical. Like a period film set.

A receptionist beamed at him as he came in. He thought she was very pretty but too young for him.

He checked the other entrances, and scanned for a camera, but they came so small now he probably wouldn't spot it.

He smiled back, not giving it much, friendly enough but not laying it on. Nothing to stick in the memory. An unusually tall man, heavy in the shoulder and darkly handsome, he always had trouble with that.

"Hi, I have a room booked. Name of Collins."

Her grin stayed in place as her eyes switched to the screen in front of her, a couple of taps on a mouse and she was turning to pick a key from the peg board behind her, a real brass one with a leather fob, no cards in this place.

"Excellent, Mr. Collins. Pre-paid. Just what we like! You're in 205."

The stairs and elevator were to his right, through a pair of glazed doors, and Button caught movement in the edge of his vision, someone coming to the bottom of the steps. He glanced sideways then quickly shifted his eyes to refocus on the receptionist. Something wasn't right.

He leaned to pick up his bag, getting a look at the person coming through the swing doors, a stumpy guy with dark hair and bad skin, but he had a look about him that Button knew well.

This was a hard man, a tough guy, maybe even an enforcer, the way he looked and held himself. Their eyes caught for just a moment and he saw the expression on the man's face, the same look of recognition.

The pistol was in the bag, he could unzip and have it out in seconds. But the guy's long dark coat had that swing to it, something heavy under there. Button, no choice, turned his back and smiled at the receptionist as she came around the front of her desk.

"I'll show you to your room, Mr. Collins. It's on the top floor, so we can take the elevator."

The back of Button's neck was prickling, but he ignored it. He felt sure this must be the man he had been sent to kill, but the guy had him cold. The receptionist was looking over her shoulder, smiling but looking uncertain.

"Everything ok, Mr. King?"

Button twisted to see, his expression carefully mild, diffident, the face of a civilian.

The man she called King was standing at the rear door, his left hand ready to push, his right hanging by his side, as if it hadn't decided what to do. He wasn't looking at the pretty receptionist. He was looking at Button.

Button gave him a half smile, trying for Hugh Grant at his most politely uncertain, dithering. King's eyes narrowed, then slid away. He turned without speaking and was gone.

The receptionist took a moment, stretching her mouth into an over-wide, deliberately forced smile that said, it takes all sorts. An apology in there too. Following her to the lift, Button said, "That was downright rude. To you, I mean."

She rolled her eyes. "It's fine, really."

Then, getting into the lift, holding the door as though she had never used one before, "I'm used to it."

Button stepped past her and turned to check if the man was coming back. The doors slid closed.

"I don't think it is fine, you know. Is he a regular?"

He wondered would she decline to comment, but she said, "No, he's American. One night only, like yourself."

She leaned in, conspiratorial, and dropped her voice. "Thank God."

Then, realizing what she had just said, "Oh, sorry, I didn't mean you, Mr. Collins."

Button felt himself flush, and knew his smile had some natural shyness in it. This was a very pretty girl, who smelled great, and he was human.

"No, that's ok."

She seemed embarrassed for a moment, then the door opened, and she hurried out, again holding it open. The top floor was also the second, and the old floorboards creaked as he followed her slim legs down the carpet to his room, which she opened.

"Well, I'll leave you to it."

Again, it felt like she held his eye for just a second longer than normal, and he said, "He didn't look American."

She laughed out loud at that, looking up at him. "What do they look like then?"

He was smiling right back at her, the two of them standing outside his room. "Ok, you got me there."

She seemed to think for a second, then said, "Funny, he was trying to put on an accent. Like he didn't want me to know he was from The States. But..." she shrugged, "Definitely American. I shouldn't really be telling you this."

"Don't worry. I won't let on."

He wanted to think of something else to say, keep her there, but that didn't make a bit of sense, what with the business he had in this town, and he was coming up blank anyway. One last smile, she had a killer smile, and she was gone.

The room was surprisingly large, and, he decided absolutely fine. Nothing was new, but it was clean, with fresh cotton sheets. His wife, his ex-wife, would have loved it, preferring it over modern hotels, the kind she called sterile. This, she would say, had character.

He wasn't thinking much about the room, though, he was thinking about King, the American who hadn't managed to hide his accent. He checked his phone, but still no word of who the hit was. Maybe King, or King might be the target's protector. Either way, he had clocked Button. It was just about possible that his Hugh Grant impression had done the trick, but he wasn't about to bet his life on it.

He had wanted to ask the receptionist, was King with another party? But that was taking it too far. He wanted to ask her out for a drink, and that was taking it way too far.

Button locked his door and took his gun out, leaving it handy on the bed. Then, he sat for a while, wondering what to do. He hadn't eaten. No sense letting himself get hungry.

He hopped to the floor and dropped, popping fifty quick press ups, then did some stretching exercises and changed into his suit. Once the long coat was on, you could barely tell he was wearing a shoulder holster. Taller than King by a good six inches, he had the bulk to hide that gun.

Unless you really knew what to look for.

***

Button nodded to the receptionist as he went out, noticing her name badge. He was sure she hadn't been wearing it earlier and had to wonder, was it there for him?

"See you later, Holly. Just going for a stretch of the legs."

"Nice suit, Mr. Collins."

"Call me Tom. Only my bank manager calls me Mr. Collins."

She smiled, "Ok, Tom it is."

He stepped through the front door and into watery sunshine thinking, what the fuck are you doing? Now she knows your real first name.

Button stood for a while, looking up and down the street, shivering despite his coat. A steady stream of cars ran either way, a few shoppers wandering around. Nobody looked at him or, more tellingly, quickly away. Nobody stepped into a doorway.

He turned right, going downhill, past a miniature museum that seemed to have Tutankhamen stuff in it. He paused, pretending to read whilst checking behind him. No King, or anybody else. That he could see.

He continued, past old banks and an older church, a street that had been turned into a pedestrian precinct, busy on this December afternoon, a group of carolers singing Hark the Heralds. He kept going, eventually turning right to find another two small museums, shoehorned into what looked like old houses. One was Terracotta warriors, the other — this made him grin — was called the Teddy Bear Museum. Another right and he was walking past yet another little museum, a six-foot plastic Stegosaurus sitting outside.

Back in the pedestrian precinct, he walked past old buildings with modern shop fronts on their ground floors — Fat Face, White Stuff, the usual. The carolers were still there, now singing Good King Wenceslas, a dozen or so people stopping to listen and drop money into charity pots. He found a café with a good view of the precinct and sat with his sandwich, watching shoppers wander by carrying their Christmas bags, wrapped up against the cold.

He was watching when Karl Weeks walked by. His old partner wearing a long dark coat similar to his own, hands in his pockets as he casually scanned the street.

A lot went through Button's mind in the few seconds it took Weeks to pass the café. Like, maybe Weeks, the guy who left it all behind to go north, set up a bar, was the target. He always was an awkward bastard, too hard for his own good, but getting on now, well over fifty. Or maybe Weeks had come out of retirement to be King's minder, if so, what was he doing strolling down the street?

Something was badly wrong here and the best, most sensible, thing to do was to walk straight to that hotel. Nod and smile one last time to the lovely Holly. Get in the stolen Audi and drive.

Button dropped money on his table and eased out of the door, keeping close to the shop fronts as he followed Weeks. It wasn't easy and he had to hang well back because his old friend was being careful, checking for a tail. Which told Button, loudly and clearly, he had a good reason to be careful. A rural town in the middle of Dorset and a serious London heavy was watching his back like a hawk. The sound of the carolers faded and here was an animatronic Santa on a full-sized sleigh, people shaking charity tins, then a violinist, a teenage girl making a decent job of Silent Night. Button couldn't help but stare at her as he passed, she looked so like Elaine, how he imagined she'd be in maybe five years. He tossed a tenner into her cap and moved on.

Weeks strolled into a department store and Button hung well back to wait. From time to time, he checked around him, so it was a surprise when Weeks leaned in to tell him, "Don't think I'm in there no more, mate."

Button turned to find Weeks was still staring hard at the department store, as if expecting himself to come out at any moment.

"I'm beginning to think I might have bailed."

Then, "Fancy a pint?"

***

They were sitting in a bar with an open coal fire and a dog that kept coming to be petted and posters advertising a Friday night meat draw. Weeks had his pint of ale and Button had a single Glenmorangie.

Button said, "Fuck's going on, Karl?"

Weeks didn't answer straight away. Instead, he looked around the bar. "Maybe I should move here, what d'you think? My place hasn't a tenth of this atmosphere. You here to off me, Tom?"

Button thought about it, then leaned back, twisting his glass but not drinking. "Honestly. I don't know."

Weeks nodded like something had been confirmed. "I got here this morning. Drove to Southampton and took the train the rest of the way."

"Yea?"

"Yea. Thing was, I saw somebody I know get on a couple of stops later."

"He see you?"

"Nah."

"Who was this?"

"Greg Hollis."

Button sat back. "Wait now. The Yank? Guy they call The Man with no Heart?"

"The fuckin Man with no Heart. Nastiest bastard I ever crossed paths with. Next thing, Tom Button is following me down the street, making a right pig's ear of it by the way. You goin to tell me what's going on?"

"What's he look like, this Hollis?"

"Not as tall as you, I'd put him about six-one. Looks like he never eats."

Button had put off sipping the whisky long enough. He sipped it.

"I think we ought to finish these drinks, Karl. Get in my car and drive as far away from this place as possible. I think we're being set up."

"What you talkin about?"

"I seen another guy, in my hotel. Little skinny bastard calls himself King, but he's got the look. Another Yank."

Weeks took a pull of his pint. "You're telling me there's four hitmen, including two from The States, just arrived in this one little town?"

"Looks that way. You waiting to hear about your target?"

Weeks nodded and pulled out a phone. Button placed his own beside it, identical. "Snap."

Weeks blew out his cheeks, looking from one to the other. "Well, would you look at that. You think, maybe we been called on purpose? It's not exactly a secret we worked for Eddie all them years."

"Maybe. Except why not say *before* we came?"

"I don't know. But you can bet your bottom dollar that Hollis or this King guy are the target. Maybe both of them."

"It's a set up."

"A fifty-grand set up."

When Button blinked, Weeks tipped his glass towards him. "Thought so. We both got the same offer, mate."

After that, the two men nursed their drinks, making them last as it grew colder outside, and dark, but making no move towards Button's Audi.

Weeks asked, "You ever think about it, how you got here? I mean doing this weird shit for money."

Returning to where they'd left off, a conversation they'd had five years ago, before Weeks jacked it in.

"How come you're back?"

"I'm no businessman, it turns out. A bar. I thought, how hard can it be?"

"It go down the tubes?"

"Heading that way. This payday could turn us around. Mary knew I was doing this, she'd be gone, for good this time."

Weeks, Button knew, was aware of a good part of his history, coming out of the army with no good prospects, ending up working doors in some dodgy places, catching the eye of Big Eddie and working better doors. Then standing side by side with Weeks, two steps behind Eddie when deals were done.

It seemed to get heavier by increments. Baby steps so you hardly noticed.

Now Button raised his glass, still with some whisky in it after more than an hour. "What I was too embarrassed to tell you back in the day, when I first came out of the Army, I was hitting this stuff hard."

"Ok."

"Worse than that. I was on the streets. Homeless. Couldn't seem to find a way to be normal, after all the shit I'd seen."

Weeks shook his head. "You? Can't picture you there."

"How I look was part of the problem. You're standing on the door, looking hard is a good thing. A homeless man, it's a liability. I'd like to jack this in, but I'm not really fit for anything else."

"Bullshit. You're educated."

"Couple of A levels, so what?"

"More than me, and I'm a bona fide licensee. You're young still, a young man. Not even forty. What about Alice?"

"We split, years back."

"Your girl, Eleanor is it?"

"Elaine. She's at a swanky private school, costs a packet. I still see her…sometimes."

Weeks went inside himself, thinking about it. Then he said, "I can see how it might work that you'd be fucked up, after what happened in Iraq. But this is now. A man like you, all you have to do is *decide*. Make it happen. Fuck the swanky school."

After that, there didn't seem to be much to say and at around four, Weeks' phone chimed once. He put his hand out, but Button stopped him. "Wait a second, Karl."

"What?"

Button sat back, his jacket was open, and he crossed his hand casually, so it was just below where his pistol waited. "What if it's my name on there?"

"You serious?"

"What if it is?"

"Who'd spend fifty grand to off you, you daft bastard?"

Button's phone chimed.

Now it was Weeks turn to sit back.

"Well. This is awkward."

"How about we press at the same moment? We can't just sit here."

The bar had filled slightly since they had arrived, and there was a background hubbub. But nowhere near enough to drown a gunshot.

Weeks said, "Fuckit. It's not like we can shoot it out in here."

"No?"

"You kill me in this nice bar, I'll never speak to you again."

He picked up his phone and thumbed the screen. Button saw his expression change. "Oh."

"Oh what?"

"Check yours."

Button scooped up the little cell and frowned. "Declan Mooney."

He looked up. "Never heard of him."

There were a couple of photographs of a pudgy, middle aged man, with thinning sandy hair.

"Currently staying at Dorchester Travelodge, room 112. That's where you're staying?"

Weeks nodded and leaned in to see. "No. I never seen that guy."

He turned his own phone. "David Meechie."

"Somebody you know?"

"Heard of him. A Glasgow hard man."

It was full dark outside and colder, flakes of snow beginning to blow through. The open shops along the pedestrian precinct were brightly lit as they walked past. This had probably once been the main through road, Button thought, wide enough to drive sheep down, which might still happen, but now closed off to cars.

Market traders were just packing up and Button saw Declan Mooney a few seconds before the man saw him, had time to take two long steps to the side, which is probably what saved him. Mooney wasn't making any effort to look inconspicuous, none at all. He was standing close to the center line of the precinct, looking crazy-dangerous and making it plain he was searching for someone. Shoppers were giving him a wide berth.

Mooney spotted Button just as he reached the brightly lit glass of Boots, and was instantly in shocking motion, sweeping around to pull an assault rifle from under his coat, right there in the open.

Button skipped behind a stone pillar as a spray of bullets shattered glass and tile in a stunning burst of shrapnel and noise. The man moved as he shot, coming for him. Button ran through the doorway, hitting the deck to scramble between aisles of skin products and dental care. Bullets spattered around him, bursting open jars and bottles.

A woman, frozen and screaming, took two in the chest and went down in a spray of blood. People went instantly from browsing to screaming and running.

Button gained his feet and pulled his pistol, for all the good it would do against an assault rifle on full auto. Slithered around another aisle as Mooney kept walking, firing as he came.

Mooney's clip ran out but, by the time Button stood to aim, had ducked away. He came up again a second later, laying down a new hail of deafening fire. Another shopper went down, screaming. Button crawled on his belly, pulling himself through broken glass and plastic as Mooney shot through the racks between so that puffs of powder and bit of stuff sprayed across Button. A line of pressurized containers burst into the air, shaving foam erupting from their ruptured sides.

A pistol shot came from near the doorway, then, exploding a pot of hand cream that had to be near Mooney's head. Mooney returned fire, blowing the doors out. Button stood, Glock at arm's length.

There was a second, less than that, when everything froze. Mooney looked at Button, and the pistol inches from his face. Had time to say, 'Shit', before Button pulled the trigger.

People were still screaming when the man went down, still screaming when Weeks ran in, gun ready. A young man bustled past, head down, half carrying a woman with blood pouring from her leg. His own face was a mask of red.

Weeks. "You get him?"

"Yea, thanks, mate, you saved me. Jesus, I thought I was done there."

"We gotta get out of here. Place will be crawling with cops in no time."

"Wait, I need to check something."

Button hurried to bend over the dead man, stepping wide to avoid the spreading pool of blood. The phone was in Mooney's breast pocket.

"Tom Button. Casterbridge Hotel room 205. What's going on Karl?"

"Fucked if I know, let's just get going."

Button couldn't hear his phone above the noise but felt it vibrate. He pulled it out.

"Jesus Christ. Michael Tambini AKA Mr. King. Hardy Hotel room 112. £250,000."

He toggled the screen. "And check this, I've been paid already. For Mooney. Fifty grand right into my bank account."

Weeks grabbed his arm, pulling him towards the front of the shop.

"A lot of good it'll do you, we don't make tracks now. We're maybe already too late. Nobody's getting out of this shit-show free and clear."

They hurried out of the shop to find snow was falling harder. People were running and screaming every which way, in confused herds. Button froze, staring down the precinct, hearing the flat pops of a high caliber pistol, maybe a couple of hundred yards away. Somebody else returning fire, a real fire fight starting up. The carolers ran by in a group, their red coats flapping.

But not everybody was running. Between them and the main street, where cars still flowed as though nothing had happened, a man in a black parka turned to look at them, a pistol in his hand. As he raised it, Button cut left, while Weeks went right.

The man loosed off a couple of snap shots in each direction, then spun away, diving behind a market stall. Weeks aimed into the stall, three rapid shots. Dodged into White Stuff when the guy returned fire, shattering windows. Button had got almost to where he could see around the back of the stall, but the guy swiveled, firing fast so Button threw himself flat. The man stepped into the open and Weeks shot him in the back, knocking him down. He walked across to him and shot him again.

Now the cars in the main street were slowing and stopping, everything coming to a noisy halt with horns honking and lights flashing as panicked shoppers spilled across the road. Button grabbed Weeks' arm, hauling him up a narrow shopping alley, signed Antelope Walk. Still surrounded by panicked runners, they sprinted, stopping at another snarled up road, snow blowing in their faces.

Weeks pulled out his phone.

"I been paid! Thirty seconds ago, I topped the bastard, and I been paid. Can you believe this shit?"

"Got another target?"

"Yea. Nobody I know. Same payday as you. Where we going?"

"My hotel's up there."

"You crazy? You got King as a target, so that means he's got you."

"I got a car there, far enough out of the center that it shouldn't be caught up yet. We get in it and drive away."

Plus, there was the girl, Holly. He told himself he was crazy and believed that was true. But then, there was nothing about this that wasn't crazy. Where were the Police? The whole place should be crawling by now.

They had been standing just inside the alley of Antelope Walk, now they paused, nodding to each other before stepping out, back to back and guns at the ready. About twenty meters away, a guy in a bulky coat saw them and spun, immediately firing his pump action shotgun, the explosion blinding in the low light. Button hauled Weeks down, feeling something smack into his shoulder, knocking him the rest of the way to the ground. He and Weeks, both on the sidewalk, returned fire, shooting fast, seeing the guy tumble back and fall, behind them somebody else was shooting and they scrambled to their feet and ran between the lines of stalled cars. Bullets shattered windscreens and dinged off metalwork, but they kept going, staying low.

Button threw down behind a Skoda. Peered over to see who was shooting, briefly sharing a glance with the terrified driver, a man in his eighties.

The shooter was a woman, wearing a fleece with a Labrador on the front. She ducked into a restaurant doorway, but Weeks shot her before she could get inside, and she went down hard.

Weeks stood, panting. "You know, I think we just blundered in between those two. Not our fight at all."

Then, looking at blood on his hand. "That guy with the shotgun tagged both of us. Any closer…"

"Come on, we got to keep going."

"Tom Button!"

Button swiveled to see a man, young and Asian looking, standing over the corpse of shotgun guy, a phone in his hand. The man picked the shotgun up and racked it, firing from his hip as he came.

Button sprinted back down Antelope Walk, knowing the guy was coming for him and thinking he looked fit. He kept going across the shoppers' street, almost going down in the growing cover of snow, and down the lane he had come up earlier. He glanced back to see the guy was gaining. Saw him stop and pull the shotgun to his shoulder. Button dodged left and the shot missed, apart from something that slapped the edge of his coat.

He went past the plastic dinosaur and slid out into the street, doubling back and running into the Teddy Bear Museum. It had looked like a house from the outside, and that's what it felt like inside too, the lobby of a big house from Victorian times, with steep and narrow stairs leading off. He took them three at a time, ignoring the shout from someone on the ground floor, asking him where he thought he was going.

Near the top step he gasped, almost tumbling down again in his shock at the size of the guy waiting for him up there.

It wasn't a man, though, this was a giant teddy bear, dressed like a Victorian father and glaring sternly downstairs. All that had happened today, and the biggest scare was from a bear in a waistcoat. This room was jammed with bears of all kinds, big and little, some in tableaus, taking tea. Another room led off, also full of bears.

He stepped to the window in time to see the Asian guy run out into the road, just as he had done. The man bent over the snow-covered ground, following the blood.

Then he was coming up the stairs, going at them fast. The shotgun went off, shockingly loud, blowing the big bear back, filling the air with flecks of cotton. Button waited, thinking to tag him as he came out of the stairwell, but the guy came out shooting. Button rolled and returned fire. The man racked the shotgun, but it just clicked. Empty.

Even before he pressed the trigger, Button knew he would be empty too.

They had closed to within feet of each other and the man tried for his pistol. Button threw his, hitting him in the chest and continuing through, punching him hard.

The guy smashed into a glass cabinet full of tiny bears, then rolled, coming up with a knife. He slashed quickly, once, twice, pulling back before Button could catch his arm.

The men circled each other. Button was bigger and had had a lot of training, but this was his first time facing a knife in earnest, and he was in a room full of toys and floating cotton. He flicked a stuffed bear at the man, following in but having to hop back to avoid the blade. The guy was fast.

He picked up a heavy hardback chair, home to an oversized bear, and threw that, following in with a solid kick to the man's knee, but again having to retreat.

The man came at him, catching his forearm as he blocked, but Button had hands on him now. He threw him to the ground and locked his knife arm.

They struggled, wrestling and punching. Button caught the severed head of the huge bear, pressing it hard over the man's face. His struggles became increasingly desperate, but Button kept the pressure on, finally feeling him shudder and spasm under his hands.

He rolled away, panting.

The room was a ruin. His forearm was gashed despite the heavy wool of his coat, and bleeding, but he could cope with that. His shoulder, where the shotgun pellets had hit, was stiffening up, which was worse.

He searched in the debris on the floor, finding his gun and reloading. About to go downstairs, he stalled, then fished in the dead man's pocket, coming out with a phone showing his own name and face.

He crept downstairs. A woman stared at him from behind a counter, eyes wide, saying nothing.

He made a face. "Sorry about the bears." And peeked outside.

To his left, the main road was a solid jam of cars and headlights. People in there looking worried, one or two getting out to look. There was still shooting someplace, though not close by, and then the sound of someone running, feet slapping hard. He stepped back as Karl Weeks ran across the little street, limping heavily, breath pluming. He hunkered down behind a small wall, right where the street joined the main road. People stared for a second from their cars and then they were moving, pouring out, running to get away. Some screaming in there.

Weeks checked his magazine, then glanced across, freezing when he saw Button standing inside the doorway. Button held his hand up and Weeks nodded, pointing with the flat of his hand, back the way he came. Then he ran amongst the traffic and got behind a pick-up truck, peering over the bonnet. He yelled, "Come on then, you pair of bastards!"

Letting Button know there were two of them.

Seconds later, a man and a woman came into view, holding shotguns but moving careful, keeping low. Button pulled back until they passed, then stepped back out and shot them, the man in the back of his head and a double shot to the woman as she turned.

Weeks limped out of cover, waving Button towards him. "I owe you. Man, we got to split."

They ran as best they could to the hotel, slipping in the snow and taking it in turns to take point, the other covering the rear. In the car park, Button unlocked the Audi, saying I got something to pick up in the hotel. Won't be a minute.

"You crazy? We got to *go*."

Button ignored him, racing into the rear entrance, pushing his gun into its holster and wiping blood from his hands. Holly was there, looking terrified, the desk phone at her ear, a cell in her hand.

"What's happening out there, Tom? A terrorist thing?"

Tom nodded at the phone. "You dialed 999?"

"I can't get through! It's crazy."

Outside, somebody was screaming, more shots were fired, the sound of people running. He saw how she was looking at him and looked down and the mess of himself, blood mixing with everything he had crawled through in Boots the Chemist. His suit could no longer be described as nice.

"Look, come with me, Holly. This place isn't safe. I'll get you out of here."

They looked at one another for a long minute and he thought, she's going to do it, then her eyes moved over his shoulder, her expression changing. He turned as King stepped into the lobby, gun coming up. Button threw himself behind a big old chair, hearing the slap of a bullet as it came through, whining beside his ear.

He rolled behind the desk and the guy was laying down fire in earnest. Holly just stood there, phones in her hands, not quite frozen, because her heels rattled on the floor, like she was running in a dream, but going nowhere. Button launched himself at her, dragging her down as a slug hit his side.

He rolled onto his back, pulled his own gun and fired fast and blind, shooting through the old wood of the desk to where he thought the man must be, hearing a loud grunt on his third shot. He stood, finding King on his backside, but already pulling himself up, bringing his pistol around.

Button shot him, once in the chest and once in the head. Then he looked down at his side. His white shirt was turning red fast. He pulled it out and found the bullet had gone through the muscle at his waist, clean through, hopefully not hitting anything. He winced as his legs briefly sank at the knee.

Holly, still lying where he had thrown her, stared up in horror.

"Who are you, Tom?"

But then she was getting to her feet, her eyes fixed on his side. She pulled a towel out of a drawer and pressed it hard against him. "Is it bad?"

He thought about telling her, you see people being shot in the movies, Bond going about with slugs in him but it hardly slowed him down, it's not real. Damage like that to flesh and muscle, once the adrenaline leaves, you're going nowhere.

But there was plenty adrenaline flowing around his system right now and, when he thought of it, that was exactly what he was doing. Like he was John McLane or something.

"Come with me, Holly. We can get out."

She shook her head, eyes wide. "I think maybe you saved my life there, but I don't know you. I don't know what's happening."

"I don't know what's happening either. Ok, listen."

He took her hand in his bloody one. "I got to go. Got to move or I'm dead. If I come back, maybe a month later, will you…"

He saw her think about it. "Maybe. I don't know."

He stepped away. "Good enough."

More shots now, this time from the rear of the hotel, the car park. He stepped outside in time to see Weeks wrestling with a tall skinny guy, both of their pistols pointing into the snow blown sky as they tussled. Even in the poor light, Button could see that Weeks' face was bloody and desperate. A hard man, good guy to have in a fist fight, he wasn't winning.

As Button speed-limped out there, the guy, surely Greg Hollis, pulled his head back and nutted Weeks, nutted him again before pulling his arm into a lock, flipping him onto the ground. As he brought his pistol around to finish him, Button shot him in the chest. The guy stumbled back but that was all he did, so he was wearing a vest.

Christ, but he was fast, getting off two quick shots that had Button sprawling for cover. Weeks, lying on his back in the snow, pulled another pistol and shot straight up between the guy's legs. the bullet came out somewhere high inside the vest, spraying red up his neck. Hollis stood baffled for a moment, then crumpled.

When Weeks struggled to his feet, Button could see that he was bleeding, a chest wound of some kind. He waved to Button, come on, hobbled to the Audi and fell inside the passenger seat.

Button climbed behind the wheel, and sat there for a few moments, breathing hard.

"Tom, snap out of it!"

Button's hand on the wheel was stickered with blood and shaking. He could feel blood under his belt, sticky, squelchy when he moved. He said, "Listen."

"What?"

"It's quiet. Nobody shooting."

Karl opened his mouth but didn't say what was clearly on his mind to say. Instead he looked away. "Oh yea."

"You think maybe it's just the two of us left?"

"I kinda do, yea."

Button turned in his seat, wincing. "I wouldn't be breathing right now, if it wasn't for you."

"No, you wouldn't. Neither would I."

"Only reason we're alive is because of each other."

Weeks was still staring at the dead man. "I shot the Man with no Heart in his asshole."

"Man with no asshole doesn't have the same ring. What I'm saying…"

"I know what you're saying. I just wish you'd stop saying it and get us the fuck out of here. Whatever this is we've fallen into, we're not killing each other, Tom."

"No, we're not. I'm glad we got that straight."

Button's fingers were on the ignition when their phones went off, both of them chiming in the same instant. Karl lifted his phone but looked at Button.

"We don't have to read this."

"No."

"We can wait till we're doing eighty and drop them out the window. Both at the same time."

"Yea."

"Cos you got to think if there's a number on there, I mean a really big number, it might, you know…"

"I know."

Weeks stared at the little screen, his thumb smearing blood across it. As he watched, it chimed again. So did Button's.

Button rolled his eyes, "Fuck it."

He flicked his thumb and the screen lit up, both men craning to see.

Weeks, his voice subdued, said, "Now. That really is a big number."

It's Only Over When the Fat Lady Sings

Tim Mendees

"That's all folks!"
—Porky Pig.

"**D**amn! That was close." Tony's rasping voice had been ravaged by years of heavy smoking and hard-drinking. He took a slug from the half-bottle of Bells whiskey that his pal, Karl, had passed him. "The fat lady was almost singin' tonight."

The robbery had started smoothly. Their inside woman, Tony's niece Veronica, had disabled the door alarms and cut the power to the CCTV cameras as planned. They had cased the building carefully and had jammed the entrance to the maintenance tunnel with a well-placed cork in the door jamb.

Tony and Karl were old hands at this, they had been breaking and entering since they were snot-nosed youths growing up on the Edwards estate. First, it was a necessity. Both men were poor, woefully undereducated and far too lazy to get jobs. What other option did they have? Later, when they had grown up a bit and had reluctantly taken positions on the various fishing trawlers that come out of the dock, it became a nice little sideline. A kind of homespun supplementary income. Later still, it was a hobby. They only took big contracts for big rewards and left the grubby little thefts to the new generation of snot-nosed kids.

The local constabulary had been thwarted in their attempts to catch the duo every single time. They were cautious, methodical. Tony loved to say that 'fools rush in' and preferred to plot the jobs slowly and thoroughly. This dedication to planning bordered on OCD but had paid off, they had never once been caught before, during or after a job.

Tonight's robbery had gone from butter-smooth to gravel-rough in a heartbeat due to an unfortunate and completely unanticipated development. Out of the blue, the curator of the museum had decided to move some of the exhibits around so the item they had been contracted to steal wasn't where it was supposed to be. In fact, it couldn't have been further away from where it was supposed to be without removing walls.

The stone idol that their client had requested they acquire had been transferred from the lower east wing to the upper west. After a fruitless search of the east-wing, Tony, the bright spark that he was, hit on the idea that there must be a plan or list somewhere. There was, it was in the curator's office. Unfortunately, so was an infra-red sensor not affected by the measures that they had taken to avoid alarms.

The museum erupted into a deafening cacophony of bells and klaxons. For once in their criminal career, luck, not planning, was on their side. Next to the glass case that contained the idol was a metal fire escape that led down to the rear of the building. They smashed the glass, nabbed the idol and were down the steps and away before the first police car showed up.

"You're not wrong," Karl grunted. He took the bottle from Tony and took a hefty gulp. Karl was a heavyset man with fists like shovels and a low beetling brow. "That's such a stupid sayin' Where does it even come from?"

"Opera, you uncultured wretch," Tony answered. He was a large man too but nowhere the imposing bulk of Karl. Tony didn't need to be, he was the brains of the operation, Karl was the muscle. "It's from some German opera that went on forever. The last bit was some fat woman dressed as a Valkyrie..."

"A what?" Karl cut in.

"A Valkyrie." Tony annunciated every syllable. "You know, big bird in armour, horned helmet?"

Karl nodded, not understanding, but agreeing.

"Anyway, this big buxom blonde would come onstage and warble for about ten minutes. The opera went on for so bloody long that people would ask 'damn, when is this bloody thing over?' and his mate would say 'it ain't over till the fat lady sings.'"

"So you're telling me that when people talk about Armageddon and say 'it ain't over till the fat lady sings' they are talking about some boring opera?" Karl crinkled his brow and puffed out his stubbly cheeks like a disgruntled pufferfish.

"It's not important. It just means it ain't over till it's over." Tony rubbed dust out of his thinning hair.

"That's even stupider! Of course, it's over when it's over! How the hell could it be over and not? It doesn't make any bloody sense." Karl sucked thirstily on the bottle then passed it back to Tony.

"Ok," Tony huffed. "What if we use something from something you like then?" Karl nodded, Tony continued. "What if we say 'it ain't over until the helicopter explodes? You know, like Die Hard three?"

"That's much better" He grinned widely, displaying a yellowed collection of higgledy-piggledy teeth, like a row of tottered gravestones.

Tony took a swig of whiskey and joined Karl's grin. A sudden wrap at the old wooden door broke the jubilant mood.

***

The old lighthouse at Barron Head had been abandoned since the early twentieth century when its larger, automated brother was constructed in nearby Betyls Cove. Nestled in a dense growth of trees and wild bracken, it was the perfect place to lie low; derelict, abandoned and forgotten.

Subsidence had turned the headland into a particularly nasty game of Russian roulette for any hiker foolish enough to follow the old coastal path. One misplaced step and your leisurely walk would swiftly become a terrifying free-fall. Not even the police were brave enough to venture past the rusty metal 'keep out' gates. Only the desperate or suicidal would dare cross the weed-choked threshold and approach the teetering tower.

One could hide out in the lighthouse for weeks and not see another soul. Karl knew this was the case, he had spent just over a fortnight hiding out here from the vicious battleaxe he once married. He was so drunk at the time of the split that he still couldn't recall the infraction that led his belligerent bride to vow to remove his gentleman's vegetables with a rusty bread-knife. It must have been a corker.

The lighthouse was the perfect spot for a couple of wily ne'er-do-wells to hide and wait for the storm to blow over. It was also a superb location to meet with clients and exchange loot. This place was their office, their stronghold, their sanctuary. A safe place away from prying eyes and inquisitive minds.

Karl jumped to his feet, displaying a nimbleness not expected from such a mass of meat, and positioned himself behind the door, lump-hammer in hand. "Who's there?" He barked, his voice like a cement mixer.

"It's me." A cultured, nasal voice answered. "Open up, Karl."

Tony had positioned himself opposite the door, a small camp-fire flickered weakly between him and the aperture, his legs shoulder-width apart and his arms levelling a lovingly maintained service revolver. "Open the door, Karl." He whispered.

The two men exchanged a knowing 'be ready' nod as the big man lifted the wooden bar and let the wind push the door open. The rusted hinges sounded like nails down a blackboard as the third man pulled the door the rest of the way.

A short, pudgy man wearing a long coat and a trilby entered the room, his hands shot up aromatically upon eyeing the pistol. Evidently, this was a long way from the first time someone had pointed a gun at him. A smirk spread over the man's fleshy lips and his prominent eyes twinkled with amusement.

"About fuckin' time." Tony spat.

The squat man lowered his hands and batted rain off his shoulders. "Sorry for the delay, gentlemen. There seems to be one hell of a lot of rozzers around tonight. You wouldn't know anything about that, would you?" His grin widened knowingly, displaying a row of sharp-looking jagged teeth. The man seemed to revel in the chaos of tonight's heist and his colleagues' slip up like he had been waiting for it for an eternity. Oh yes, he was enjoying this.

"Piss off!" Karl grumbled. "You bring the cash?"

"It certainly sounds like your luck is running out and no mistake," The man giggled.

"The money," Tony said levelly, waving the gun at the man's coat pocket. "If you please."

"Okay, okay." The man chuckled, waving his hands in a 'calm-down' motion. "Here you go." He removed a large brown envelope from his pocket and tossed it to Tony. "It's all in there. Count it if you must but please be quick. I parked my car on the trail and I'll never back the bugger out if the rain gets any worse, it's already a mud-bath out there." He removed his hat exposing his bald head and shook the water from the brim.

"Not so fast, Art," said Tony. "I will count it if you don't mind, you don't know who you can trust these days." He smiled wryly and produced a note-checker pen from his pocket. "This will only take a minute." He said. "Sit. Why don't you have a drink while you're waiting?"

Art brushed the seat of an old, filthy deckchair sending plumes of dust into the air and parked his sizeable rump. Karl rattled the bottle of scotch on his collar bone, Art took it and put it to his lips. "Yeah," he wheezed after imbibing, "I heard that the fat lady was almost singing tonight."

"Oh for fuck's sake." Karl hissed under his breath.

Tony's eyes twinkled with mischief as he carefully checked each bank-note one by one by one. "Hey Art," He smiled, "What opera is that about again?" Tony could never resist an opportunity to needle Karl.

"Götterdämmerung or 'downfall of the gods' by Wagner. It refers to when, after an eternity, the Valkyrie, Brünnhilde, comes on for the finale." Art spoke with all the emotion of a radio 4 presenter. "She was a large woman, so hence 'the fat lady sings' putting an end to 'Der Ring Des Nibelungen' and the suffering of the audience."

Tony clapped as Karl muttered oaths under his breath.

"Have I missed something?" Art asked with a smirk.

"Nothing to worry about, Art. My partner here hates the phrase, that's all. I think he hates the concept of a portly woman singing being the herald of Armageddon. I think it reminds him too much of his ex-wife doing karaoke. That was always pretty apocalyptic." Tony chuckled.

"You can piss off as well," Karl growled, his heavy jowls wobbling like a turkey's wattle. "I just think it's a stupid, outdated phrase that's all, why does it have to be a fat lady, not a skinny lady, or a fat man, or a skinny man come to that."

"Tradition!" Tony chirruped.

"Bollocks to tradition," Karl muttered sulkily.

"Well, whatever the phrase, the bell nearly tolled for thee tonight." Art said mockingly, gesturing at Karl with the bottle. "The modern world of sensors, camera's and DNA coding are moving too fast for you two dinosaurs."

Karl bristled, his fingers tightening around the shaft of his precious lump-hammer, it had been his grandfather's, he had been a blacksmith. Karl said it brought him luck. People cherish all manner of totems from horse-shoes to rabbit's feet so why not a lucky lump-hammer?

"Easy Karl," Tony commanded. He was the only person on planet earth that could get through Karl's thick skull when the red mist descended.

"I wasn't trying to be offensive," Art pleaded. "Anything but. I was about to offer you, two fine gentlemen, an opportunity."

"What opportunity?" Karl hissed.

"A once in a lifetime one; that's what." Art smirked. "An opportunity to keep the tolling bell in the distance, to slow the clock, to give Brünnhilde an even longer song!"

Karl snorted, "Oh yeah, and how do you reckon you can do that then?"

"I have this book..."

"Karl stopped Art mid-sentence with a bark of "Fuck me!" He turned to Tony and motioned towards Art with his hammer. "You didn't tell me he was born again. He's goin' to start thumping the bible in a minute."

"Not that book." Art asserted petulantly. "This book is much more powerful." He pulled a leather-bound book from his other inside pocket. It was worn, well-thumbed and worm-eaten. Karl detected a hint of the smell of corruption about it; like festering refuse.

Karl snatched the book from Art's fingers and puzzled at the embossed title. "O Terreno Baldio De Ger'igguthy?" He moved his lips clumsily around the words. "What the fuck is that supposed to mean?"

"Roughly translated it means Ger'igguthy's wasteland." Art replied.

Karl flicked through the pages, blanching at the strange etchings and symbols. "Who the fuck is this Ger'igguthy then?" He asked with a hint of malice.

"A god!" Art proclaimed. Karl snorted derisively. The man continued. "You see, everything has a god if you look hard enough, a patron saint or whatever. Ger'igguthy is the god of the outcasts, the ones with wasted lives, the fallen and discarded. He feasts on the refuse of humanity, growing stronger, ever stronger. You would be perfect acolytes, outside the laws of men, above them even."

Karl shot his big hand up to his face and placed a sausage-like finger to his cracked lips. "I didn't ask for a fucking sermon." He bellowed. "This thing is all in bloody Spanish or something, I can't make head nor tail of it.

Tony snatched the book from Karl and fixed his eyes on the beady eyes of Art. "You appear to be a hundred short." He spoke with the calm sort of threatening tone reserved for the truly dangerous.

Karl cracked his knuckles and toyed with his hammer. "How many pounds a finger, eh, Tone?" He grinned. This was his favourite part.

"Hold on a minute gentlemen," Art stammered, "The deal was 'no police.' I will have to keep the idol well hidden until the rozzers have given up looking for it. This causes me great inconvenience. You know that as a 'collector' of strange theological artefacts, I will be the first on the list of suspects. I merely docked you a token amount."

"You fucking prick!" Tony spat, losing his cool for the first time in years. "Next time you have some old crap in a high-security building to pinch, ask some other idiot!" Art tried to argue but was cut off, "No! Not another word. Now, take your idol and piss off!"

Art stood, replaced his hat, gripped the idol and held his hand out for the book. Tony smiled, baring his teeth like a shark and tossed the book into the fire. "Fuck you and fuck your book." He hissed.

Art didn't flinch, didn't try to rescue the book from the hungry lick of the flames, he merely smiled. It was a pitying and knowing smile. "What a waste." He shook his head, turned and walked to the door with the stone idol tucked under his arm. "What a terrible, terrible waste. You could have proved infinitely useful. My lord always needs craftsmen such as yourselves." He clicked his tongue against the roof of his mouth and pushed the door open. "What a bloody waste." He muttered with a sinister smirk as he walked into the sodden gloom of the night.

***

The wind rattled the rotting shutters of the upstairs windows. Lightning flashed intermittently, casting unnerving shadows caused by the debris of the crumbling structure. Everybody knew that the lighthouse wasn't long for this world. One good storm could send it sprawling into the sea. A storm like the one currently raging outside.

Tony sat and split the money as Karl drained the last of the whiskey and tried to simmer down. He was born with a dangerously short fuse, one that had caused more than one run-in with the law. He had never been charged with anything, however. His justified reputation for breaking bones saw to it that witnesses were less than forthcoming.

Tony suddenly became alert, his neck craning and his ear cocked like a startled meerkat.

"What is it?" Karl asked, reaching for his hammer.

"Dunno," Tony whispered. "Sounded like a car."

"Shit!" Karl yelped. "I bet that slimy little fucker, Art, has called the pigs on us."

"Nah, they'll nick him too. He might be a wanker but he's not a stupid wanker."

The faint rumble of the engine became a deafening roar as someone slammed their foot on the accelerator.

"Bollocks!" Tony cried in alarm.

Suddenly, the lighthouse was rocked by a catastrophic crunch as the car connected with the doorway.

The building shuddered violently. Beams, plaster and the dust of ages rained down from the ceiling. Floorboards from the floor above clattered down, clanging off the rusty old generator. The doorway crumpled in upon itself. The opening choked with stone and splinters.

The cloud of dust rushed into their nostrils and stung their eyes. The car horn blared into deafening life, playing the kind of irritatingly jaunty jingle that you normally associate with the mini Cooper. As they coughed and spluttered, the car door opened and they heard the voice of Art sing out...

"What a terrible waste!" He giggled maniacally. "I knew you were the ones!" Art started to chant. His tongue twisted around strange unholy words. The chant built into a fever-pitch then stopped suddenly. Apparently complete. Art fell silent.

This betrayal was beyond the pale for Tony. He was a principled, gentleman crook of the old-school who believed in honour amongst thieves and an unspoken code. What Art had just done was tantamount to treason in his eyes and he would be punished accordingly.

"Art!." He screamed. "When I get out of here, you snivelling little shit, I'm going to skin you, turn you into a book... No! A whole library of books all called 'the downfall of the back-stabbing weasel.' Then, I'm gonna' set fire to the bloody lot!"

On hearing nothing from outside except the violent thrum of the rain, Tony bellowed again, "You hear me, Art!? You little fucker! I'm GONNA KILL YOU!!"

For once Karl was cast in the role of peacekeeper. Like most level headed and patient people, when Tony's fuse blew the effect was akin to a nuclear explosion. "Hey!" Karl snapped, gripping Tony by the shoulders. "Let's figure out how to get out of here before we decide on just how much we are going to kill that little scrotum, Okay?"

Tony took a deep breath and unclenched his fists. "Okay." He breathed.

The two men surveyed the room around them. The dust was beginning to settle. The headlights of the crashed car shone through the gaps in the rubble, catching the thousands and thousands of dancing dust-motes in their bright beams.

Karl poked and jostled the stones covering the entrance. "I can probably shift this lot but some of this stuff is wedged tight. Have a look around for something I can use as a lever would you?"

"Yeah." Tony agreed. "There must be a crowbar or something lying around here somewhere. I'll have a look." He turned and surveyed the room, he had been here enough times to know that there wasn't anything on the ground floor, so he would be forced to investigate the stupidly unsafe upper floors.

***

Karl was concentrating on shifting heavy stone and barely noticed Tony mounting the rusty metal staircase. Every footstep clanked and clomped. The tired and corroded bolts heaved and strained with every shifting of his weight, causing a strangled squeak to rasp and wheeze around the circular interior.

The first floor had been a modest kitchen. The old iron stove sat lopsided on the twisted beams. If the restraining bolts ever snapped the entire kitchen unit would slide out through the wall and clatter to the ground below as the impact of the car against the lighthouse had caused the stones under the window to dislodge.

Tony scanned the room. There was an old broom-handle that looked rotten and a smashed table. Neither object would be of any use to the task at hand. He eyed the hole under the window, it was large enough for a man, even one as big as Karl. If he could find a rope or a ladder, they could slip out that way, then pound Art into the mud and be home in time for breakfast.

Tony smiled at the thoughts of bloody vengeance followed by a greasy fry-up and turned to exit the room. Thunder boomed above him, the cylindrical structure acted as a superb echo chamber and his head rang with the decibels of the rumble. He steadied himself on the rusty rail and mounted the steps to ascend to the second floor.

Tony could only guess at how miserable life must have been for the men who once resided within the cramped tower. There had been four of them judging by the bunks. They were uncomfortable-looking things. Merely thick, unyielding boards supported by a cold metal frame. Orange-tinged water seeped through the ceiling. The smell of filth and metal was stifling.

Tony eyed the beds, he reasoned that he could break off one of the bed legs to use as a crowbar given enough force. He was sure that Karl would loan him the use of his precious lump hammer if he asked nicely. This was an emergency after all.

Before making his way down two treacherous flights, Tony decided to check the lamp-room for a rope or maybe a metal bar he didn't have to fight with. As he started to climb the rickety staircase a flash of lightning and a mighty gust of wind caught the tower.

Tony felt the tower shift, move and wobble. He gripped the rail for dear life as a fresh shower of dust and debris rained down. The lighthouse groaned. Stones ground against stone. Metal buckled and twisted.

Tony nearly lost his footing on the slippery metal. It was slick from years of rain and rust. Finally, he reached the lamp-room. The circular room was a mess of broken glass. The huge lamp had long since shattered, along with the convex glass that magnified the illumination.

As the tower swayed under the force of the wind, Tony looked for anything of use. Using the metal support rails, he shuffled crab-like around the circumference. He had reached halfway when a violent gust caught the roof of the chamber. The force of the gale lifted the roof like a hat and sent it sailing into the sea below.

Tony shook as the freezing rain whipped at his face, driven by the howling wind. His eyes were drawn upwards, defying the downpour. The moon hung above the lamp, bloated and leering, it was though the clouds had parted so it could peer down and mock the insignificant little man on the toppling tower.

A rush of blue flame, like a gas eruption, rushed from the staircase in a huge pulsating ball. It caught the lamp and flowed into it, around it, and through it. The lamp began to spin faster and faster as the blue flame built in intensity. Eventually, it burst, sending a searing column into the sky and towards the hungry beckoning of the moon.

His feet moved marionette-like around the rail and he clomped down the stairs in a panic. He reached the second-floor landing in a daze and rushed into the room and began kicking at a bedpost like a man possessed.

He roared in frustration as he stomped the ancient welding to oblivion. A teeth-rattling screech of rending metal announced that the leg was free. He picked it up in his hand, weighed it then tested its durability by taking a ragged chunk of worm-eaten timber out of the door frame. It was solid.

Moving to the door, Tony came face to face with a prime specimen of the genus Rattus Norvegicus; the brown rat. The feisty rodent bared its vicious-looking teeth and let out a squeak of rage that was akin to the hiss of some primordial serpent. Tony smiled at the creature's bravery then smashed its tiny skull to paste with the metal bar.

As he descended the now rain-slick stairs, a strange hair-raising chittering sound echoed from above. Tony craned his neck and looked behind him. A writhing mass of strange insect-like creatures swarmed from the exposed lamp-room. They fell in a terrible mass upon the broken body of the proud rat. Gnawing, tearing, and feasting on its remains like a swarm of ungodly locusts.

Tony cried in horror as his foot slipped on the steps, the momentum of his twisted posture catapulted his legs out from under him, he spun ungracefully through the air and came down hard on his coccyx. The sudden burst of searing agony knocked the wind from his body and sent his vision reeling.

***

Karl was oblivious to everything except the straining of his muscles and the grind of stone. The pain from his lower back sparked a warming wave of endorphins and a burst of adrenaline flowed through his massive frame. He gritted his teeth and pulled harder, sweat beaded on his wide brow.

So engrossed was Karl, that he failed to see the blue flame building in the embers of the fire. The downfall of dust and detritus had extinguished the blaze down to a few orange cinders that smouldered ineffectually.

First, there was a vague flicker, then a spark, then the coiling flames began to build, conjoin and become. Once the unholy fire had reached critical mass, it split from the embers and spun off towards then up the spiral staircase.

Karl's hand slipped and the stone crushed his thumb, he growled in pain and the bell tolled. A large, booming, hollow sound of a dolorous bell rattled in the big man's bones. He jumped in alarm as the bell tolled again, again and again.

Wind punched the wall of the tower with immense force, causing more dust and filth to rain from above. He stared in horror as the wall facing the sea began to buckle. He returned his attention to the pile of rubble blocking his exit. Swearing with rage, he heaved at the rocks with renewed vigour.

As the bell continued to clang its mournful tone, a heavy clock began to tick. It ticked quicker and quicker until another sound joined the din. A faint whir of blades that gathered in speed and volume; the helicopter was about to explode.

Kari Bellowed "Nooo!" At the top of his tattered lungs as yet another noise echoed around the chamber. A Low wail with a skillful vibrato raked through his ears like a length of barbed wire. It gathered in pitch and intensity with every second. The wail was deafening, Karl tossed the rock aside and clamped his hands over his now bleeding ears.

The ground below his feet shook and reverberated, every stone in the tower, every plank, every rivet and bar, shook independently of each other in destructive resonance.

A blinding flash of brilliant blue blinded Karl's eyes as he spun around. There she was, over in the corner, Brünnhilde. Her arms were raised and her head tilted towards the heavens as she belted out the words. The powerful song rushed from her gaping mouth.

Karl hated that woman with a passion born from terror. She was his harbinger. Herald of the end of days. Karl gripped his hammer firmly in his right hand. She was attractive in a strong, matronly way and the way the blue light played on her armour was mesmerising. Karl nearly lost himself in the drifting tune for a second. He slapped his face sharply with his free hand in an attempt to bring himself back to life.

He had to stop her singing. It wasn't over yet. He could keep going, keep living, as long as he got Brünnhilde to stop singing. If she finished her song, he was done. It was over. These thoughts raced through his fear crazed mind as he raised his hammer and lunged towards the singing Valkyrie.

"Karl! NO!!" Tony yelled as the big man's big hammer connected with the supporting joist, cracking the aged, brittle metal like an egg. Tony fell down the last of the stairs clutching his backside in pain. The scuttling horde wasn't far behind him.

"Where is she!!" Karl demanded, madness dancing in his eyes.

"Who?" Tony yelled back in equal fury.

"The fat lady of course!" Karl yelled, his roar becoming a frenzied cackle that morphed into sobs of despair. "Can't you hear her Tony? She's singing. The fat lady is singing! You have to make her stop!"

At that moment the wall fell inward with a deafening roar. The land below them cracked asunder and slid forward like a wave of earth, bringing tons of stone and metal down upon them.

***

Only the debris of the doorway and part of the wall remained of the lighthouse the following morning. The rest of the tower had fallen into the sea, finally defeated. There would be no corpses to recover, the scavengers would see to that.

Art reversed his battered car and stepped from the vehicle into the punishing storm. With a calm that belied the situation, he carefully traversed the remaining spot of land from the tower interior.

With the tip of his boot, he kicked aside a pile of plaster and wood-splinters. There below the rubble were the remnants of the fire. He reached a leather-gloved hand into the remains and retrieved the book. It was intact, undamaged, no scorch nor scuff. It looked in as good condition as it always had been.

Art smiled and placed it in his coat pocket. He had done fine work and his lord would be pleased. He had promised sacrifice and he had delivered in spades. He shook his head as he peered down at the wreckage of the tower. All that wasted potential. All that wasted talent. All those wasted opportunities. All that wasted life. Yes, his master would be very, very pleased.

He knew that telling his friend Dave to give the museum a face-lift would do the trick to set the cogs into motion. All he had to do now was return the idol to its rightful place in his study. It was his, after all. He knew that loaning it to the museum would pay dividends in the end.

As he turned to leave, he spotted something else among the ruins. It was a brown envelope stuffed with cash. Art grinned, pocketed the money and returned to his car.

Dolls and Trolls...

Sergio 'ente per ente' Palumbo
Edited by Michele DUTCHER

The area was covered by a mesh of undergrowth, while the water of the small river below looked like liquid sandpaper that had been scratching the surface below them for a very long period. All the more reason to pay attention while moving on. The 30-year-old man put his foot on a large boulder and told the younger girl who followed him, "Let's get going, the terrain gets easier from this point on..."

The other nodded in silence and then continued. Sweat was on her pale skin and the bulky hiking boots she wore made her appear slower than she might have been otherwise, though it was a false impression. The look of fatigue had already settled on her features. Apart from this weariness, surely any man would have been delighted by how beautiful she looked in the outfit she wore. Likewise, she certainly enjoyed the attentions of a lover like the man she followed, the same as many other women commonly did.

Northern Norway consisted of three counties — Nordland, Troms and Finnmark — covering about a third of the country. Some tourists in summer favored busy ports such as Bodo or Tromso, and primarily visited a few sheltered coves or straddle islands along the coast. But others like Augustin and Hulda preferred to go inland off the beaten track, staying overnight in one of the many national parks where bears and wolves still roamed freely. It was a little more dangerous, and you had to be prepared to face rain, cold, and difficult trails, but taking chances often proved to be worth it if you dared to hike a little deeper into the wild. The great scenery, combined with the sun that stayed high in the sky during this season, and the many possibilities of challenging outdoor activities, was what made this part of Norway so appealing to travelers.

People came here to fish in the rivers, to go bird watching and walk through the endless caves. For example, Svarthamar, that was one of the largest caves in northern Europe. People could also take trips into the mountains and simply enjoy a vacation in a cabin somewhere. In the national parks you could go just about wherever you liked. In fact, as long as the land was uncultivated and you followed a set of easy rules, you were allowed to go hiking, camping or riding more or less wherever you wanted. Besides, there were more than 230 mountain peaks above 6,560 feet within this country, so you had many breathtaking possibilities ahead of you.

After the railway line ended at Bodo, that was situated about 40 miles from the town of Fauske (Norwegian for 'old trees') - the two had travelled along a very long narrow road. In fact, Bodo had been the last small urban area where they had spent the night in a real bed. Then their true trip across the mountains had started. Although there were several tourist lodges in the surroundings, they didn't stay in any of them, as a small tent and a good camping site was better than anything else in their point of view.

This area was located inside the Arctic Circle and had 24 hours of daylight from early May to the beginning of July - the present month. Average temperatures were below freezing from mid-November to the last part of March, but the ice-free Skjerstadfjorden usually made the snowy climate more moderate. Southwesterly winds brought thaws anytime in late winter, but not in the mountains, which usually got large amounts of snow. A traveler wouldn't see many tourists here during that period, as it was the summer season that extreme travelers like these two preferred most. Hikers enjoyed this wild region in the heart of the county interspersed between lakes, large ice formations and massive boulders here and there along the trails. *How could it be different, after all?*

The eastern terrain was punctuated by peaks rising to 5,577 ft, while further west — exactly where they were heading for now — there were wide mountaintops and forested valleys. The current footpath they were following had probably been kept-up by ancient farmers so that people from northern areas could reach their villages to trade goods. Though the trail didn't appear to be in good condition at present - unless you were a goat capable of easily climbing such higher zones covered in thick underbrush… Augustin and Hulda kept going with all the effort necessary and made it through, in the end.

Here around, the few villagers you might stumble into, if ever, still wore the Nordland *bunad*, the traditional costume, that was originally blue, but also came in greenish shades at times. Based on a 200-year-old fabric from Vefsn, the bag for women that accompanied the typical clothing matched the color and pattern as their skirt. The large migration of rural people to the towns had made the *bunad* itself a symbol of their identity and for many an important link with their home village. Its use wasn't just meant for festivals and was reputed to have become increasingly popular in such places. Not that the two young hikers were researchers of ancient traditions, though it might always prove useful to have knowledge of such customs, of course.

At a particular moment, the young man pointed at a spot in the distance and smiled. Lying in the shadow of a much higher mountain, the secluded point Augustin had chosen looked like an elevated small meadow that was dwarfed by the towering rock formation which stood nearby. Not much sunlight reached its surface, but the site seemed to be well protected from the winds. Walls of sedimentary stone rose steeply on both sides as they continued walking with much difficulty, while making their way through the forest trees, until they got to the place the man had selected.

They sat on the ground to rest for a while. Their end destination was not that far away, but they couldn't get there without stopping from time to time. As Hulda took a beverage out of her daypack and then started savoring some food prepared for the trip that morning, Augustin slowly laid down in the meadow and started reciting something, with a serious look in his eyes. "Did you ever hear about that fairytale? In a hole in the ground there lived a..."

"That is the beginning of *Shrek*, am I right?" the girl completed the phrase, interrupting him.

"That was an Ogre, but I was thinking about a Troll..." her man replied, making a face. "Okay, how about this one: not a nasty, dirty hole, filled with..." Augustin said after a moment.

"I know what that is...the start of the *Hobbit*, or *Lord of the Rings*, and..." the girl spoke again, seemingly incapable of staying silent about this.

"Stop it...will you allow me to tell you this tale or not?" the young man asked, poking fun at her. But he appeared to be incapable of being angry for all of her interruptions, and he understood why as soon as he turned his eyes to her.

The heart-shaped, fitted bodice she had on at that moment, with a stand-up collar and a full skirt from the waistline perfectly outlined her beautifully slender figure. Two matching bluish hiking boots with a yellowish trim highlighted the ankle joints. The young man knew that

Hulda had chosen those colors on purpose to please him, in a way, as they reminded him of the national flag of the country he was from: Sweden. In fact, that was the stretch of land directly bordering the part of Norway where the girl had been born 23 years ago.

She wore a colorful headband from which her blonde curly hair fell down on both sides around her ears. That stood in clear contrast with his own dark chestnut head of hair that showed off a boyish style which looked old-fashioned, but still was very attractive to most of the girls, as he well knew. Of course, the cut-off shorts with cuffs he commonly used for hiking displayed his muscled athletic legs, which the girls also liked. After all, with a strong build and good-looking features like a thin nose and those deep eyes the azure of a summer sky, he had been naturally gifted with good looks so how could things be any different?

Augustin's hiking equipment was well suited for the trip, as he had a lot of training and a great knowledge of the area itself, so he knew what to bring here and what to leave at home, indeed. He was very experienced and would have never embarked on a trip he wasn't qualified to complete, the same as he wouldn't forget to listen to the forecast and respect the weather. More than that, the young man was very good at maintaining his stamina as long as necessary.

With his outer-wear white long sleeve T-shirt and an open light gray windproof full zip jacket over it, the man dressed exactly according to what all the travel guides required for such outings in the high ground, given the season. He also had a cool-head visor, mitten gloves and a classic daypack that was very comfortable, conforming to commonsense practices. The only exception he made was about long underwear, and long pants, that were always suggested for anyone who went walking in the wilderness, though he preferred to wear his lightweight shorts instead of those when hiking in the mountains with his girlfriend, as he liked to look sexy during the trip. Call it what you want, it was his way of being flashy during a vacation in such places.

"Of course, darling, please go on…but I must warn you that, as a Norwegian-born citizen, I do know about fabled Trolls more than you might think." The girl made a huge smile while eyeing him.

"Are you sure? Maybe you don't know this one yet…" the young man replied.

"This country is full of ancient legends about them. I can't say I remember of all of them, but…" Hulda objected in an uncertain tone.

"So, let me tell you this tale, and we'll see if you have already heard it." Augustin challenged her with a more serious expression in his pupils now.

"Ok, darling. I'll listen quietly," the other nodded, turning silent.

Augustin started telling the tale again and the girl listened to his words with an attentive look. It was a story of high mountains, of old huge Trolls, of dark caves below the ground and of unbelievable treasures, of course—riches of great value that not many men might ever say they had seen before. The recount didn't leave Hulda very surprised, in the end, though some details had certainly attracted her attention.

"So, what do you think of my fairy story?" the young man asked her when he completed the tale.

"Oh, well, darling, I really don't know…I've previously heard so many legends about such creatures since I was a child that I couldn't say this was the scariest tale I've heard. But I really loved the way you narrated it, and all those beautiful descriptions you put into. It's almost as if you really underwent such experiences, as if you actually visited such dark places before…"

"Do you think so, my dear? Come here and let me kiss you…" Augustin invited her to come into his arms with a wide gesture. She acted accordingly, and they lay next to each other on the ground in silence for a while, as they enjoyed the moment in the wonderful site.

He made his fingers run across her skin as she remained silent, with a pleasing look. After some time, Hulda interrupted all that stillness that seemed to have fallen around them. "I love this place!" she stated. "Yes, it's far from any town, and we had to come a very long way to finally get here, but look around: it's really great! You know how to bring a girl to such wonderful, scenic spot and allow her to make the most of it, certainly…I'd never go away, if it was up to me, certainly! When will we come back here again?"

The other said nothing, his face deeply buried in the gold of her hair as she was lying on the meadow.

"Talk to me, Augustin!" the girl said. Her lips were redder than blood, seemingly, or maybe it was just the way that they appeared to him. "When do you think we can come back here?"

"I don't know…it depends…" were the only words she got from him in the end. The young man looked pensive, as if something else was presently on his mind, and he was making a lot of effort not to think about it.

The two stood there, partly unclothed, for some time more. Then, the moment came to get dressed again. They stood up, took their daypacks and got ready to continue their trip for that day.

"I'm going to show you something really unusual…" Augustin told the girl as she was following him. "We have to go that way, it's a short climb from here, but there's a narrow rock that will give us a beautiful view, next to a precipice."

"Ok, I'm right behind you…lead on!" she incited him.

It didn't take them long to get to the spot where the young man wanted to be, even though it required a little more effort and there were visible scratches on their hands and arms from climbing over the rocks. The couple finally found themselves on the edge of a wide cliff, beyond which the mountain dropped off so abruptly that it seemed they were standing on the verge of an unending world of trees and rocks below them.

"Beautiful, isn't it?" he asked, while pointing at the amazing scene below.

"Yes, you're right! It is so beautiful…" the girl smiled in agreement, with her heart full of appreciation and interest.

And it was at that time that the young man, without thinking twice of it, spun her around with all his strength.

Hulda began to cry out, more from surprise than from true pain; but she looked back at him in disbelief and he said nothing in return, though there were, maybe, hints of tears in his eyes. Trying to regain her balance, which she couldn't do, and clearly incapable of grasping something to keep her on top of the cliff, there was nothing else she could do except follow the inevitable path downwards at full speed.

Just a minute or two went by, then Augustin approached the steep precipice to finally have a look. Her body had hit the ground below more or less precisely where he had predicted. His previous experiences and his knowledge of the place — achieved over the course of years — had made him very capable of getting the exact result he wanted. Now he just had to wait for what he knew would happen next.

It didn't take long before something started moving, coming from an unseen part of the mountain and heading straight for the corpse of the poor girl who had fallen. It was a huge figure, much taller than a man, probably double the size of Augustin himself. Many strange low grunting sounds were clearly emitted out of its wide, fierce mouth.

Unlike the common fabled depictions of wild Trolls in the northern lands, and especially in the Scandinavian countries, that tall being had an intimidating massive though well-muscled overall shape which was very different from what you might imagine a Troll to look like. The creature's legs, face, and arms resembled a bear or a big cat more than a traditional Troll's. Its large strong paws ended with very pointed fingers — appearing to be rigid and deadly — and it certainly made the creature appear to be a beast used to digging, actually. Truth be told, such legendary beasts had a very destructive disposition as they were used to forcibly making their way through narrow caves and cumbersome rocks in the depths of the mountains, and so their bodies were endowed at birth with all the tools needed for that work.

The creature's pointed teeth along with its always-alert angled eyes and huge ears, made you understand at once that it was a carnivorous monster with an aggressive look and full of ferocity, ready to become violent and eat whatever came too close, whenever the opportunity presented itself. Its big stomach was perceived as being empty all the time by its small mind, for sure, which forced the monster to go searching ceaselessly for new prey in the surroundings when its nose caught the smell of anything alive.

The creature turned its thick-skinned head with its sizeable chin quills to the right and to the left, so it could be certain that there were no other predators nearby that might want to start a fight. Then it kept walking through the shrubs with its huge tail held straight until it reached the dead body of the girl. As it took her, some other growls were heard nearby, and the Troll seemed worried. There were visitors not far from where it stood…

Hurriedly, the monster moved on and disappeared behind a big boulder with its prey still in arms. Its lower intelligence let it believe its goal had been accomplished for the day and there would be no reason to go hunting until tomorrow. However, this was provided that it might distance itself from the others of its own species that had also smelled the blood of the same corpse and were catching up to it. Besides, what had been taken looked really delightful, and its mouth would keep it busy for some time by savoring that tasty human female as it liked to eat such meat, given its previous experiences. For sure, the Troll wouldn't regret having left the remains of the food it was eating before it got to that point in the forest, as now something fresh was at its disposal, and such young prey appeared to be much more appetizing certainly. Keeping this simple fact in mind was something even the stupid monster could certainly do...

From above, Augustin was able to view the whole scene. Soon the other two Trolls reached the first predator that had gone through the trees nearby, and a cruel fight did break out. As the creatures were battling each other over the right to be the first — or the only one — allowed to eat the tasty meat of the girl, the young man took the opportunity to go down the slope, unnoticed, and enter the caves where the Trolls lived. Then, he started searching for the object he wanted.

Augustin reminded himself of the first time he had discovered such things. It had just happened by chance, in frank words. He had always loved exploring darkness. In his free time, he lowered himself into the underground world of hidden caves to navigate the crevasses of a very different environment, and it was that day, four years ago, that he saw it. The man was spelunking with his girlfriend of that time, and they spotted a shiny golden object in one of the most well-hidden sites in the same cave. As she had moved in for a closer look, the two had found several ancient coins stashed inside wooden chests, along with swords, shields, gems and other valuable belongings. Those artifacts were probably ancient treasures, put in that place and left underground from the Middle Ages, or maybe even earlier, and that sight had greatly aroused their interest. Then, they had discovered who those caves belonged to — and the creatures that lived in them. *Trolls,* some real Trolls from the ancient legends...*how was it possible? Why did they really exist, and stay in that site?* So, probably those goods were something that came out of many bloody robberies and assaults the ancestors of those Trolls had perpetrated in the past, that had remained in there until today.

Or perhaps it was these same creatures that had taken those objects from human beings and brought them here — *after all, who knew how long those legendary monsters might live?* Otherwise, it might also be that such treasures had been hidden in the caves — in the hope of better days — by local residents in the past, or by Vikings, who moved elsewhere and never returned to collect them. Until the Trolls came and took over the caves for themselves.

Augustin and his girlfriend had entered there seemingly unnoticed, as the Trolls were asleep at that time, and started picking-up valuable objects while trying to not be discovered. Which didn't happen, in the end. As is prone to happen when stealing someone's property, some noises they made attracted the attention of the fierce creatures that rose to their feet at once and started chasing them, until one of those Trolls grabbed the leg of the poor girl. A bloody battle had begun among the three monsters in order to keep that food in female human form for themselves. Augustin had finally made it out, only by luck, and he had run away with only some little golden coins with him, but there had been no hope to save his girlfriend, or to retrieve her corpse that had been completely eaten in a matter of minutes by the eager Trolls.

Later on, the young man's decision had been a difficult one. He wanted to inform the police about what had occurred in those caves, and about his loss, but he doubted anyone would believe his story. *Trolls in recent time in Northern Norway, get real!* Come to your senses now… More than that, he didn't want to share the location of his find with anyone else because he didn't want to lose a single object from those treasures that lay hidden underground. *He wanted all of them for himself and for himself only!*

So, the young man had come back to that site, another time, bringing a rifle to get rid of those creatures from afar before trying to enter again. He couldn't trust hiring professional hunters to do that job, given the chance they might take all that gold for themselves afterwards, or spread the word about his search, which might prove even worse. But none of the Trolls had been killed by his shots because the skin of those monsters was too thick, simply put, the hits didn't kill nor wound them at all.

He even tried to distract those creatures, throwing game to them that he had killed before, but only one Troll grabbed it, while the others remained in the caves. It was clear that they liked such food, but that was not enough to start a bloody fight among the three and to make them all get distracted for his own purposes. And he needed all those Trolls to move away from the mountain for a while before he might dare enter those caves safe, and alone, certainly…

'*What can I do now*?' Augustin had considered. He knew he couldn't forget about that gold, he wanted it all for himself! And then he had thought about what had happened the first time he found those creatures — and of his loss. It appeared that such monsters found the meat of a freshly killed human body very tasty, especially a female one — for some unknown reasons he could not figure out. The only time he had tried to let them have a poor local peasant's corpse instead of a young woman's, it had turned the same way as when he threw game. Over the course of the following years he discovered that his guess was true, unfortunately.

The image of all those golden coins, along with glittering pieces of jewelry, including rings, bracelets and earrings, meant to be hidden and unfortunately left to those creatures, troubled Augustin's mind for a long time. He really wanted to become rich and bring those treasures home to Sweden — where he was from — until the day he decided to follow a completely new course of action. With all the consequences involved, anyway…

From that moment on, every year, he headed for this area with a new girlfriend of his, though he had to wait for the end of winter, when nature came back to life. It was not difficult to make Norwegian girls fall in love with him. After all, he was a very handsome young man, and young women like Hulda liked him at first glance, usually, and were eager to spend time with him. They were also eager to hike with him in the mountains of the north, even though they didn't appreciate going to such places at first. You had to convince them and choose the right ones: interested in hiking and an exhausting vacation; with no parents alive; and with no next of kin who might seriously start searching for them after they disappeared.

So he had to bring his girlfriend to this area, lead her near to the Troll's caves, and let those monsters take her and start fighting between each other to get the right to eat the tasty human meat. After that, he had to be fast and enter the caves to plunder as many old valuable objects as he could every single time and move away from there before the Trolls themselves came back.

By the time those returned, after stuffing themselves, Augustin was long gone, safe, with his bags full of riches for himself, certainly. It was the tactic of 'eat and run', in a way, *even though it was his current girlfriend that was eaten in the end, and it was the young man who did run away with the gold.* Using this strategy, it would take some time before he might get as rich as he desired, but it was a good start for the moment, undoubtedly. He had already done this exact thing eight times so far and still hadn't gotten caught.

Once the young man had collected the riches he was after, and thought that it was enough for today - as he couldn't take away too much loot back up the slope, he distanced himself from the cave in order to climb to the top of the precipice. As he started moving away, heading back for the town of Fauske, which was about five days from here on foot, his thoughts turned again to the face of Hulda, the poor dead girl he had left in this place, in the hands of the Trolls that were eager to eat her as their preferred food. He knew the thick forest would swallow everything soon… If she was alive when the creatures came for her, he would probably have heard her cries asking him: '*Why did you do it?*'. A better question would have been,'*What did you get for killing me?*', after all.

It was really a pity actually, Augustin considered. He had dated many girlfriends so far — it would be almost impossible to exactly remember all of their names - but he believed he might have developed a deep feeling for this latest one, if their relationship had lasted long enough. He liked her peculiar face, those delicate eyes and her voice, he couldn't deny it. Even her style in clothing was great, the same as her interests and education.

But he had always loved valuable objects and treasure more than the golden curls of a woman. Those things surely lasted forever and made you happy, he knew it very well. On the other hand, the prettiness of the girls, even the most beautiful ones he had dated, disappeared as fast as the gusts of the cold wind on a warm summer day.

Perhaps love could be thought of as a short dream of warmth and sunlight in a very long winter. But it was the rest that truly counted… It was, in fact, the icy months that mostly ruled over his own northern country during the year, exactly as his ice-cold heart controlled all of his actions. And his icy emotions had also shaped his mind.

He didn't even know why he had told her that old tale, which was connected in some ways to the caves of the Trolls themselves, and to what lay in those depths. Maybe it was just a feeble attempt to warn the girl, to make her be suspicious about the place they were really going; to the destination he was leading her to in the end. Or maybe it was something he felt in his heart, something that couldn't be helped.

Did he really want to prevent the girl from reaching the site he was leading her to? Did he love Hulda so much that he wanted her to be safe without ending her life that cruel way, as many others before her had? It was hard to say. Heart and mind, they are not always well connected, you know…

But there was no way he could have acted differently. There was no way to keep the girl alive or prevent her from going to that sad end. People say that we pay for our mistakes, every single time we make one. As far as the young man knew, you could call them mistakes if you liked, but he claimed that he had ruled his actions with wisdom, as they had always given him great value in return, by all means.

Addicted to The Night
Alexander Marais

If you were ever to call me pretty, I'd laugh at you. I'd fucking laugh at you. That is, until my more diplomatic instincts would kick in and have me making you wish in a variety of ways you were dead. I don't appreciate boys, men, girls, and women who lie. Never have. Never will.

If I were to tell this story in chronological order, you wouldn't get the half of it. I mean, you'd *obviously* get the technical flow of the unsightly events that would befall me after my sixteenth birthday. But you wouldn't get it the way I now understand it. Which, as far as I am concerned, is the only way to *really* get it because I'm me and you're you.

As I said before, it all started after I hit the sweet age of sixteen. The age where, allegedly, you gain empathy as a teenager for the first time. I guess I got a C minus in *that* class. Probably a bit more of a B, by now. Yet as I look back at everything that has occurred, well, really *fallen* would be the better word, I'm shocked while simultaneously a little cocky about the fact I haven't entirely lost the small amount of regard for others that I just began to possess myself. And just began to possess when shit splattered, and I mean *splattered*, against the fan.

I always was bound to snap. You'll learn a little later why in these pages. The home environment I was from, privileged as it may be, proved to be the most surprising — if luxurious — of prisons. The old saying is true. Money can't buy you happiness. And the folks who raised me, *happening* to be my parents, were pretty unhappy people. Yet I hesitate, pondering whether or not the word *snap* really describes what happened to me. Prior to this whirring cyclone of shit, I didn't have a history of mental health issues. Of course, I was told constantly that I did. But I didn't. I *really* didn't. Never saw any files. Never was able to be told explicitly what indicated the nature of my "ailment." I was just continually brainwashed via the black magic of constant, negative reinforcement. Which, as I got older and started to ask more questions, needless to say got worse, and worse, and worse.

I'll formally begin my story's narrative with waking up.

Dirty. Scared. Alone.

I had become a rather feral creature in my own eyes, rising only in the early hours of night after a long day's sleep inside my dumpster. When you reside and hide in such a place long enough, the usually nose-pinching aromas become like old friends. Covering myself with seemingly infinite bits of waste and shredded paper didn't even trigger an afterthought. I could only imagine the bewilderment of those who lived their whole lives this way seeing the life I used to lead. Needless to say, though, it appeared to be all over for now. *Or so I thought.*

Several years of living on the streets taught me one thing. *Embrace your unpreparedness.* Don't expect to make it through the night. Just go through the motions of someone trying to survive, and well…do your best *to* survive. I was surprised at how seemingly easy such a thing appeared to be, but learned the hard way time and time again you didn't disappear into the night without earning it first. Sleeping in dubious concealment during daylight hours seemed the safest of all unsafe options. The freaks and the truly heinous — much like myself — were creatures of the night. Somewhat paradoxically, I had decided it would be best to be awake when they were. To be prepared for such encounters, rather than avoid them. To be ready to run when danger truly was present, lavishing the few and filthy splendors of safety when able.

The abandoned warehouse I called home was never a place safe to inhabit. During the day, due to its close proximity to an artist colony some yards off, there was minor supervision of comings and goings courtesy of the armed guards before the chain-link fence. Night, however, was when residents of the former military units were told to deadbolt their doors. Management could only do so much, or would. Needless to say, such hours proved to be go-time for the crawlers, bottom feeders, cutthroats, and those who enjoy burning both people and things.

The fact my dumpster was never touched, day or night, I considered to be a great blessing of impossibly metaphysical proportion. My residency amongst the colonists proved undisturbed for quite some time. To say I was content would be a statement of seventy-five percent accuracy. I had forgotten what happiness was years ago, and coupled with external reinforcements it showed no signs of soon returning. But oddly enough, I found solitude and purpose in my life being homeless. It was more real to me than anything I had ever experienced. Until I met Dom.

He was working outside his pale white apartment, his hands covered in thick, wet clay. There was nothing particularly extraordinary about him, not that my allegedly troubled mind was attuned to such distraction. Silhouetted against the red, evening sun, his life was the epitome of what I had always imagined for myself. A life free of convention, yet conventional to those who shared it. The life of an artist, a poet, a creative person. A life beyond the Siddhartha effects of my societally acceptable, yet undeniably bizarre rearing.

He saw me before I saw him. Like I said, my mind was not fixated on things such as romance. *Obviously.* Sauntering cautiously out of my unstable haven, the hairs on the back of my neck prickled almost instantaneously as I grew parallel to the colony. *Someone has seen me.* My first instinct was to run, quickly made secondary by my turning to judge the witness. He simply stared back at me in response, never once moving his hands from the rotating device sweating sheets of gray.

"Hello."

My head snapped at the sound of the greeting. I had grown accustomed not only to my own silence, but simultaneously the stillness of others. When the words managed to reflux into my throat, I was shocked to hear how much my voice had changed. "You gonna bust me?" It was deep and gravelly, my tone somewhat threatening.

Dom frowned, for the first time moving one of his hands away from the spinning machine. "No," he said finally, eyes peeled for what he must have deemed potential threats. "Should I?"

"No." The word escaped my lips with an even greater fire, fear momentarily overcoming my hardened exterior. Then I remembered. *The guards have gone home. This belongs entirely to me.*

"Very well then," he said, instinctively glancing in the direction of the chain-link fence. "I will not bust you."

"How long have you been around here?" I interjected, still terse.

Dom raised an eyebrow. "Here?"

"Yes, asshole. *Here.*"

"About eighteen months."

Now it was my turn to raise *both* my eyebrows. "Eighteen months? Huh. You like it so far?"

"It has its advantages." His eyes were focusing back on the clay formations, and for the first time I began to feel a flicker of mortification. *He's no longer looking at me.* "You can stop staring now. Unless you want to come up here and help."

My eyes bulged. *Was this man insane?* "Help you?" the words barely escaped my mouth, complete with hardboiled egg formation.

Dom merely shrugged in response, leaving me in maddening silence again to contemplate my next move.

"I'll help you."

When he didn't respond, I began to turn around and walk away. I couldn't help noting in that moment the girl I used to be. Several years ago, I would have been bold enough to challenge this by walking straight towards the apartment and smashing his device. Things now, however, had changed me along with them.

"Hey!"

I kept walking, yet slowed my pace. After several more steps, something within me broke through the ice — forcing me to turn around.

He stood, continuing to be framed against the magnificent sunset, arms outstretched. "What happened to helping me out?" His tone was the perfect mixture of baffled and inquisitive, complete with a cloying if not unworldly sincerity.

Helping him, as it turned out, lasted about two months. During this period, I finally began to recoil at the filth and shit that once coated my tongue. What he saw in me, at that particular moment in time, is anyone's guess. My hair was long, ragged, and unkempt. My teeth were yellow. And I was said to have had glowing eyes in the darkness — a small but significant adaptation to my usual routine. I ultimately never asked him, and he never proceeded to tell me. I started living with him as the ultimate opportunist, in complete awe at his actions while wondering what the hell his shtick was. On a certain instinctual level, such thoughts were deemed irrelevant. Sliding back into a life with a few creature comforts was like a slow but steady addiction. It became transcendently surreal to rediscover what "good" food was, the feeling of water hitting my skin, and soft fabric touching the back of my head. Yet it always remained disconcerting to feel clean, cool clothes touching my naked figure. Such revelations made the truly new things, like Dom's lips pressing into my own, that much more revolutionary. My parents had always said such things would be out of my paygrade. *How wrong they were...*

It was our own, private world — his apartment being its facilitator. Surrounded by tall, exotic, and sometimes frightening shapes Dom crafted with clay. Like me, he was the ultimate outsider in his youth. He just found a way to make money with it. To be something *because* of it. I always envied that about him. But more than that, I envied his open heart. Granted, I had now seen enough to make me never smile again. Yet the pain of rejection, in any context, is what can make wrists bleed. But not Dom's. His wide-eyed stares and bright smiles contained no inkling of sardonicism.

He was the yin to my yang. Someone who chose to believe in the good of the world, overlooking any indicator of *bad to the bone*. That was the only time we would fight, our little universe threatened with breaking apart. He would accuse me of affecting his art courtesy of my cynicism, my retorts equating him to a bastard with no spine. Making up often consisted of some of the best sex I've ever had in my life. His innocence seemed to become undone every time. A darker side of the man would emerge — shining and feral. He would pin me to the bedclothes, digging so deep inside it felt like I'd burst. Needless to say, the mortality vibe to such carnal moments made the occasional shatterings that much sweeter.

Such pleasantries were never things I could find myself getting used to or taking for granted. Something else connected to what drove me wild about him. He never was able to comprehend that, despite knowing my story better than anyone. It was too easy for him to suffer vexations courtesy of my night terrors; to slam glasses onto floors when I'd be in one of my many moods. He simply didn't have the patience for a girl used to life on the streets still incapable of a steady step in modest means. Something, I would come to understand, that lay the foundation for what ultimately caused us to suffer our worst fight — for the hundredth and final time.

He came home late that night.

The thought beat and beat relentlessly against my thick skull as I surveyed the icy waters.

He would have come home earlier if I hadn't fought with him.

Why I chose to blame myself in this instance is anyone's guess. Perhaps it was easier than the truth. It felt better to blame myself, rather than both of us or him. Such self-loathing seemed to delay the impact of realizing my new life was gone. Almost as quickly as it had begun.

Dom had been followed. Dom had been followed, and it was all my fault.

You should never be outside past the unspoken curfew after the guards return home.

It's all my fault.

The devils always come to dance the moment authority disappears. That night was no exception…

It is all my fault.

My hand instinctively moved between my legs. I winced twice, first upon the impact my fingers made with the damaged tissue. Then again when retrieving them I saw they were covered in blood. A broken cry erupted from the furthest depths of my throat — the most painful thing about it being its failure to communicate the entirety of the anguish within.

Taking one last look at this wretched world, I cursed it quietly under my breath. *Hopefully the next place is better.*

And with that, ignoring the painful throbbing, I closed my eyes — waiting for the sea's harsh embrace. It came, but not in the sense that I hoped.

It is all my fault, it is all my fault, it is all my fault.

I continued to let the words dance through my head as I made slow, heaving motions onto the sandbank. The water stunk of pollution, the smell embedded deep within my sinuses and making every breath arduous. Shore was just a foot or so away. I couldn't help letting out another, agonized wail. Even Death wouldn't stay.

At long last, I felt the entirety of my belly make contact with the lukewarm surface. Closing my eyes again, I proceeded to breathe in as much reek as I could.

Maybe this could stimulate his return.

Yet all it did was jerk me further into the present, courtesy of a familiar nausea. "Oh God," my words subsequently escaped. "Is this my burden? Is this my curse? To continue to carry a most unpleasant weight of the world upon my shoulders?"

If there was a God, and he was merciful, this would have been his time to answer. To reassure me this was just part of the journey. That all this was a test of my strength, in an effort to maximize the redeeming qualities of my character. I laugh at such thoughts now. As if he really were merciful…

Perhaps the ensuing silence is what finally drove the final shaft of pain into my heart, blackening it forever. Accompanied by the stink and filth that I knew so well. The familiarity was the most potent aspect. It formed the grail from which a new kind of feeling emerged — one terrifying in its implications, but so very enthralling in its promises.

Walking around the endless megalopolis only cemented this new sensation. Much like a tentacled parasite, it spread across my body until I could almost swear I felt as if I were growing bigger. Badder. Smarter. Yet there was still an undeniable air of melancholia. It wasn't as if the gratification and adrenaline freed me from the origins of its existence. It was as if I had become synonymous with my pain, this newfound persona a child of that marriage. While I no longer felt disenfranchised enough to wander complete with psychologically induced limp, every confident step now taken *depended* upon my awareness. *Awareness of the damage. Awareness of the disillusionment.* Awareness of my own, innate drive to self-destruct. Not that it was entirely of my own making…

"Remember, sweetheart. You are ill. *You are ill.* Now repeat after me, *I am ill.* I am *ill.*" Those words became the mantra of my household role. Routinely coupled with dubious feedings of multiple medication. My birth trauma planted the seed of the seemingly endless paranoia. Plus, I made no eye contact. I preferred being in a world of my own. Worst, I didn't care to please — such traits deemed especially damaging for a girl. The oddities performed on me, unpleasant as they were, all were done in the name of "love." Or so they called it. The means was to an end titled *not losing me,* and from there the list went on and on. I may or may not have had measles, dyspraxia, and motor dysfunction. Needless to say, it was hard to tell where the condition ended and the side effects began. I never feel well as a general rule.

Call it a blessing or sheer dumb luck that I was a block away from the soup kitchen. Every single sad sack flocked to their charity, often trekking from miles away. Getting an actual meal from the place equated to winning the lottery. So naturally, in spite of my short-lived comforts, I gladly wolfed down everything they gave me. The entire time locking eyes with the server, staring back at me blankly. *Had it really been so long?* Molly was just a grade above me when we both attended high school. Was my appearance alien enough to her that she truly did not recognize me? I still wonder.

Following her home proved easier than I thought. She had the awareness of a child looking through a keyhole. For that reason alone, her very presence after the initial shock irritated me. It must have been very stimulating for her to do a bit of volunteer work. Seeing "the real thing" for twenty-four hours made her an expert in her mind, I am sure. Yet not enough to understand leaving one's door open, regardless of seconds, is an easy way to the hereafter. She was lucky in that the interloper was only me. A "damaged" young female after twenty bucks in her precious, sequin-coated wallet.

Buses wouldn't run for the next couple of hours, so I squatted in her closet for a small eternity. It was a relief there appeared to be no man in her life. The seemingly endless piles of ladies' underwear and bright pink bras confirmed it. When sounds dissipated and the apartment grew dark, I finally mustered the courage to half-slither my way from the smelly quarters. Rifling around in the darkness was easy. I had grown used to it in my street formative years. Making my way through the small kitchen towards the door, my finger pricked a corner of newspaper. I proceeded to grab at it, instinctively. *Something to remind me of the other world is always welcome.* Outside, the air was cool and crisp. The kind that could quietly creep up on you and leave the unlucky dead by morning. I paid it no heed as I continued walking towards the nearest station. The stink of dried diesel left itself in my wake. Pity the fumes weren't enough to cause anything more than a headache.

Sitting down amidst the dim fluorescent light, a particular article caught my eye. Not the writing, so much. The ten to twelve-point font was little more to me than dots. It was the photograph, framed beneath text too large to see. I blinked several times, part of me tempted to stick a cuticle in my left-dominant eye. The photograph matched Dom's face. In every way. The cliché in films at this point depicts the heroine crumpling up the newspaper and falling to the ground. But I had fallen many times over the years, and even in the face of this had no plans to do so again. Catching a breath, I squinted in the hopes of turning the small print to information.

Dominic Larson. Twenty-five years old. Believed to be the victim of a homicide involving the Pelphry Gang.

I could interpret little passages. Such a trait is the closest I'd get to howling in despair. Being reminded of a tragedy I wanted to forget seemed like the universe's ultimate *fuck you.*

He is survived by his mother, Angela Larson of Point Pleasant, New York, and his father, Arthur Prescillio of Mill Valley.

Edit my comment on clichés. Forget the bullshit I just wrote. The name *Arthur Prescillio* did not hit me slowly. It drove a freight train into my chest. *Running over my heart.* The paper fell out of my hands, splashing messily in a puddle by my feet. *What did this all mean?* Arthur Prescillio was the name of *my* father. *In* Mill Valley. Here, in the northern part of the state of California.

What did this all mean? A painfully naked sob escaped my lips when the answer cruelly flashed itself, in hideous glory. My small-time love, albeit necessary affection, was my half-brother. The infamous, unspoken child of my father's "other" family. What didn't hurt me was the incest. It was the realization of the profound irony. *Dominic wasn't good enough for my father's form of child-rearing. I was.* In a way, looking at it now, you could say he was blessed. Blessed because in spite of a life of luxury, I was a prisoner in a golden cage. While he rose, I had fallen. The small nexus that was our romance proved the ultimate cruel joke. For us both, *equally.* Only I was further cursed by living to see the results.

After I boarded the transit, I decided not to ride the bus toward the Oregon border. The same demeanor overtaking me after I jumped had other plans. I was returning to Mill

Valley. There was a score I could not bear leaving unsettled. My knuckles were white balls entrapped within walls of skin. My jaw was so tight, I was surprised my teeth didn't crack. Over the grief had spread the plasma of a wrath I couldn't have contemplated — even in the presence of already such revelatory moments. As the doors slowly closed and the vehicle began to chug along the dimly lit streets, the ethereal nature of my predicament began to film. *He didn't choose him. He chose me.* The words angrily played out, over and over, beating evenly on either side of my head. My father had chosen me. Chosen me as a superior target to break. The only thing worse than the epiphany was my own self-doubt that followed. Perhaps everything I now felt was the ultimate marker of *why. I am weak. I am vulnerable. They have won.* I blinked hot tears back around my eyeballs. There was no denying it, least of all to myself. *Congratulations, father. If nothing else, this is how you have succeeded with me.* The fire that had engulfed my heart would not break. The damage caused could no longer be undone, if it ever could have to begin with. They had won. And through winning, they had created a monster. A creature of the ultimate malice, as you will no doubt understand the further you delve into my story.

"Excuse me, miss?"

I slowly turned with a brazen stare. Needless to say, I was unhappy to be yanked away from my critical and depressing thoughts.

The voice belonged to a figure next to me, reaching out with a gnarled hand. His face was completely obscured within the depths of an olive-colored hood. No matter how hard you squinted, there was no telling just who...or *what*...was in there.

"Yes?" My voice was calm, but my fists were cocked. Not that it would have been a fair fight. *Yet nevertheless...*

"Are you hurt?" The words were maddening because of the bizarre calmness with which they were spoken.

"No." My tone now communicated impatience. You told it like it was. That, or played the game. The latter was not an option for me right now.

"I didn't mean *physically*."

I slowly turned to face him again, finding the hood cocked at a funny angle — almost levelling with my right tit. "What's the matter with you? You want to fuck me?"

The hood moved up and down slightly as a hollow laugh emerged from its depths. "Not particularly. You're not my type."

"Then fuck off." I was not in the mood for games. Yet, in spite of the harsh words, I found myself literally unable to look away.

"Be careful with what you do. Don't regret what you wish for. And remember above all else, *tread carefully in the darkness*."

My eyes didn't widen, despite wanting to. Frozen, my mouth moved without my consent. "What do you mean by that?"

The figure laughed again, silhouetted slightly against the growing blue light outside. "Exactly *what* I meant."

"No," I found myself able to blink, regaining some control. "What do you mean *tread carefully in the darkness*? What does *that* mean?"

The figure simply stared back in silence. "You should be fully back in control in several seconds," the voice – almost a separate entity due to the visual disembodiment — finally spoke.

I blinked again. "What?"

The figure folded its arms across its chest as it reached its punchline. "Then you will understand all that there is to comprehend."

Despite my best efforts, my eyes were beginning to close – sleep covering me with its bitter sheen. The only thing I can remember was the figure flickering slightly. Yes, *flickering.* And I know it wasn't because of my trembling eyelashes.

When I awoke some hours later, he had vanished. I was being roughly shaken by the driver — a pig-faced man displaying apparent disgust. "Time to get out, time to get out," he was saying.

"Where are we?" I yawned in reply, rubbing my eyes with my fists.

"Mill Valley," the man replied curtly. "Now scram before I call the fucking cops on your bum ass."

"Mill Valley?" I sat up slowly, looking around me. "I thought this bus was headed to Humboldt County." Despite the reassurance of not having slept through getting home, I was struck by the odd disconnect — *plus* the hooded figure — all in one night.

"Don't know where you heard that," the driver spat. "But I'm not fucking around. I'm going to count to three, and by three you better make me feel sorry. Get!"

Finding my way home was an odd experience. One would think after so many years I'd forgotten the way. Yet my feet knew exactly where to go, my conscious mind in tow. The pavement was terribly hot in the autumn sun. The soles of my feet felt like burnt leather every step of the way. Yet I had been through enough pain that I had developed an elaborate system of clouding. Shutting in everything sensory and otherwise until I reached the present goal. But in that moment, such a habit fluctuated in its effectiveness. I grit my teeth as the feeling refused to go away, instead merging with the overall tapestry of misery. *This will only make it harder...*

Before I knew it, though, I was home.

Looking around me, I had forgotten just how beautiful everything was. *The spacious two-story house, atop a large hill, overlooking the great mountains ahead.* A soft breeze rippled through the trees, touching the back of my hair. Cocking my head as my eyes closed, I couldn't help feeling for just one second like the young, wide-eyed girl I used to be. It was as if by being here, I could finally mourn what I had lost. *Even if just for a moment...*

It wasn't long before the stink of diesel signaled the return of my newfound character. Eyes opening, I proceeded to lock such reek inside the furthest confines of my heart. Taking several steps forward, I knew exactly where I would seek refuge until the new night fell. The garden my mother and I had planted felt like an old friend. It was bleak-looking and rotten in places, just like me. Waiting there proved to be so much of a comfort. There was nothing too beautiful to remind me of what I had been missing.

When the right time finally came, my lips were chapped and sore while my head felt it would burst. It was an all too familiar feeling, intense in its being suddenly alien. Despite consuming so little for many years, being home spoiled not only my mentality but also my senses. It was as if physically I had undergone a transformation. What normally I could take I found myself oddly averse to. It was hard to cloud this particular pain, or to make it another motivator for what I was about to do. But looking upwards, my newfound demeanor burned fire in my throat. They needed to pay for what they had done to me. And they would.

Climbing onto the roof no longer scared me. Back in my days of privilege, I had suffered bouts of severe vertigo. I couldn't even ride in elevators. *At least that's changed.* I scuttled without hesitation towards the far left of the house. From there, I could safely jump onto the upstairs deck. If they were anything like how they used to be, my mother and father would have left the sliding glass door open. They preferred that to AC. On such a hot night, the faux worldliness of this made me stifle a hooting laugh. *Fucking ridiculous, as always.* Sure enough, the door was open. Walking towards it proved easy. It was as if I had never left. Yet I froze the moment my front permeated the space within its frame. Terror welled up in the back of my throat, like a flapping second tongue. In the darkness, the grandiose nature of our living room was bizarrely intimidating. Perhaps it was the large, pointed chairs – resembling monstrous entities writhing before me. Or maybe it was the large painting of my grandfather – eyes staring directly into my soul. It took a lot of willpower, boosted by my revelatory ferocity, to finally put one foot in front of the other – returning to a world I had known intimately for so many years. Looking back on it now, I wonder if I was feeling the superior mortal fear of a guilty executioner. Someone needing to be intimidated by anything they could conjure that was greater than themselves. Needless to say, it would have made perfect sense to whatever sliver was left of my former self…

There was only one other time I approached their bedroom in this fashion. It was twelve years ago — and like today, I planned to kill them. Of course, I was a lot more naïve then. I thought I could strangle them both with my bare hands, bless me! Almost turning the knob, I regret irrationally in retrospect chickening out. It would have been the perfect scene for making the ultimate point. Not that they would have understood, of course.

Heavy moaning had emanated from within, creating an uneven paradox. *Brutally dying while in the highest state of life. Maybe even while creating it.* Yet such sentimentalities mean little to me now. The memories of such a feeling only hardens the grail of my *un*feeling cruelty. I suppose my need to note this adheres to an overall sense of protectiveness. I spent the first three quarters of my existence living a hideously cauterized life. A life that ironically subjected me to the very things my parents claimed to protect me from. *Manipulation. Sexuality. Death.* Needless to say, there were many reasons for my finally turning into what they proclaimed I always was. For my *needing to be* such a person. But such details are stories for another time.

"What are you doing?"

For a second, I thought the voice in present time was my own. Thinking out loud was one of my many weaknesses. The crack beneath my parents' bedroom door emitted no visible light. It was late enough so both of them must have been asleep. Then I jerked into the moment when I remembered my voice wasn't that high anymore. Turning slowly, I found myself further floored at the sight now lying before me. She was a beautiful little girl, about eleven to twelve years old. Dressed in pajamas reflecting the precociousness of Generation Z. Eyes shining in the darkness — *just like mine.* There was no mistaking it. I was looking at my new, little sister.

Neither one of us moved for several more seconds. It was as if we were both judging — then subsequently regretting — our roles in this scenario. Hers being confronting me at all. Mine being the cold pragmatism surrounding what I was now compelled to do. It was just a question of who would act first. Her, or me. The girl did not disappoint. Turning on her heel, she ran with surprising speed down the stairs. My eyes gleamed. *I knew the way.* There was only one place she could be headed. Racing after her down to the house's first story, my eyes locked on the closing door of what used to be my bedroom. *No,* the fire burned. *My bedroom. It's mine. It's rightfully mine.* The outrage accompanying this epiphany increased my already fearsome stride. My left foot jammed itself between door and frame, the ensuing pain prompting me to use my right to kick it hard. There was a shriek from the other side, indicating the back of it probably hit her in the face. As the door swung violently open, my assumption proved correct. The girl had been knocked into a sitting position, eyes wide with fright, blood escaping her nose. She wasn't one to play victim too long, however. I couldn't help smiling as she grabbed at a fluffy toy — admiring her grit. *It reminded me so much of myself.* The stuffed animal proceeded to harmlessly bounce off my left breast. I cocked my head slightly. "Never hit a woman there, young lady." Even I was struck by the loss of innocence in my thick, ragged tone. A feral cry escaped the child before me. Seeing she was out of options, my little sister wasn't going down without a fight. She came at me, utilizing everything she had. The teeth were the only effective parts — two especially sharp incisors sobering my initial amusement. With a roar of my own, I proceeded to grab ahold of the young girl's throat, slamming her onto the gray-colored carpet beneath us. "You think you know how to fight?" The demeanor was all I had now.

"Fuck you," my sister wept. Even displaying such naked and childish vulnerability, her magnetism never faltered.

"Do you know who I am?" I said, something in me bridling slightly at the sight of fresh tears.

"No," the girl said, closing her eyes slightly.

"I'm your sister." The words escaped my throat right as the revelation caused it to close. Whatever shred of humanity that was left was being used up courtesy of this encounter. "I'm your fucking sister, that's who."

"I don't have a sister." The girl's voice was weak. Clearly all the stress inflicted upon her was taking its toll. She looked like she could barely stay awake.

"Is that what they told you?" The demeanor reared its head again, the tears slowly running out of gas.

"My sister..." the young girl struggled, "is dead." Her eyes opened right after she said this, as if such a statement reinvigorated her own fire.

"So that's what they told you," I assessed, slowly moving my hands away from her neck.

"Why are you here?"

The question was simple enough. The diabolical answer caused my tongue to waltz and my blood to sing in my veins. Yet looking into her face, the response became so complicated to word. However would I do it justice? The young girl stared at me, armed with an expression best described as vehement curiosity. "I...I don't know," I finally said. This reinvigorated my own tears. Yet it remained unclear to me whether their existence depended upon her or myself. Several seconds of this newfound grieving passed. Then my sister proceeded to break it.

"Get off of me."

If the words weren't so demanding, weren't so…*entitled*…I might have complied. But as a response to her tone, my face hardened while hers subsequently crumpled. The fire in her eyes was beginning to dim. Childish hopelessness and childish submission were beginning to make their entrances.

"*Please*," the young girl begged. Stripped of her mane, her plea came wrapped in excessively sweet sincerity. Yet to no avail. Whatever chance she had to reason with me, she had wasted.

My hands began to close themselves around her throat, naturally her breathing beginning to quicken at this.

"Please, don't." More tears. More slightly stifled cries. Now more *stifled* cries. "Please don't. *Please don't.*"

Yet looking into her petrified face was cherry on top of the visceral sundae. In it I saw something even worse than Dom's scenario. This was someone who was kept. Someone who was spoiled. Someone who, in *this house*, wasn't groomed for a life of shattered stability and lost hope. As her life began to escape, the words the hooded figure spoke to me suddenly flashed to mind.

"Be careful with what you do. Don't regret what you wish for. And remember above all else, *tread carefully in the darkness.*"

My hands went limp, the process suddenly interrupted. Beneath me, the young girl struggled for breath — her cheeks slightly blue. Her eyes were completely stripped of their power. Wild and terrified, they stared at me with the circumference of saucers. I simply proceeded to stare back, coldly. When my mouth formed the words, I realized her life was the last roll of the dice I had had. The last chance to *trust* and to *spare*.

"I'm not here for you," I heard myself say. "I'm here for them."

Tread carefully in the darkness.

The Brother
June Trop

The Eighth Year of the Reign of
Nero Claudius Caesar Augustus Germanicus [Nero]
62 CE, Mid-March
Alexandria *ad Aegyptum*

It was almost noon on the Ides of March when my house servant, Minta, recognizing the frantic jingle of bells as those on Phoebe's litter, rushed into the late winter chill to greet her at the entrance to our townhouse.

"Miriam! Miriam!" The urgency in Phoebe's voice rang through the house.

A moment later, my best friend was plunging through the ceiling-high, double mahogany doors of my study. I looked up from my desk and had to remind myself to breathe.

Her cheeks flushed, her shoulders rigid under her crimson *stola* and the matching silk himation, she stared at me with wild eyes before dropping into the *sella* opposite me. To calm my own blood hammering like a clapper inside a bell, I focused on the scent of alarm in her perspiration.

"Tell me, Phoebe."

Wringing her hands together, she squeezed out the bitter words. "It's gone, absolutely gone. Menander's *Dyskolos*. The edition Bion brought me from Athens. We'd been keeping it on display in the shop to attract customers. You remember—"

For an instant I caught a nascent glitter in her eyes as she reminded me that Bion had picked out this play for her because in the story, Sostratos falls instantly in love with Knemon's daughter just as he fell in love with her.

"When, Phoebe? When did it disappear?"

"I'm not sure. I hadn't been to the shop lately. I only went this morning to help rearrange the shelves for a shipment due this week."

And then with tears flooding her cheeks, her eyes a little bigger as they fixed me with a searching look, I felt the question in her gaze.

"Of course, Phoebe. And we'll find it. That I promise you."

I entered the shop on a shaft of afternoon sunlight slanting under the *stoa*'s portico. Bion, maneuvering his paunch with the skill of a sea captain, sailed around the half-empty boxes of scrolls and stationery supplies to greet me. His easy smile turned his gold-flecked eyes into fringed slits and his chubby cheeks into pomegranates.

When Bion met Phoebe, he was a public slave repairing scrolls in the workshop of the Great Library. Eventually he was sold to a Jewish sandal-maker and bibliophile in Caesarea who liberated him after six years as is the custom with our people. Along with the quitclaim, his master gave him enough money to establish a business repairing and selling rare scrolls. Now Bion owns a thriving *bibliopōleion* in the agora, where he deals in rare classical manuscripts as well as the contemporary works of scholars like Thrasyllus of Mendes and engineers like our very own Hero.

"Oh, Bion, I'm so sorry!"

"I see Phoebe's already told you. She mentioned when she was here earlier that she'd stop by to see you. She's quite upset. Actually, we both are. But let me show you where it was displayed."

I followed his stubby shadow as it looped around the stacks of manuscripts and knots of customers buzzing about the counters, tables, and shelves until we reached the empty vitrine at the front of the shop.

"How much could that scroll be worth today?"

His voice dropped to a whisper. "About 2000 drachmas, enough to buy the grandest house."

A fishy reflux rose in my gorge.

"Quite rare," he continued. "An almost complete edition of what is still regarded as the best example of Athenian New Comedy."

I pinched my lips. *By now, it could be on a ship headed anywhere.*

"It was right here." Bion, in a characteristic gesture, pointed with his chin. Then he threw up his hands in despair.

After swallowing hard, his face softened, and he jerked his head toward the young man walking toward us. "But wait. I'm forgetting my manners. Let me introduce you to my new apprentice, Varius. Surely Phoebe's told you he and his brother are lodging with us."

Rare for me, I had to look up to meet the deep-set dark eyes of the trim, immaculately dressed man before me. Cleanshaven, baldheaded, and with the immovable face and bearing of a military officer, he exuded the somewhat sweet leathery scent of the labdanum that oiled his body.

"Welcome to Alexandria," I said.

He seemed pleasant enough. When I asked him how he happened to come here, he answered that he and his brother were eager to escape the stench of Nero's Rome. "It hovers over the city like a fog, enough to make even the dogs sneeze." He spoke our Greek smoothly but with the limestone-edged consonants of a Roman.

"So how did you find Varius?" I asked when Bion and I had taken our usual places in his office behind the scrim at the back of the shop.

We were sitting across from each other at the rosewood table that stretches across the room. Facing the marble-topped cabinets that frame the lone, east-facing window, I had a chance once again to admire the tidy elegance of his office. No careless piles of scrolls or sheets of papyrus shingled its surfaces. Instead the busts of classical dramatists, poets, and philosophers peered out from their niches.

"Actually, he found me. He answered the ad to let our upstairs apartment that Phoebe had posted at the East Gate. He wanted it for himself and his brother, and when I saw how learned he was, that he'd even studied rhetoric and grammar with the disciples of Pliny the Elder, I invited him to be my apprentice as well.

"You know Thoth and Galen have been with me for years, ever since Caesarea, but I just felt we needed the energy of someone younger. Even with Phoebe's occasional help, we barely keep up with shelving the new supplies as they come in. As you can see for yourself," he added with a rueful smile and a sweep of his arm.

"His brother had been staying at The Pegasus—"

"Oh, no! Not that slimy box of depravity-"

"—And working as the night watchman at the warehouse behind the Flamingo's Tongue. Actually, I've never met brothers more different. There's a family resemblance to be sure—both tall and swarthy—but otherwise they're completely different and not just in appearance but in personality and accomplishments too. Dario—that's his brother's name. Did I already mention that?"

I offered Bion a crisp shake of my head, but with unfocused eyes, he was already organizing his impression of Dario.

"He carries his head cocked to the right as if he were balancing a barrel of henket on his left shoulder. And, oh yes, his hair is thick—like a hedge of curls—and grows low on his brow before crawling down his cheeks and flowering out of his nostrils and ears. And—forgive me for saying this—he smells like a stable.

"Well, Varius signed the lease for both of them on the calends, and they moved in right away, Dario sometime that day and Varius that evening."

"Let me ask you this, Bion: When did you notice the manuscript was missing?"

"I wish I could say for sure—I've been in and out of the shop arranging credit for the next shipment—but surely within the last couple of days. *Hmm*." And then pausing with half-closed eyes as if reading the information on the inside of his lids, he declared. "Yes, it was yesterday. Had to be. That's when I told Phoebe."

"And is there a key to the vitrine?"

"Yes, four, one for each of us," he said, ticking them off on his fingers. "Phoebe and me, Thoth and Galen—No, make that five. Varius has one too. I had a key made for him just this week. And, of course, we kept the cabinet locked. Besides, my regulars knew the manuscript wasn't for sale, and it was much too expensive for anyone coming in off the street."

I nodded.

"Please, Miriam, do what you can to find it, especially for Phoebe."

"It'll be okay. You'll see," I said in that phony singsong I use whenever I want to sound more confident than I feel. I knew it wasn't going to be easy, but I could never have imagined what was in store for Bion and me.

It was the next day when looking up, I saw Bion standing at the threshold of my study framed in the bloom of late-morning light.

"Miriam, something bizarre has happened."

I put aside my reagents—I'd been perfecting the fabrication of pearls—got up from my workbench and slid into the chair behind my ebony desk. Bion flopped into the *sella* across from me.

He looked past me for a while, beyond the purple-tied-back drapes, as if intent on watching the light finger its way between the columns of the peristyle. He didn't speak until the incessant squawking of a crow punched the stillness.

I hinged forward.

"Listen, I'm sorry to bother you again, especially after yesterday, but Varius told me this morning that Dario didn't come back from the warehouse after his nightshift. That's when they have breakfast together." Confusion and worry competed for purchase on Bion's face. "Do you think this could have anything to do with the manuscript?"

"I think you need to alert the authorities."

Bion sighed with exasperation.

"You were loitering outside a brothel this afternoon." The twinkle in Judah's luminous green eyes belied his flinty tone as he regarded me over the rim of his wine goblet.

"Well, yes, and not just one." I replied, leaning forward, raising an imperious eyebrow.

"Look, I knew when I married you that you were *unusual*—"

"I hope you mean—"

"Okay. I should have said *special*, but I hardly expected to hear that you'd be passing your afternoons outside brothels, saloons, latrines, soup kitchens—"

"Oh, that must have been Aspasia who spotted me. For a while this afternoon, I was near her apothecary. And then she must have stopped by your shop."

"Spoken like an astute detective. But don't you send Phoebe to do your undercover work?"

"This time I couldn't. Bion needs her in the shop right now. Besides, he doesn't want her involved in our latest investigation. Too upsetting."

I saw through the windowpane shadows of the leaves shivering in the wind as Judah and I sat in our dining room. Waiting for Minta to serve us boiled capon in a honey glaze with a platter of cucumbers garnished with dill, we snacked on a tray of olives and deviled eggs. A spike of pepper tickled my tongue and sharpened my memory of that first encounter with Judah, that unexpected ache when I'd walked into his jewelry shop to collect the mortgage payment he owed my father. As he leaned toward me to hand me the envelope, close enough for our air to mingle and for his hand to brush against mine, he ignited my embryonic fantasies of love. Now, sixteen years later, his eyes are still framed by a dreamer's lashes, but his wreath of black, glossy curls is lit with silver.

"So, tell me about your investigation."

"Bion and I are trying to recover a scroll stolen from his *bibliopōleion*. At the same time, the brother of his new apprentice, a night watchman at one of the warehouses, didn't return home after his shift last night."

"You suspect a connection?"

"Well, I don't believe in coincidences, and his brother could have known about the manuscript and, at least indirectly, had access to it."

"So, you and Bion went searching for the brother today."

"And Varius—he's the apprentice—he checked some places too."

I gave Judah a thumbnail description of Dario based on Bion's report, that he's hairy, cocks his head to the right, and smells like a stable.

"Well, with a description like that, he shouldn't be too hard to find."

"Spoken like the deputy to an astute detective," I said, "especially when you have a friend like Aspasia, but I believe Dario must have absconded with the manuscript by now."

Such was my opinion at the time, but I couldn't have been more wrong.

I waited anxiously for any news of Dario or the manuscript. I heard nothing, not a word despite slogging every day through the tide of vehicles, dodging bullying oxcarts and getting trapped behind clots of hawkers and gawkers. Nothing, not a word despite my daily rounds to every barber shop, tavern, brothel, soup kitchen, latrine, moneychanger's stall, and port official. When I went to the warehouse behind the Flamingo's Tongue with Bion's description of Dario, even the guards claimed not to know him.

But I got an update a week later when Bion stopped by to tell me about the two granite-faced soldiers who'd swaggered into his shop.

"They barged in, flaunting their red-crested helmets and iron cuirasses as if they were going to arrest us all. I heard only their hobnail boots scrape the tile floor—which they carpeted with filth by the way—until one of them summoned me by name."

Bion described him as pear-shaped, the other as lanky. The pear-shaped one handed him a cylinder of parchment sealed with a puddle of wax bearing the magistrate's signet. Then Bion watched the backs of their scarlet capes billow and snap as they passed under the portico, mounted their horses, and vanished in a geyser of dust.

His fingers trembled as he tore through the seal to read the memorandum and then pass it to Varius. The substance was that Dario's body had been found floating in the canal that crosses the *Rhakotis* quarter.

"'Oh Jupiter, how can this be?' Varius asked, his hand to his cheek as though he had a toothache. 'And where on Earth is this canal and this *Rhak*—whatever-it-is?'"

Bion then explained to his stunned apprentice that *Rhakotis*, our oldest residential quarter, is in the western section of the city, where most of the Egyptians who work in the shipyards and on the quays live. He tactfully refrained from adding that the quarter is blighted by poverty, pestilence, and violence and that murderers lurk there to prey on the nameless and dump their corpses in its malignant canal.

"But," Bion added, "it was even harder telling Varius that the authorities wanted the next of kin to identify the body. I thought he'd want to—you know, his chance to say good-bye, his filial duty and all that—but no, he boggled as soon as I mentioned it.

"'Could you do that for me?' he asked.

"My mouth hinged open. 'Look,' I said, 'I'm just his landlord, and not for so very long at that. I saw Dario a few times running down the steps, rushing to the warehouse—oh, and that one morning when he came to the shop to tell me you'd be late—but as his brother, your word would be beyond dispute.'

"'But you know him—I mean *knew* him,' he pleaded. I tell you, Miriam, his voice was pitiable. 'And I can mind the shop while you're gone. Really, I can. I just don't think I can bear to see my brother like that.' His hand felt like a claw as he gripped my wrist.

"Well, you know what a pushover I am. I told him I'd do it providing I could get you to accompany m—"

"Me? You must be kidding."

"Miriam, dread was consuming him like a fever."

"You want me to vouch for the identity of a man I've never seen?" My voice came out like the rasp of metal on stone.

Bion's cheeks turned crimson. "Listen, the truth is corpses surface in that canal every morning, more than anyone can count, let alone investigate. I was notified simply because I reported Dario missing. But that doesn't mean I can make sense of a body that's been putrefying maybe for days in that nasty scum. That's why I need your help, you know? Besides, you're a Roman citizen, so I figured your statement would be more persuasive than mine alone."

"Well, I do want to get to the bottom of this—at least to recover the manuscript—and Dario, or what was once Dario, may be our only clue. So yes, I'll go with you."

And then, as the corners of my mouth lifted, I asked with a hint of mischief peppering my voice, "If we hurry, do we still have time to get to the morgue today? It's inside the Palace of Justice."

Bion pointed his chin toward our side street where his litter waited.

We cruised southward and then westward in a grim silence. Blades of the late-afternoon sun spilled through the colonnades, porticoes, and arcades; stabbed my eyes; and forced them to the pavement, where I saw torch lighters refreshing the wooden staves with a mixture of sulfur and lime.

Knowing the importance of spectacle, the Romans had designed their Palace of Justice to be a perfectly proportioned repository for their official records. From the vine-covered, wrought iron gate to its twin marble columns, we mounted the long flat steps to its double-arched doors.

An albino guard in scarlet livery squinted at the fibula that distinguishes me as a Roman citizen and scrutinized the seal on the parchment Bion presented. Then he called to a flat-faced soldier to escort us to the morgue. Crossing a grand hall redolent of exotic perfumes, pomades, and unguents, we passed the high arched windows that splashed long slants of sunlight across the mosaic floor and dusted the clerks with glitter. Finally, we followed the soldier's easy stride through a tangle of corridors to a narrow flight of stone steps. Claiming two portable lanterns from a stand in the landing, igniting them with his fire steel, and handing one to Bion, he opened the thin sheet of mica on his lamp to direct an amber beam down the steps and into the low-raftered chamber that was the morgue.

The thud of his military boots and the rhythmic clang of his sword against his thigh filled the stairwell.

The air exhaled a chill.

The stench, a hideous brew of decay and human waste, rushed up the stairwell, growing closer and heavier as we made our way down. A fit of retches ripped through Bion, his face turning a bright pink before he covered his nose with the tail of his himation. My own skin turned clammy as a foul taste collected on my lips. Worsened by underventilation, the stink of decomposition hung over the chamber like a mist.

Excusing himself in a coarse Latin, the soldier left to fetch the body. The click of his heels on the stone floor returned a feeble echo. Otherwise we waited in the gloom watching the lantern lick at the darkness while the time passed with appalling slowness.

My heart fluttered with expectancy as he rolled the gurney toward us. The corpse lay on his back. First, I checked the tag tied to his toe. It read *Rhakotis*, the day, and Dario's name.

His flesh was half gone. What remained was bloated, bloodless, and bleached to a pale yellow with clumps of algae in his eye sockets. The cause of death was not obvious until I lifted his skull and found the rear portion had been crushed into a spongy mass, the result of a savage blow. One-by-one I called out these observations to Bion, who was standing behind me, his shoulders bunched, still recovering from his fit. The soldier stood in a far corner rocking on his heels.

"I need you here, Bion. Tell me whether you recognize Dario."

Bion edged up to the gurney on trembling legs, coughing as he tried to suppress another retch. "You know, I don't think there's enough left of him for me to know. *Hmm.* The build seems right, though. Can you straighten out his limbs so I can get a better idea? Here, I'll help you lift him."

"Look, Bion. He's missing a hand, his left. Was Dario missing a hand?"

"No. Certainly not. But maybe he lost it when he was killed."

So, I examined the stump and removed what was left of his tunic to see whether he'd suffered other traumas. Meanwhile, Bion stared at the ceiling, now and then closing his eyes.

"The scarring around the stump is old. Look how white it is compared to the rest of his arm. Not even any redness, which means the injury occurred years ago."

Bion pinched his face and nodded.

"And here's something else. There's a fuller's mark on his tunic."

"So?"

I turned to Bion with a single nod. "That must have been how the authorities identified him as Dario. They recognized the fuller from his mark and then checked his customer list against your missing person's report. Still, regardless of the fuller, I'm convinced this man couldn't be Dario, not with that missing hand."

"Me, too. So, I'll call the soldier. Let's sign the statement, and then we can tell Varius the good news."

"But now we have two new questions: What happened to Dario? And why was someone else wearing his clothes?"

We folded ourselves back into the litter and headed toward Bion and Phoebe's house and Varius's apartment. Our shadow crawled alongside us as we passed arcades and monuments flecked with the last shards of daylight. I wrapped my arms around my chest to fend off the evening chill and clamped my jaws shut so my teeth would stop rattling like a backroom dice game. At the same time, a bead of sweat trickled down my spine. And then the bearers stopped and lowered us to the pavement in front of a three-story limestone townhouse, prim, solid, and respectable, with a dim yellow light shining through a window veiled in lace.

My arms swung with lightness as we carried our good news through the red marble atrium, its walls veneered in the latest style and its mosaic floor patterned with scenes from *The Odyssey*.

"Where's Phoebe?" I asked.

"Her shift tonight at the soup kitchen. Let's go right upstairs to see Varius. The news is worth interrupting his dinner if we have to." I could hear the relief that had seeped into Bion's voice.

He took the oil lamp from the window and led the way up the curved marble staircase to the second floor. From there, we took a narrow wooden staircase to a hallway punctuated by the thick oak door that was the entrance to the brothers' apartment.

Bion knocked gently at first, but with no response, he became more insistent until he was pounding on the door, calling Varius by name.

"Gee. Where could he be?" I asked.

Another shrug, this time in despair. "He should have come back from the shop already, and it's too early for the saloons, not that he's the type. He could have ordered dinner from a cookshop, but surely he'd have brought it home to await our news."

"Do you have a key?"

"Oh, Miriam, I couldn't do that, invade his privacy like th—"

"He won't even know," I pressed. "We don't have to touch anything. I just think these are exceptional times. And if something did happen to his brother—and I'm convinced it did—that same thing could be happening to Varius."

Bion put up his hand to stop me, but I could see him debating with himself.

"I don't kn—"

"And look. He is, after all, more than just your tenant. He's your apprenti—"

He threw up his hands. "Okay, okay. I'll unlock the door."

We entered the apartment like thieves. Holding our breath, dragging our shadows behind us, we tiptoed along the polished oak floor of a square room tucked under the eaves of the house, its one heavily draped window facing the harbor. The mournful ring of a buoy and the groan of an oxcart slipped through the drape.

Bion's lamp painted the gloom with a watery light.

"*Whew*! What is that?" A menacing stench was seeping into my nostrils.

"Holy Isis, that's an animal stink."

"Have they been keeping animals here?"

"Not that I know of. Why would they?"

We looked at each other in bafflement as Bion swiveled his head from side to side. His eyes widening, his words tumbled out in a thin, high pitch. "This place is all but empty, just the furniture that comes with the apartment. Look, even the shelves are bare."

"Only one sleeping couch?"

"They're here together only at breakfast. But did you hear me? The place is empty!"

And then I felt a pinch in my gut and could taste the tang of acid in my throat. "Wait! What's that?" I gasped, pointing to the washstand, my arm twitching like a branch in the wind.

"What? This? The head? It's a wig holder. Made of wood. Phoebe has several."

I exploded with barks of laughter that I could stop only by stuffing my knuckles in my mouth. "Yikes, I thought it was Varius, his head I mean. But didn't you tell me Varius is bald, and Dario's hair is thick? You said 'like a hedge of curl—'"

"Quick, Miriam!" He gestured me toward him with a series of arm rolls. "Over here, by the cooking furnace. The smell is even stronger."

"Oh, Lord!" I slapped my mouth with an open palm as I edged toward the counter above the furnace. "These are hoofs. They've been making glue from the hoofs of horses!"

"But why?" Incredulity spilled from Bion's voice.

"We have to search the apartment."

"But they have rights under their lease. You said we wouldn't touch anyth—"

"The manuscript is here, Bion. I know it is. You search the washstand, wardrobe, and sleeping couch. I'll check the rest. And don't forget to look for hiding places in the walls and floor around them."

I found nothing in and around the shelves and table and chairs, so I hunkered down and inched along the floorboards, oscillating my head, my eyes raking the strips for any gap, any disruption in the grain of the wood. My palms extended, my fingers fanned, feeling the sting of dust chafing my fingertips, I paused only to pick at a drop of dried spill and dislodge some grit from the corner of my eye.

Then staggering to my feet, wiping my palms together, calming my skirt, and brushing the grime from my hem, I rapped on each wall, my ear flush with its surface, listening for any hollowness. At the same time, I heard the dry complaint of the wardrobe doors as Bion swung them open and their wheeze as he slammed them closed.

"Miriam, the wardrobe is bare, like they were never here and never coming—"

"Take your time around the sleeping couch. Check under the bed linen, mattress pad, and pillows."

Between the slaps of my own footsteps, I heard the crack of his knees as he skirted around the sleeping couch, his weight shifting as he snapped the sheets, his himation swishing as he beat the blankets and pounded the pillows.

Bion took a step back. "Nothing," he said, with a hiss of exasperation.

"Are you sure? It has to be here. Let's move the wardrobe."

"No, I'll do that. It can't be very heavy."

A creak and then a whine as Bion slid the wardrobe away from the wall.

Blinking slowly, he caught his breath and released a sigh so extravagant that the track of lamplight trembled in the gloom. "Oh, bless me, Isis! I can't believe it! It's here, been here all along, hanging from a hook behind the wardrobe. And look, its sheathed in the very same linen I stock."

Silent tears streamed down his cheeks as he pulled me toward him. "Miriam, how did you know? How did you know the manuscript was here? And that Dario took it?"

"There is no Dario. I found that out when I went to the warehouse. No one knew him. Also, Varius claimed his brother was working there when he rented your apartment, and I knew that was impossible because the ports had yet to open. True, some days have been mild this winter—that's probably what misled Varius—but the ports never open here before March 10th."

"If Dario never existed, then who was the other man staying with Varius?"

"There was no other man. Varius assumed both identities. And by claiming they were brothers, he could account for any resemblance. But if you think about it, their differences were superficial, something Varius could create with a little glue and a lot of imagination."

"So, he planned to steal my manuscript all along! I feel so foolish, but why, after all that deception, did he leave it behind?"

"He knew he was in danger when the authorities found a body they thought was Dario's. See, Varius had staged his brother's flight so he could blame him for the theft. That's why he threw away Dario's things. Of course, we'll never know, but my guess is a one-handed beggar took the clothes and was wearing them when he was killed.

"But I'm rambling. To answer your question, if Varius had been found with the manuscript, he could have been accused of murdering Dario to get it. So, he had to leave it behind. And he left the wig holder behind because it was too conspicuous to carry along with the rest of his things. Besides, he didn't need it anymore. Anyway, seeing the wig holder and finding the glue confirmed my theory."

Bion stared into space and then furrowed his brow. "Well, should we just let the scoundrel go?"

"Well, at least we got the manuscript back, and he's gone. But, unfortunately, without proof, we can do nothing more. Let's just hope he thinks we identified the body as Dario's. That, more than the authorities, ought to keep him running for a long, long time."

Purge
Victoria Greenaway

*Y*ou'd *better stop lying because one day you won't know you're doing it.*

Standing in the bank, the words floated like flotsam from the depths of Daisy's sub-conscious. Her mother's words. The teller was telling her there was not enough money. Not enough money in her *account*. She only had fifteen hundred. But the nasty man had asked for two thousand. And there was still the rent to pay. The rent never got paid late, because questions might get asked. And then people might *know*.

Don't tell people your business.

More of her mother's words. But telling people her business was Daisy's compulsion. She told her business so much that by the time she was a couple of years into school, both kids and teachers had started to avoid her. She remembered clearly the day her teacher had rolled her eyes, turning away from Daisy's coma-less monologue about the cat. That eyeroll had stung like a wasp. Adults loved her stories, didn't they? But here was one who clearly did not.

That day, Daisy realised she might have to make her monologues more interesting. That day, Daisy started lying.

The teachers became worried about Daisy and had contacted home. Mortified, her mother said for the first time: *You'd better stop lying because one day you won't know you're doing it.*

But Daisy hadn't stopped. The school never phoned home again.

Growing up, Daisy's mother had told everyone who would listen about the time she had to turn down a small part in a soap opera. She never used to add the part about it being because she was pregnant with Daisy. She'd told Daisy, though. Her mother kept saying that maybe Daisy could take up where she had left off. So, she did the plays at school because her mother had convinced her that she could. But instead of red carpets, Daisy got a bottom-of-the-rung office job and the occasional small role in the local drama society. She spent her wages like the red carpet existed, though. When her mother died, she spent the proceeds of the sale of her mother's home on red-carpet stories. For a little while, they were real.

But now the bank teller was telling her she couldn't have two thousand dollars. How was she supposed to pay off the nasty man? The teller simply didn't understand her predicament. If she didn't pay the nasty man off, he would tell everyone at work that she didn't have cancer. When Daisy had heard the word come out of her mouth that morning in the break room, she felt it was *right*. People had to listen to cancer stories, even those who had stopped listening to all the others. Occasionally she forgot that she didn't actually have it.

But the nasty man didn't believe her. He thought he knew more about it that she did.

'Where is it you're having that chemo?' he had asked in the break room as he dunked his tea bag.

'At the hospital. It's really awful.'

'The local hospital? The one up the road?'

'That's right.'

'You don't look like you're having chemo,' he had said with a hovering grin.

People weren't supposed to say *that* about chemo. What if she actually *had* the disease? Which she did. She did have the disease. She was having chemo twice a week. She said she was. If she said something was a thing, it was already done.

'I've got a good nutritionist. She's doing all the macros with me—'

'I know what chemo patients look like, because my wife's an oncologist up at the hospital. I asked her and she's never heard of you.'

Daisy had started to flannel, to say: how dare you say I haven't got what I say I have!

But the man had put his hand up to stop her. 'What kind of sick lie is telling people you've got cancer? *Everything* you say is shit. I don't believe your dad's a billionaire in America. I don't believe your mum was a famous actor who died on set. I mean, *look* at you. You're just a dumpy frump. You *really* need to understand that.'

Daisy was quirky and cute, not dumpy and frumpy. Confronted with someone's actual experience of herself outside of her own head, she had been close to panicking.

'I'm going to tell everyone you're lying. Jill's husband died of cancer last year. So, she'll be very interested to hear what I have to say.'

Daisy had begged him not to. But he had a mean streak, and kept glaring at her when someone asked her about her health. He'd poke and prod with knowing glances, and drop disturbing hints in group emails. After a week of torture, he told her if she gave him two thousand dollars he'd keep quiet. He seemed to think he was being funny. Funny or not, Daisy promised he could have it.

But he couldn't. The bank teller was saying to her that she could not have two thousand dollars. Because there wasn't two thousand dollars to have.

'Fix it,' she said, staring at the glass in front of the teller's face. Not the face itself.

'I…I can't fix it.

'There's a mistake.'

'There's no mistake. It's probably because your personal loan, car loan and credit card all came out at the same time.'

'But—'

Daisy stopped talking. She turned abruptly and left.

Outside on the footpath as the summer sun punched rays into the concrete, she searched fervently for a solution. She couldn't find another job. She had no savings and too much debt to go without income while she found another job. Could she make up a story and get him fired? No, that wouldn't work. What would people think of her? She walked home, her steps fast with anxiety.

Unlocking the front door and stepping inside, the flat this afternoon looked less like the waiting room of greatness and more like a cheap shit-box with a laminate kitchen. A prison of inadequate wages and billing cycles. She went and stood at the sink, gazing out at the identical block of flats next door. And the one next to that. And the next. And the next. There was nothing magical about the dominoes. Her eyes dropped to the dish drainer. A knife lay there. The good one she'd spent a lot of money on when she'd started to watch cooking shows. The one that sliced through meat like butter and cut through bone.

The next day at work, Daisy went up to the man. Without meeting his eye, she said: 'I've got it at my flat. The money. It's at my flat.'

He paused as he poured in the milk. He laughed. He looked up at her. 'You're serious?'

Daisy told him six o'clock, nodded, and walked away. She didn't talk to anyone that day. She did her work, plugging accounts into her computer. On a different day, she might have imagined herself working for the CIA, trying to hack some un-hackable system. But today, she had to concentrate. She didn't even say goodbye to people in the office.

Getting home, she put down her bag and got changed. Having spent the previous evening cutting up sheets of photocopy paper taken from work, she counted off twenty $100-sized pieces and stuffed them into an envelope. She sealed the envelope, feeling the heft of it. That should pass. She checked the clock and quickly cleaned up the left-over bits of photocopy paper.

Then she went to the kitchen draw. She slid it open. She would like to have been a mobster's girlfriend whose safe house had been tracked down by a rival family.

You'd better stop lying because one day you won't realise you're doing it.

But today she would concentrate on the job at hand. She withdrew the knife, a continuous piece of razor-sharp German-engineered steel, weighted well, and 30 centimetres long. Sliding the knife into its plastic scabbard, she tucked it into her clothing and sat in her armchair to watch the clock. The short hand moved toward six.

The doorbell buzzed.

She jumped and blinked, staring at the door for a moment. Pushing herself out of the chair, she retrieved the envelope from the dining room table. Knife hidden against her skin, she went back and opened the door.

There he was. The nasty man.

'Come in,' she said and stepped aside.

The man entered and briefly cast his eye around the flat. Lounge, dining and kitchen all in one with nothing but a breakfast bar to delineate the cooking from the living. She saw the sneer on his face, as if he had expected nothing more.

Daisy held out the envelope. 'Here's your money.'

The nasty man burst out laughing. But it was odd. It was like he felt bad to do so. 'I don't want your money.'

Daisy fell into confusion. 'What?'

'I just…I don't know, I feel a bit bad. I just wanted to see if you'd do it.'

'Why would you *do* that?' she said, horrified.

'Why would you tell people you have cancer? Although, everyone knows you don't, because I told them. Like, I told them last week.'

Daisy stared. That wasn't *fair*. He'd let her think she had it in her hands to prevent this catastrophe. She listened to other people's lives all the time. She knew how people lived. Holidays, parties, that Christmas when so-and-so got so pissed they fell on Grandma who was asleep in the corner. Such hilarity. Such camaraderie. Youthful adventures and painful romances. When life dished up nothing but endless mediocrity and cheap mundanity, a person had a *right* to make it up. It wasn't fair if she couldn't.

She dropped the envelope. She reached into her clothing and unsheathed the knife. The nasty man's face flashed from triumphant to surprised.

'What the fuck is that?' Then he smirked. 'You're a fucking psycho.'

Daisy stabbed the knife forward. She'd looked it up on the internet at work. You don't stab overarm, you stab underarm. The knife went in and out as if through butter. The man's eyes bulged. He looked down at the blood, spreading rosy fingers over his t-shirt. The nasty man's face went from surprised to terrified. Daisy smiled, smiled wide. His hands dropped to his stomach. He screamed once. Daisy slashed with the blade and caught him in the jugular while the wound in his guts had him distracted. He arched away, spraying hot, arterial blood over Daisy and up the wall in a gory parabola. He collapsed on the carpet with a soft sigh and a thud. Daisy gazed as he bled out, watching the stages his body went through. The twitching and the final gasping.

She was particularly fascinated by the eyes as they saw the growing pool of their own blood.

She swept up the envelope with her free had and emptied it in front of him.

'It's photocopy paper. You nasty man.'

His breath laboured for a second or two. Then stopped.

Then there was nothing.

Daisy's body began to relax. Her eye saw the smear of the blood of the nasty man up the length of the knife. She went over to the sink and washed it, dried it, and put it back in the drawer. The laminate bordering the front edge of the sink was covered in blood. How did that get there? She looked down. Her t-shirt was soaked. Her track suite pants were soaked. She looked back at the lounge room. Red soaked the carpet. The wall dripped, smeared near the height of the arc by the man's attempt to stay upright.

She came and stood over him, happy with the thing she had done. Picking up some of the fake 100s, she started skimming them at his glassy, dead eyes.

'Here's your money. You nasty man.'

Everything would be alright now. She would keep the body here until it turned to bones. How long would it smell for? Not *that* long, surely. She went to the spare room, a guest room for all the friends she'd have over now that her mother wasn't around. Friends who would come over because she was so interesting to hang out with. But the spare room was nothing but a clutter of boxes-full of gewgaws that sat unpacked for years. Useless things that no longer excited her. Daisy looked at the mattress propped against the wall. It had never had sheets on it. Didn't matter, though. The body would fit behind it. She'd let the nasty man dry out like beef jerky. She could open the window, and get air fresheners to hide the smell.

She shoved aside the dusty boxes, lowered the mattress, and went back out to the body. Grasping the ankles, beads of sweat oozing from her temples, she dragged the remains of the nasty man into the spare room. She rolled the body flush against the wall and, grunting, leaned the mattress over him. From a certain angle, though, you could still see the feet. Cover it with a towel. That'd work.

Walking on bare feet over the fresh trail of blood, she went to the bathroom for a towel. She caught herself in the mirrored cabinet. She arranged her features, arranged them how she did when she was telling herself a story.

'No, I've not seen him since I left work on Friday. Maybe he can't come back because he's told lies about me. I have cancer. It's not right to question people with cancer.'

She told the lie again.

'No, I've not seen him since I left work on Friday.'

And she didn't know she was doing it.

SHEA of Pink
Marcus Cook

People say that stripping is a classless job, for trashy crack whores who just want to fuck and drink. I say to those people, Fuck off. Stripping makes me more in a day than a retail cashier in a week. Those women who are cracked out looking for fast cash, and a quick fix, are not getting their money dancing and working the pole. They are in the alley blowing a cheating ass drunk for twenty bucks.

I get the money by knowing how to bend over at that right time as my body flowed with the music. On stage, I dance to *Metallica*, *Poison*, *Aerosmith*, and *AC/DC*. I'm hot and I know it. Tonight, I'm in a leather and studded G-String. The zippered boots are a highlight as they travel up my legs, gripping my calves, and hugging my thighs. These guys go gaga when I unzip them. I love my haircut; I shaved the back and sides and gave me that mop top look. Pink is a fantastic color.

"Alright let's welcome to the stage, Shea!!" the DJ announced as Aerosmith's "Sweet Emotion" started to play. I adjusted my costume then stepped through the curtain. The air was warmer due to the venue being packed. Men and women staring at me as I sauntered over to the pole. I leaned up against it and slowly wrapped my leg around. In a swift move I let my body swing around, the crowd started to cheer. I gripped the pole just above my head, flipped my body up, and wrapped my legs around the pole. After one spin around, I released my hands and removed my top. I may have tiny tits, but I haven't had any complaints. Everyone gazed in amazement as I stuck with my chest out just as the song ended, the money came flying onto the stage. Sweaty and catching my breath, I grabbed my top and cash before I slowly walked off stage as the crowd's cheers died down.

I walked back through the curtain and immediately felt a tight grip around my arm, "Where do you think you're going? The crowd wants to see that snatch of yours." Bruno said.

Bruno was the manager of Perky's. It's a nice club, hot girls, good drink deals and one of the best Blooming Onions I've ever tasted. The one thing he lacks is people skills.

A girl has to protect herself, which is why I had my fingernails filed really sharp. My left hand was free, so I immediately grabbed him tightly around his testicles and squeezed. He released me quickly, "I have a thing I need to attend too. Depending how it goes, will determine if I return here. I must say the week has been very pleasant, until this past moment."

I released my grip and he dropped to his knees holding his crotch, "I'm sorry. I hope you come back." Bruno replied with a slight tear in his eye.

"If not today, maybe next time I'm in town." I answered with a pat on top of his head while I continued to the back room.

I walked into the locker room where the girls were getting ready for work. I opened my locker and undressed. I placed the money in a waterproofed fanny pack and wrapped it around my waist. I then grabbed my shampoo and entered the showers.

I recognized the two girls showering together as Mims, and Poi. Mims was tall and tan with long pink hair and her "partner" Poi was a small Asian girl with long dreadlocks. I was positive neither one had natural hair.

"Look Poi, the new girl has a fanny pack." Mim mocked.

"What's you got in there? Drugs?" Poi asked.

I started to lather up, "More money that you two bitches wish you made in a month."

"Bitches! Who are you calling a bitch? Me and Poi are VIP dancers, we make rolls of money."

Mim exclaimed as she and Poi stepped up to me, "And since you're washing your hair, you better wash out that cheap ass dye job. I am the only one who wears Pink here."

I let the soap wash off my body as I stared the girls down. I didn't blink, so it was a surprise when I snatched the pink wig from Mim's head. At the same time, I whipped Poi in the face with it, which caused her to slip and take the both of them down. They were in shock.

I bent over and replied, "I was addressing you two as bitches, VIP here means Very Inexpensive Pussy and rolls of dollar bills are nowhere what I bank. I love my hair color, but since I'm leaving, you and your Halloween wig can stay. Next time, either of you two get in my face again, I'll blow it off your skull."

I left the water running as I stepped over them, leaving the shower. I tossed t-shirt and sweatpants on before I exited the club. There in the parking lot stood my baby, the love of my life, A red 1969 Ford Boss 429. Under its hood was a 375 horsepower 429 cubic inch V-8 engine. It was a speed demon and I used just about every penny of my dancing money to get it purr-ing.

I heard the yelling and bitching behind me and knew the girls weren't done with this fight. I hurried over and opened my trunk, keeping my back to the club entrance.

"No bitch disrespects me like that! Do you hear me! Nobody! I am going to cut you so de…"

Mim was interrupted by the barrel of my shotgun in her face.

"You're going to what?" I asked as I slowly squeezed the trigger. I looked down and saw a small puddle of urine underneath her. Poi has already booked it back to the club.

"Whoa! Let's be civil here. I was just blowing off steam, I wouldn't really gut you." Mim stated.

"Hmm, well I would have no problem pulling the trigger. I have nothing to lose and who's going to call the police about a dead stripper?" I asked.

I think the puddle got bigger.

"Okay, Okay, I'm sorry. Please let me go back into the club and I'll never bother you again. I promise on my alcoholic mothers' soul." Mim said as tears rolled down her cheeks.

I pulled the shotgun out of her face and smiled, "Fine. If you promise to never wear the color pink again, you can go."

"Yes!" Mim shouted as she slowly backed away, "If I can bleach my vagina I will. I promise."

I fired into the air and Mim sprinted away like a jackrabbit. I'm such a bitch.

I got into Zvira (yes, I named my car) turned the ignition and let her scream out through the parking lot. My seat vibrated as it idled so hard, I became wet, I looked at the time and knew I had no time to play, so I dropped it in gear and sped off down the highway.

The desert sand swirled across the road as the sun started to rise, it was going to get really hot, real soon. I saw signs for my destination, Chucks Lube. It was a gas station converted into a bar. I pulled into an empty parking lot. As I stepped out of Zvira, a couple of motorcycles rolled in and parked beside me. I locked the doors and headed in.

The bar was simple, decorated with neon signs and old license plates. The highlight was a 1964 red Ford Mustang Coupe hanging from the ceiling. The bartender was nowhere to be seen as the mini-biker gang sat at the bar waiting to be served.

"Look boys, this place has a stripper!" a large man with a thick, long, white beard said to his buddies.

I looked behind me and then back at them, "Oh where?"

The man chuckled, "Girl, you scream stripper."

I smiled and walked up to him with a very seductive smile, "You have an amazing judgement of people." I snatched his beard and yanked hard, slamming his head into mine. He looked stunned as I followed up with a knee to his groin, then caringly caressed his head, "I'm sorry that looked like it hurt." I said before ramming his head into the bar. The man dropped to his knees bleeding from the forehead and mouth. I noticed a large knife strapped to his back.

"Bitch we're going to ruin that pretty face. Boys get her!" the man yelled.

I snatched the knife and held it across his throat, "They touch me, I end you."

"What the hell, Shea!" a man's voice yelled from behind the bar. I looked and saw an older man holding a case of beer.

"Hi, daddy." I replied with a smile.

"Shea, let Gus off the ground." My father instructed.

"I'm keeping the knife." I whispered as I stepped away. Gus got off the ground and joined his friends.

"This is you daughter, Chuck?" Gus asked as he wiped the blood from his face.

"Yeah, and I guess you weren't playing nice with her." Chuck replied as he placed the beer on the bar.

"He called me a stripper, dad." I said.

"Get out!" My dad pointed to the door.

"Excuse me?" Gus questioned.

"He said get out." I repeated my father's command.

"The club will hear about this. Your business is done." Gus replied as he stormed out with his men.

"Jesus Christ, Shea. Why are you here?" my father asked.

"I'm here for the race."

"No."

"Excuse me? What do you mean no?" I was beside myself.

"I mean no. You snorted away your chance to race." My father's eyes pierced me hard.

I couldn't believe my own flesh and blood would hold that against me as mind raced back six years.

I was in my trailer at The Daytona International Speedway excited to be in the Daytona 500. I was even predicted to place in the top ten. Unfortunat2ely, I had done well on the previous year's NASCAR Circuit and created a fan base. I let it get to my head and started to act like a rock star. I partied hard in the off season and became addicted to cocaine. There I was with a rolled up hundred-dollar bill sniffing lines of my girlfriends' bare tits. By the time I got my pit call, I was high as a kite and jacked to race.

Once the green flag was waved and the race had officially begun, I believed I was driving an unstoppable vehicle. After the fifth lap, a driver lost control and hit the wall and bounced in front of me. Instead of maneuvering around, I pressed the gas thinking I'd go right thru. I hit it so fast and so hard I flipped the car in the air, before mine went into a barrel roll. I pulled myself out and staggered over to the other car. The other driver was bent like a pretzel. They pronounced him dead and I spent three years in jail, another year in and out of rehab, along with a life-time ban from any professional vehicle race.

"I did my time for that. I'm ready to get back to my life." I responded to my father.

"Well, you aren't getting it back today." My father replied.

"Okay, dad. I guess I'll drop an anonymous tip to the ATF hotline and let them know your bar runs an illegal car race." I began to leave. "Love you dad, maybe we can get together for Christmas. You should be out of jail by then."

"Hold it. Are you really going to play that card?" My father asked.

"Yep."

"Damn, you are your father's daughter. You're in."

"Thank you, daddy." I ran up and gave him a hug.

I followed my father a few miles through the desert, until we came up to a pop-up race staging area. There were several tents with cars parked underneath, some port-a-potties, and large screen for spectators to watch the race. I parked Zvira under one of the empty spaces and then joined my father for the grande tour.

A Spanish looking man sat in the flat back of his 1979 Chevrolet El Camino. Under its hood housed a 350 cubic inch V-8 and an Edelbrock four-barrel carburetor. Not much of a challenge for Zvira.

"Shea, this is Peligro Tortuga." My father introduced.

"Is that your birth name or are you horrible with creating names?" I giggled.

"It is my birth name." Peligro replied.

"You might as well just give me your pink slip now." I replied as I walked toward a small gentleman dressed in striped shorts and a green tube top.

"Shea, this is Scivoloso Donnola." My father introduced.

I looked past the man and straight at his cherry red, 1974 DeTomosa Pantera. This was a slim beast with a 351 cubic inch V-8. She handles well, if she has the right driver. Judging by the size of the man, he will need a booster seat just to steer. Will need to watch him closely.

"Ciao, Bella." Scivoloso said as he kissed my hand.

I let it go for now as I pulled my hand away and continued towards the final loser.

I didn't see the driver, but I did see some competition. 2019 Dodge Ram 1500 Rebel 4-wheel drive, air suspension, and a Hemi V-8. It's got speed and muscle. I exhaled.

"Yeah, she is a beast. "a Texan accent whispered in my ear.

I stepped up, before I turned around to see a tall, muscular, blonde hair, blue eyed man. When he smiled, his teeth sparkled in the sun.

Noah William-Brown, this is my daughter, Shea." My father finally introduced.

"Shea O' Sullivan. Ranked 35 in the pro circuit before you flamed out." Noah replied as he held out his hand.

"Wow, you're a groupie." I stated as I turned my attention back to his truck.

"I'm no groupie! I just a fan …" Noah replied.

"So, you're a fan. Got a marker? I'll be happy to sign something." I interrupted knowing I was getting his goat.

"Of NASCAR! And you are nothing, but a black mark on the sport!" Noah said in a heated voice.

I wasn't sure if it was the truck or the passion he radiated, but I was turned on. I looked around and saw everyone was occupied. "Black mark, huh?" I quickly kissed him firmly on the mouth. It took ten seconds for him to respond by lifting me in the air and pinning me against the hard metal frame of his machine. It also wasn't the only thing that was hard against me. We dropped under his truck and had a quickie, before we started to hear the roar of engines. I quickly crawled back from under it.

"Wow! That is a long exhaust pipe you have got there." I said as I wiped myself off.

"Yeah, it is impressive." Noah answered with a big Texan grin.

"There you two are. The race starts is in a half an hour. Any prep you need, I suggest you do it now." My father announced.

"Thanks daddy." I answered as my father walked back to the bar.

"That was a close one." Noah whispered as he grabbed my ass.

"Whoa there. Slow down, Tex. We're not going steady now. I just relieved some stress from the day." I said as I started to walk back to Zvira.

"Maybe we can do breakfast sometime?" Noah asked.

"Maybe, if you survive the race." I responded as I waved good-bye without looking back.

I arrived back at Zvira and popped open the hood and trunk. In the trunk I checked my nitro cannister and the battery. Then grabbed my shotgun and a box of armor piercing shells. I closed it up and walked over to check her levels and clean up the spark plugs. Sand had already started to fill in every little nook and cranny. A desert race such as this one will be brutal on one's vehicle. One of modifications I added to her was a backup water reserve. Can't have the radiator go out on you.

Once I went through everything, I closed it up and got into the car and loaded up my shotgun. I've been following my father's races for years; there aren't many survivors.

I was startled by a knock on my passenger window, I looked, and it was my father. I unlocked it and he got in.

"What can I do for you dad?" I asked.

"I just wanted to wish you luck." My father said as I could tell he had been crying.

"Yeah, well I hear luck doesn't win you this race, skill does." I replied.

"And knowledge." My father added, "I run an honest race, just remember this. When you hit the cliff drop down in gear before the turn. That's all I'm going to say. Good luck, hope we can have dinner together tonight." My father let himself out as I watched him walk over to the Italians car. Is he sharing the same hint? Probably. When it comes to his daughter in competition, he believed everyone gets sprinkles on their ice cream not just the winner.

"Attention Racers! Please make your way to the starting line." My father's voice came over a PA unit.

I turned the key and Zvira roared to life. I could tell she was as hungry as I was to win, "Alright baby, we been waiting for this moment. Now it's time!" I patted the dash, dropped her into reverse, and peeled backwards. I guided the car backwards all the way to the starting line and as I approached, I hit the gas, spun the steering wheel, putting the car into 180 stopping in between Noah and Scivoloso vehicles.

"I once saw an ape drive a taxi once just like that. It was far more impressive." Scivoloso chuckled.

"I saw a woman stick her whole fist up a donkey's ass once. Would you like to reenact it?" I replied as Scivoloso quickly stopped laughing.

"Racers welcome to Cardera De La Muerte. It is a six-mile race where you may not survive. You will begin the race as you head toward the wall of burning tires. Vision will be tough, but beware it ends just shy of a cliff. That will lead to a ten-mile drop. The turn is tight so drive smart." My father started with the instructions.

If that's the hardest part of the race, then I got it in the bag.

"The next stretch with put you through a cactus maze and finally the death stretch. Hottest stretch of road over fresh asphalt.

This isn't going to be a ride in the park, but not the first time I've taken on three men. I ended on top every time.

"Racers start your engines…"

I flipped on the ignition and Zvira let the others know she was here.

"On your marks,"

Just like when I dance, I need music to guide my movements. I popped in AC/DC's "Thunderstruck."

"Get set."

I put my sunglasses on and fastened my seatbelt.

"Go!"

That was the last thing I heard as I pressed on the gas. Zvira sped out into the desert sandwiched between The Dodge Ram and the Pantera. It felt like they wanted to jam me, until I lost control. Boys, I'm always in control. I tapped my brake and dropped down in gear letting the two vehicles speed ahead. I noticed the El Camino was bringing up the rear. Quickly I slammed my foot back on the gas and back in gear, Zvira accelerated as sand and dust flew onto my windshield. I was gaining ground when clouds of black smoke suddenly skewed my eyesight. We had arrived at the wall of burning tires.

The smoke was blacker the closer you drove to it. Noah pressed ahead and Peligro seemed to slow down, it was Scivoloso's strategy I was curious about. He was driving away from the tires at the same time creating a large gap in the race. I sped ahead with my wipers and headlights on. I kept my eyes focused on the trucks backlights using them as a beacon. I waited to see him make the turn.

My car jerked hard as Scivoloso's car slammed up against me hard causing me to knock into the wall. I know that ass just scratched Zvira. I quickly dropped into high gear and sped faster toward the Pantera. I could tell Scivoloso was trying to cut me off. I turned into him locking my bumper into his. We were now stuck together. My steering was tight as I finally saw Noah's light make a hard right. I pushed the gas petal to the ground. I could see Scivoloso panicking as he tried to break away. I hated what came next, but he started it. I counted to five and as I hit five, I jammed my foot on the brake and turned my steering wheel hard to the right. Zvira made the tight turn, unfortunately Scivoloso continued straight over the cliff. I'd shed more tears if he didn't scratch my baby.

The next stretch of the race route was short, and I was still eating Noah's dust as The Rebel kept a nice lead. I knew I would catch up, the question is when? Ahead I could see The Rebel disappear into a wall of cactus. I wasn't sure how tight it was going to be in there, but I knew it would be wider once Noah drove through.

I sped for the entrance when I was jolted from behind. I gripped the steering wheel tightly as I peered through my rearview mirror. The El Camino was now ridding my ass. We approached the wall quickly and it seemed Peligro's goal was to drive Zvira into the wall. I made a quick decision as I yanked the steering wheel to the right, until Zvira spun around and I ended up behind the El Camino. I hit the gas and rammed his back bumper hard. Peligro seemed shock as I jammed on the brake. I stopped and the El Camino continued straight into the cactus wall. I drove slowly passed and looked to see a branch of a cactus smashed through the windshield and impaled on Peligro's head. Not a great way to go.

I spent too much time with Peligro as I pressed hard on the gas and shot through the tight entrance through the cactus field. I could hear the needles on the cacti as they scratch Zvira's body, I could no longer see Noah, so his lead was longer than I wanted. I dropped the car into fifth gear and sped through, until the cactus limb smashed through my windshield. Tiny shards tore into the left side of my face as a large piece penetrated my left shoulder. I slammed on the brake and came to a complete stop. Blood leaked from my shoulder; I knew if I pulled it out, I'd bleed to death before I got to the finish line. I lost. I leaned back frustrated. This was my one chance to get the life I loved back; I guess I go back to stripping. I looked in the rearview mirror; my face was shredded. As I stared at myself, I knew I couldn't give up. That if anybody could come back and win, it was me. I lifted my legs straight up and kicked out the cactus limb. I ran on adrenaline as I put the car and gear and continued out of the cacti field.

The desert was wide open again as I passed by my last cactus. I could see the sand spurting into the air, letting me know how far Noah was.

"Alright Zvira, let's give you some real gas." I said as I flipped the nitro button. I could feel the fuel ignite as I am launched through the desert. The landscape around me had become a blur, but the Rebel was coming into focus. As I got closer, it seemed that Noah's truck was slowing down as I see smoke rolling from under its hood. It then stopped.

I pulled up beside him and pulled myself out the driver side window and sat there watching him scream and throw a tantrum. I honked my horn and he looked over at me, "What's wrong?"

"I don't know! I just lost oil pressure and then she stopped." Noah explained as he noticed my wounds. "Holy shit! Are you okay?"

"Huh. Yeah, it's only a scratch. Now let me give you some words of advice." I smiled, "When you're having sex with a beautiful woman. Keep your damn eyes open!" I flung his oil plug over to him.

I blew him a kiss, got back in the driver's seat and peeled away to the finish line. Long live the new queen of underground racing!

OTHER HELLBOUND BOOKS

The Toilet Zone
"Restroom reading at its most terrifying!"

Compiled and edited by the grand master of 80's schlock horror, Bret McCormick, each one of this collection of 32 terrifying tales is just the perfect length for a visit to the smallest room....

At the very boundaries of human imagination dwells one single, solitary place of solitude, of peace and quiet, a place in which your regular human being spends, on average, 10 to 15 minutes - at least once every single day of their lives.

Now, consider a typical, everyday reading speed of 200 to 250 words per minute - that means your average visitor has the time to read between 2,500 to 4,000 words, which makes each and every one of these 32 tales of terror - from some of the best contemporary independent authors - within this anthology of horror the perfect, meticulously calculated length.

Dare you take a walk to the small room from where inky shadows creep out to smother the light and solitude's siren call beckons you?

Dare you take a quiet, lonely walk into… The Toilet Zone

Blood and Blasphemy

If you enjoy your horror dipped in buckets of blood and sprinkled with generous amounts of blasphemy, then you've come to the right place!

Blood and Blasphemy is a collection of over thirty of the most sacrilegious horror stories ever written.

Within these irreverent pages, you will encounter a priest that keeps his deformed spawn chained in a root cellar, a convent where a poisonous species of salamander is worshiped, a demonic altar boy, possessed religious relics that kill, blood-drinking clergymen, a Son of God who feeds on sin, an unsuspecting couple who run afoul of religious lunatics in a small town, the divine (and deadly) turd of Christ, and other terrifying tales guaranteed to make church ladies faint and nuns clutch their rosaries.

Schlock! Horror!

An anthology of short stories based upon/inspired by and in loving homage to all of those great gorefest movies and books of the 1980's (not necessarily base in that era, although some do ride that wave of nostalgia!), the golden age when horror well and truly came kicking, screaming and spraying blood, gore & body parts out from the shadows...

This exemplary 80's themed/inspired tales of terror has been adjudicated and compiled by one Mr Bret McCormick, himself a writer, producer and director of many a schlock classic, including *Bio-Tech Warrior*, *Time Tracers*, *The Abomination*, *Ozone: The Attack of the Redneck Mutants* and the inimitable *Repligator*.

Featuring stories from: Todd Sullivan, Timothy C Hobbs, Mark Thomas, Andrew Post, James B. Pepe, Thomas Vaughn, Edward Karpp, Jaap Boekestein, Lisa Alfano, L. C. Holt, John Adam Gosham, Brandon Cracraft, M. Earl Smith, Sarah Cannavo, James Gardner, Bret McCormick, and James H. Longmore.

Graveyard Girls

Female authors + Horror = something spectacularly terrifying!

A delicious collection of horrific tales and darkest poetry from the cream of the crop, all lovingly compiled by the incomparable Gerri R Gray! Nestling between the covers of this formidable tome are twenty-five of the very best lady authors writing on the horror scene today!

These tales of terror are guaranteed to chill your very soul and awaken you in the dead of the night with fear-sweat clinging to your every pore and your heart pounding hard and heavy in your labored breast…

Featuring superlative horror from: Xtina Marie, M. W. Brown, Rebecca Kolodziej, Anya Lee, Barbara Jacobson, Gerri R. Gray, Christina Bergling, Julia Benally, Olga Werby, Kelly Glover, Lee Franklin, Linda M. Crate, Vanessa Hawkins, P. Alanna Roethle, J Snow, Evelyn Eve, Serena Daniels, S. E. Davis, Sam Hill, J. C. Raye, Donna J. W. Munro, R. J. Murray, C. Bailey-Bacchus, Varonica Chaney, Marian Finch (Lady Marian).

**A HellBound Books LLC
Publication**

http://www.hellboundbookspublishing.com

Printed in the United States of America

www.ingramcontent.com/pod-product-compliance
Lightning Source LLC
Chambersburg PA
CBHW021323190726
48288CB00003B/935